CRAZY RICH CAJUNS

BOYS OF THE BAYOU BOOK FOUR

ERIN NICHOLAS

EN FICTION, INC.

ISBN: 978-1-7338901-5-1

Editor: Lindsey Faber

Cover design: Angela Waters

Cover photography: Lindee Robinson

Models: Joshua Flaugher and Julianne Gentile

1

"Good morning, Miss Landry."

"I've been on hold for fifteen freaking minutes, *Mr. Baxter*."

Bennett grinned. She'd been on hold for four minutes. He knew because he'd been watching the time on his phone. He always kept her on hold for at least a couple. But he'd known to expect her to be dramatic about it no matter how long it was. Kennedy Landry wasn't really the patiently-wait-on-hold type of woman. Kennedy Landry was, however, the type of woman that made a man want to take what tiny semblance of control he could find and grab onto it like it was a lifeboat in the midst of a hurricane.

Kennedy Landry was absolutely like a hurricane, and she'd already pulled him under and drowned him in lust and amusement and fascination and...

Shit, he was half in love with her, and if the only way he had to remind her that she didn't *always* have the upper hand in every single one of their interactions was to make her wait on hold on the phone for a few minutes then yeah, he'd do it.

"Well, I've been waiting for the reports from last week since Monday," he told her. "Seems waiting is something we should both get used to." It was Thursday. She always made him wait until Friday for the reports she was supposed to send on Tuesday.

In part because that meant he'd call her about those reports on Wednesday and they'd fight-flirt for a few minutes. Something they both enjoyed far more than really made sense.

In part because her sending him the reports was ridiculous. He didn't really need them—he was just curious—and she knew it.

Kennedy hated being told what to do. But she worked for the Boys of the Bayou, the swamp boat tour and fishing company in Autre, Louisiana, and part of her job was to schedule the tours, deal with the customers, and keep track of the payments and receipts. Another part was to compile reports about the number of tourists—where they were from, ages and other demographics, and how much they brought in through tour tickets but also extra purchases such as T-shirts, stuffed alligators, snacks, and so on. And now, part of her job was to send those reports to Bennett, the only one of the five owners who didn't live in Autre and eat most of his meals at her grandmother's bar across the street from the tour company's office.

She hated sending the reports, but only because it meant that she was answering to him on some level. She didn't like that because she didn't have him wrapped around her little finger like she did every other man she dealt with on a regular basis.

As far as she knew.

Bennett had been very careful not to let on just how tightly wrapped he already was.

"This call could be about an emergency," she said in a bored voice that indicated: one, it was not an emergency, and two, she was trying really hard to sound bored and not like she was gritting her teeth.

Bennett loved that he rubbed her the wrong way. It only

took about ten minutes around Kennedy to figure out that she ran the show with the men in her life. The only daughter and granddaughter in a family of outdoorsy, hardworking, loud-cussing, Louisiana born-and-bred men, Kennedy not only kept up with them on the hardworking and cussing thing, but she got away with murder. Her oldest brother, Sawyer, tried to make her toe the line, but even he was a sap for his baby sister, and it was rare that Kennedy didn't get her way.

She knew how to handle blue-collar Cajun men, that was for sure.

Bennett wasn't a blue-collar Cajun man.

Well, he was Cajun, on his mother's side. But she'd married into money—a lot of money—very much on purpose and had long ago given up things like crawfish sucking and cursing in French. She had married into a white-collar, British-descended family in Savannah, neck-deep in politics and law and class and wealth and snobbery, while Kennedy had been neck-deep in, well, the Louisiana bayou. And everything that went along with that.

Bennett fucking loved the bayou. And everything that went along with that.

Especially the sassy, goth-dressing, impossible-to-impress Cajun girl who thought that the fact he couldn't fix a transmission, butcher an alligator, or bait a hook was downright embarrassing.

"If it was an emergency, you would have hung up and called back. Over and over again. Leaving progressively more and more threatening messages about what you were going to do to me when you did finally get a hold of me," he told her, signing off on the bottom of the letter he'd just finished and moving it to the side.

"I would never do that," she said.

"No?" When she *did* finally send him reports, it was always in folders that were named things like *I'm Not Your Fucking*

Secretary and *If You Ask Me to Get You Coffee It Will Definitely Have Turtle Shit in It.*

"If I really needed your attention, I'd start texting. Photos. Naked photos."

His entire body reacted to that. He cleared his throat. "I would definitely—"

"Of my grandfather."

Bennett paused. Then groaned. He knew her grandfather. Leo Landry was a great guy. Funny, down-to-earth, honest, loyal. And someone that Bennett absolutely did not ever want to see naked. Ever.

"You're an evil woman."

"Remember that."

He grinned, glad that they weren't Skyping. She amused him. And turned him on. But having her know that for certain was probably not a good idea. Though the naked photo thing wouldn't leave his mind completely.

"What do you need from me, Kennedy?" Did he purposely drop his voice and make it a little gruffer? Maybe.

Or maybe it just happened around Kennedy naturally.

"I'm being sued. Or maybe arrested."

Neither of those answers particularly surprised him, actually. "There's a difference."

"Are you suing me or arresting me?" Kennedy asked, clearly to someone else in the room with her.

"She's arresting *me*," Bennett heard a man say.

That was Leo, Kennedy's grandfather.

Bennett heard a scuffling sound and realized that she'd turned the phone to speaker and had set it on the counter.

Bennett frowned. "Ken—"

"She's arresting *me*," a woman's voice said.

That was Tori, one of Kennedy's best friend's and her brother Josh's girlfriend.

"But I'm not arresting *anyone*," another woman's voice said. This time a non-Landry.

Bennett sighed. He knew exactly what was going on.

"Ma'am, can I have your name?" Bennett asked. Loudly. Because loudly was the only way to get heard when there were two or more Landrys around.

"Bailey Wilcox. I'm with the Louisiana Department of Wildlife and Fisheries," the woman told him.

Okay, it was the same woman who'd come down to Autre to investigate the report of a rabid otter. Bailey was a young, beautiful, environmentalist who seemed to have her heart in the right place. She'd just had the misfortune of being assigned to working with the Landry family.

"This is Bennett Baxter. We met the last time you were down," he said.

"Of course. Hello, Mr. Baxter."

"Bennett Baxter, my *attorney*," Kennedy added.

Bennett rolled his eyes. He didn't think that was necessary. Bailey was just doing her job and would surely be reasonable about the animals she'd discovered. She'd believed them when they'd explained that Maddie, another of the Boys of the Bayou partners, had come up with the rabid otter story to keep a flirtatious tourist at bay. They'd also claimed that they hadn't seen the otter in a few days, and after an hour or so of looking around, Bailey had let it all go.

Of course, it wasn't true that they hadn't seen him. The otter's name was Gus and they'd hidden him from Bailey when she'd been there investigating. But after she was gone, Gus didn't want to move out. He decided that he liked living inside, cuddling with pretty girls, and getting hand-fed treats more than he liked living outside in the bayou. So yeah, he'd kind of become a pet. So they needed to keep him away from Bailey this time, too.

Of course, Bailey would have probably never come back to

Autre, if not for the fact that while she'd been looking for Gus, she'd discovered a gray wolf pup. And his brothers and sisters. And mother. Curled up in the closet in Leo's trailer where the Landrys had been attempting to hide them, too.

The new mom had been injured and Tori, a veterinarian who had been getting into trouble all her life on behalf of animals, had been nursing her back to health. Along with a bald eagle that had a broken wing. Which had also been found in the trailer. Tori had plans to re-release *all* of the animals. It just hadn't been time yet. But more than having them in pseudo-captivity, the fact that they'd been hiding them had been...well, frowned upon by the Department of Wildlife and Fisheries.

Clearly, Bailey was now back to see if the re-release had happened.

And clearly, the Landrys had decided on a strategy for dealing with her.

Not that it was a good strategy, or a particularly well-thought-out strategy, but the Landrys were more the follow-your-heart types of people than they were careful planners.

Bennett almost snorted out loud at that. That was an understatement.

The Landry family was crazy. He meant that affectionately, mostly, but it was true. They were unpredictable and, as this woman was about to find out, united. She was never going to be able to find out who, exactly, was responsible for housing the endangered wolves. Kennedy, Leo, and Tori were all going to take responsibility, and Bennett knew there were about a dozen more people who would also step up to help confuse things. No one would ever turn on anyone else, and there would be no material evidence that it was one versus another. This woman would either have to fine or arrest all of them, or none of them.

Bennett didn't really think Bailey was going to arrest anyone. The wolves weren't in danger and were back in the shed where the mother wolf had first chosen to set up house. Clearly Tori had been taking care of her and she was better off than before the humans had intervened. The wolves were also free to leave whenever they chose.

All of which he would argue to, well, whoever he needed to argue it to on behalf of the Landrys. If it came to that.

Bennett pulled up his email. He had some people he could contact about this. People who would call Bailey off. But he hesitated. He wasn't so sure that the Landrys actually needed his intervention.

"Well, Mr. Baxter," Bailey said. "There's really no need to involve you. I'm not here to arrest anyone."

"You're not?" Kennedy asked. "You said that it's illegal for me to keep my dog."

"That's not a dog," Bailey said. "It's a gray wolf. Gray wolves are threatened species and it's illegal to have them as pets."

"But I didn't know it was a wolf," Kennedy told her.

Bennett rolled his eyes. That was bullshit. They all knew it was a wolf.

"I told you it was a wolf the last time I was here," Bailey said.

Bennett could sense her exasperation. The feeling happened to a lot of people who hung around with the Landrys.

"I don't remember that," Kennedy said, "I thought it was a dog."

"You mean *I* thought it was a dog," Leo said. "Had a friend back when I was growing up who had a dog that looked just like that."

"Me, too," Tori piped up. "I've seen lots of dogs like that in my veterinary practice."

Bennett didn't even need to see the woman to know that her expression clearly said, "Bullshit."

"Then I am here to inform you, *again*, that it is a gray wolf and it's illegal to keep them in captivity," Bailey said.

"So you *are* here to give us trouble," Kennedy told Bailey. "Do the people who work for the great state of Louisiana not have anything better to do than to harass good, hardworking, animal-loving people who—"

"Ms. Wilcox," Bennett cut in smoothly before Kennedy could complete that thought out loud. "What do you need from us?"

"I'm just following up from last time." She sounded tired. "Just making sure that the wolf has been released as instructed."

He was ninety percent certain that Bailey Wilcox had actually wanted to stop by last time to see Chase Dawson again. Chase had spent a couple of weeks in Autre with the Landrys, especially Mitch Landry, learning about airboats, fishing...and Louisiana girls.

Bennett wasn't sure how they'd met, but Bailey had asked about Chase when she'd come to check on Gus and had seemed disappointed to find out that he was now back home and in medical school. Bennett thought maybe he was the only one to notice Bailey's preoccupation with Chase, however. She'd come across as a nerdy scientist who was all about rules and regulations, and the rest of the family had regarded her as the enemy out to get Gus. Bennett thought maybe she was just a girl with a crush looking for a good excuse to hang out along this part of the bayou. But Bennett knew better than to judge a book by its cover, so to speak.

After all, Kennedy Landry seemed like a sassy spitfire who thought she had no use for a guy in a suit. But Bennett thought she'd had some dirty thoughts about his neckties in actuality.

And one of these days, he was going to make her admit it.

"You're referring to the dog that looks like a wolf?" Bennett asked. He was going to cover for the Landrys. In part because he really liked them and knew they weren't doing anything wrong. They hadn't captured the wolf and they weren't keeping it captive. They were caring for it, for now. But also, because this meant he was about to enter into a contract to serve as Kennedy Landry's legal counsel. Which meant she would owe him.

He already knew how she was going to pay her bill.

"Mr. Baxter," Bailey said, with some obvious exasperation. "You know it's not a dog."

"Actually, I don't. I've never seen the animal." That was true. He'd seen Gus, but he'd only heard about the wolf and the eagle. "And even if I had, I'm certainly no expert in dog and wolf breeds," he said. Also true. "Furthermore, I would, in any case, defer to the expertise of Dr. Victoria Kramer who is, after all, a doctor of veterinary medicine. She's far more qualified than I am or, I would guess, you are, to make a judgement about this, wouldn't you agree?"

There was a long pause.

Finally Bailey said, "You've got to be kidding me."

"Are you going to charge anyone with anything?" Bennett asked.

"I'm..."

He could practically hear Bailey taking a deep breath.

"I'm issuing a warning. Again. But a formal one this time. In writing. Gray wolves cannot be kept as pets. Anyone who does is subject to fines, community service, and yes, even jail time."

She wasn't wrong about any of that.

"But you would have to prove that a gray wolf was, in fact, knowingly being kept as a pet," Bennett told her.

Again, there was a pause. "Yes."

"And you would need to see the animal actually in confinement on someone's property," Bennett added.

"Yes."

"Which would require a search warrant," Bennett said. "Do you have a search warrant with you right now?"

"I do not."

"Then I guess, for today, this is settled."

"Mr. Baxter," Bailey said. "I'm not here to cause trouble."

"You're just doing your job," Bennett agreed. "And I'm doing mine."

"That's right."

"So we can assure everyone there that no one is being sued or arrested," he added, with a smile.

"I can—"

"The wolf is mine!"

Suddenly a male voice came booming over the phone line.

Bennett groaned. Owen Landry had just joined the group and was trying to be helpful.

"So it *is* a wolf?" Bailey asked.

"Well, it's a— Ow!"

Bennett heard scuffling noises.

"Fuck! Dammit, Kennedy! What the hell?" Owen bellowed.

"Sorry," Kennedy said. Her tone lacking any contrition whatsoever.

"You fucking *threw* a *shoe* at me!"

"I saw a spider," Kennedy told him.

"On my *face?*"

"On the wall behind you."

"You missed the *wall* and hit my *face!*"

"I was just trying to get you to move so it didn't jump on you," Kennedy said. "You should be grateful!"

Bennett sighed. Did he really want to get involved with this woman? With this *family*?

"You hit me in the nose on purpose?" Owen asked.

"I was aiming for your crotch," Kennedy told him. "Guess I hit the bigger thing."

Bennett could picture her smirk and felt the familiar urge to kiss it right off of her, even though he wasn't there in person.

Yeah, he wanted to get involved with her. He couldn't explain it except to say that his family had been very...*un-Landry-like*. Maybe it was his Cajun roots, something in his genes or his blood, that drew him to the bayou and the craziness of this family.

"You weren't spanked enough as a child," Owen told Kennedy.

"You're probably right."

Bennett could also picture the way she lifted one shoulder in an adorable and infuriating so-what gesture.

"There's still hope she can find the right guy to do it," Leo piped up.

Owen snorted, Tori laughed, and Bennett scowled. Hard.

They were joking. Giving each other shit was how the Landrys showed love. Well, that and food. But there was no way anyone in this family would stand for a guy laying a hand on Kennedy.

Hell, none of them actually believed that the right guy even *existed* who could spank Kennedy Landry.

But even the thought of it really pissed Bennett off. Which made no sense.

Kennedy definitely hadn't been told no enough. She was absolutely a handful. She was...Leo's granddaughter who he loved dearly and he'd never want someone touching her inappropriately. Not that spanking was *always* inappropriate, of course. Between consenting adults who were into that kind of thing it could be very appropriate. But this all insinuated that they thought Kennedy needed someone—or that someone had missed their chance in the past—to intervene to change her behavior. That there was something they wished was different about her.

That was not okay with Bennett.

And he needed to cool the fuck down.

It was a joke. He knew that. Kennedy knew that.

Him getting worked up on her behalf over something that wasn't even serious was ridiculous.

"Yeah, maybe, but if it's discipline, I don't think the person you're spanking is supposed to *like* it," Kennedy said, in her typical smart-ass, you'll-never-make-me-blush way.

Bennett usually grinned at that attitude of hers. Not now. For a new reason. *This* all insinuated that some other guy had spanked her and everything in Bennett rebelled at *that* thought as well.

He *definitely* needed to cool down.

Instead, he sent a quick message to his assistant that he was heading to Autre in an hour. Getting to Autre would typically mean flying from Savannah to New Orleans. That trip on a commercial airline could take four or five hours with a layover in North Carolina, but thanks to his family's private plane and a small airstrip outside of Autre, Bennett had been making the trip much faster and more easily over the past couple of months since becoming an owner in the tour company.

Today would be even easier. He'd been working in New Orleans on and off for the past month, hoping to transition his work from Georgia to Louisiana permanently. He was only about twenty minutes away from Autre at the moment.

"You're a brat," Owen told Kennedy.

"Wow, news flash," Kennedy replied.

"Okay, so I'm going to go," Bailey said. "Um...just...yeah, so you've got your warning. And stuff."

She definitely didn't sound like any kind of badass officer of the law, and Bennett relaxed a little about her pursuing the wolf thing. Hell, she might not want to come back to Autre at all. Chase Dawson wasn't even here anymore, and even if he was, he might not be charming enough to make it worth putting up with all of this crazy.

Of course, that didn't mean that she wouldn't send someone else.

Dammit.

As soon as he heard the door shut on the other end of the line, Bennett said, "Kennedy."

"Yeah."

He could tell she'd picked the phone up and taken it off of speaker.

"Have you been spanked before?"

Okay, that was not what he'd intended to say first. Or maybe at all.

She clearly hadn't been expecting it, either. It took her a moment to reply.

"You'd have to catch me first, Baxter," she said.

That would not be a problem. "That's not what I asked you."

"*One* time, Bennett," she said, her voice low, almost as if she was trying to keep others from hearing. Which was very unusual. Kennedy always wanted everyone to hear her. "You try to spank me *one fucking time*, and I'll take your balls off with a snapping turtle."

Exactly. *That* was the woman he knew. The woman without one damned submissive bone in her body. The woman that needed the right man to appreciate her, to *encourage* her, to never try one thing to change her. "So that's a no on it happening before?"

"Bennett... I swear to God..."

"It's a yes or no question, Kennedy," he snapped. Jesus, the woman was so fucking difficult.

"No. And you absolutely do *not* have an invitation."

"I'm not asking for one," he said shortly. "God, that's the last thing you need."

There was a pause on her end as if maybe—holy miracles

of miracles—he'd actually made her speechless. For a second or two.

"The last thing I need?"

"You ever met a gator that *stopped* fighting just because someone got a good hold on her?" he asked. "No. Some things are just wild and will fight no matter what. Trying to hold them down is not how you handle them."

"Surely you're not comparing me to a big, ugly, stupid lizard."

He smiled in spite of the fact that he still felt, however irrationally, pissed off. "A fucking badass predator that everything else is, rightly, damned scared of."

"It's weird that you're so attracted to me if I'm so scary, isn't it?" she asked after a moment.

He almost laughed. She wasn't shy, that was for sure. Not that he'd ever hidden his attraction. "Not weird at all."

"You probably feel it takes a guy with pretty big balls to think he can take on a girl like me."

"Maybe I find the fact that you're a fighter who doesn't let anyone else tell her who she is or how she should be, pretty fucking hot."

She paused again. Longer this time. Bennett gave himself big points. Twice in one day was unprecedented, he was sure.

"It's *really* too bad you wear a suit and tie to work and don't know what to do with a crankshaft and piston."

Yeah, Kennedy had made a big deal out of the fact that he wasn't her type. Supposedly.

"You keep telling yourself that."

"I will."

He shook his head. "You're welcome for saving your sweet ass with the wildlife lady."

"Oh yeah...thanks."

"And, Kennedy?"

"Yeah?"

"Next time someone shows up like that and you *do* actually need my help, text me. I won't leave you on hold." He felt kind of shitty about that now.

"Oh, I know I could have done that."

Okay, that was good.

"But this way Bailey had a chance to hear about the growth Leo had removed from the back of his neck," Kennedy said.

Bennett frowned. "Wait, Leo had a growth on his neck?" That didn't sound good.

"No."

Bennett sighed. "Got it."

Yeah, there was no way Bailey was coming back down here to face this group. Unless she had a specific mission. Or someone with her. Tori and the rest weren't out of the woods for sure, but they'd definitely scared Bailey off for today.

"And you making me wait also made you feel a little bad, so that was like sprinkles on top," Kennedy added.

"Not bad enough not to expect payment for services today," Bennett told her. "In case that's what you're thinking."

"Payment? You're not on retainer or something?"

"Not for this." He wasn't on retainer anyway. He was a partner in the business, for God's sake. Their legal issues were his. And he was trying not to think about that too hard because the Landrys were a bunch of wildcards, to say the least.

"So how much is this going to be?" Kennedy asked.

"We'll talk about it when I get there."

"You're coming here? When?"

"Today."

"Oh."

He could picture her expression now, too. She was trying to look annoyed because she was trying to convince everyone around her—and herself—that she *was* annoyed. But it was mixed with a bit of anticipation, because they both always enjoyed their flirtation and banter, along with a dash of mischief, because she loved to give him shit and was trying to think of ways to do that when she saw him.

"I'll see you soon," he told her, making sure there was a hint of promise in his voice.

"Lucky you."

He hung up, chuckling. And definitely in a hurry to get to Autre.

2

GUYS IN SUITS WHO USED MULTIPLE FORKS AT DINNER AND WHO were referred to as "Mr."—unsarcastically—just weren't her type.

But damn, when Bennett Baxter went all lawyerly and came to her defense, it was kind of hot.

It was also very hot when he showed up in Autre in jeans and T-shirts.

So, it was helpful when he tried to do things like use power tools or fish. Because then Kennedy was reminded that he might be very nice to look at and very fun to flirt with, but he was, in the end, of no real use to her.

Kennedy sighed as everyone cleared out of the office and she tried to go back to work. And ignore the butterflies in her stomach at the knowledge that she was going to get to see Bennett in a few hours. The damned butterflies that made her realize that the whole useless-around-the-bayou thing was becoming less and less an issue. And her attraction to him was becoming more and more an issue. But she would admit that only when she was alone. And only in her weaker moments. Like right before lunch when her blood sugar dropped.

But, low blood sugar or not, there was definitely a spark between them that made her feel that they could have some amazingly hot sex, and it had been a long time since she'd done that. Incidentally, that sex had also been with a guy who was all wrong for her. Not at all in the way Bennett was wrong for her. More in the your-grandmother-hates-me-and-I'm-going-to-end-up-in-jail way. Bennett wasn't wrong in that way at all. Her grandmother loved him, in fact. He was just very different from her.

She lived on the bayou. She worked on the bayou. Her entire family lived and worked on the bayou. Bennett loved the bayou, but in a fascinated-outsider kind of way. A guy who knew the legal statutes around...okay, she didn't know a single legal statute to quote as an example...but who couldn't rewire her ceiling fan or get the wasps' nest down from the eaves of her grandmother's house or fix the engine on airboat number two in time for the afternoon tour really wasn't helpful at all.

That didn't mean she couldn't enjoy him for a sweaty night or two though.

If he'd just been some tourist down for a swamp boat tour or a fishing expedition, she would have had him pushed up against the office door and his clearly newly purchased blue jeans around his ankles in no time.

But she'd resisted because he was a friend of her brother's. Both of her brothers. And her cousin. Not because they were protective and would throw a fit. They *were* protective, but they loved Bennett and they found his effect on her quite amusing.

And *that* was why she'd been resisting him. She didn't need her family giving her any shit about how she lost her train of thought when Bennett was around and how he was the only guy who'd ever struck her speechless or made her blush.

Blush for fuck's sake. A girl who grew up around fishermen and roughnecks, with all male siblings and cousins, in a family that didn't believe in filters of any kind, didn't blush.

Worse, if she dated a rich guy like Bennett, she'd have to listen to her family tease her about trading airboats for yachts and asking if she thought she could get through an entire conversation without using the word fuck.

She didn't need the teasing. And she wasn't, actually, entirely certain she could make it through a conversation without saying fuck. So there was that reason to maybe not date Bennett, too.

Oh, and he was kind of her boss.

Well, he was actually very much her boss. One of them. She had five. Which was four too many. Or maybe five too many, honestly. But he was definitely one of them.

Still, she was beginning to care less and less about all of that. She could take her family's teasing. If it wasn't about Bennett, it would be about something else anyway. And Bennett was fun to flirt with. He had a great sense of humor. He was very smart, quick on his feet, and had fallen easily under the spell of her family. A lot of people did.

The Landrys were fun and over-the-top and made everyone feel like long-lost friends when they walked into the family bar or onto the Boys of the Bayou dock. But Bennett had gotten to know them beyond what most of the tourists did, and he understood them. He regarded them with the mix of exasperation and affection that was required. He seemed to know when to take them seriously and when to absolutely *not*, and that was a skill that took many people years to hone.

Bennett had caught on quickly and Kennedy gave him points for that.

She also loved—no, *appreciated* (that was a much safer word) —that he had their backs. Like today. She *appreciated* knowing that she could call him and he would jump in to help even without knowing the entire story. He'd take their side and then figure it all out later.

He was sharp. She liked that about him.

And she liked the way he made her feel like he'd had some very dirty thoughts about her. The way he looked at her and talked to her often sent sizzles of heat buzzing through her bloodstream and she loved that feeling.

Sure, she knew that a lot of his attraction to her was that she was a part of this completely-different-from-his-usual-life bayou package that he was so enamored with. She had jet-black hair with dark red tips, multiple piercings, and tattoos, and she dressed in black ninety-nine percent of the time. She wore shorts and skirts and tank tops—it was Louisiana, for fuck's sake—but she paired them with her black combat boots or her black Converse. She also loved her goth makeup. Oh, and she could deal with her own wasps and be her own handyman. She wasn't great with engines, but she could do other airboat repairs, if needed, and she knew everything about their computer system.

She had to be as different from the women that Bennett usually dated as he could get, and she realized that was a lot of her appeal to the guy.

Didn't matter. She still liked flirting with him and she wanted to sleep with him. Definitely.

It wasn't like they were ever going to actually *date* or anything.

"I want you to go to Savannah with me this weekend."

Kennedy whirled around on her stool so fast she had to grab the counter to keep from ending up on her ass beside it.

"Holy shit, Baxter!" she bitched when she saw him standing on the other side of the counter. "What the hell?"

He gave her a grin. "What? I told you I was coming today."

"That wasn't even an hour ago!" Kennedy glanced at the clock.

"I was in New Orleans."

She frowned. He'd been that close? What had he been doing? Why did it bug her a little that she hadn't known where he was and what he'd been doing? "You didn't tell me that."

"Do I need to tell you where I'm at?" He looked amused.

He also looked hot. Not sweaty-working-outside hot like the other guys she'd seen in and out of the office today, but brainy-in-charge hot. He was wearing a button-down dress shirt, open at the collar with his tie still on and tied, but loose, and his sleeves rolled up to his elbows. He was in dress slacks with a leather belt and scuff-less leather shoes. And glasses. Damn. Those always got to her. It was this whole picture of a guy who was totally opposite of what she was used to but still made her stomach flip that completely threw her off. Because he looked like a nerd. The kid who studied on Saturday night. The guy who sat in the front row and asked questions of the professor. The guy.... No. Fuck. He looked like he *was* the professor. And like he had some creative ideas about his extra credit opportunities for her.

That was what it was. It wasn't how he *looked*. It was how he looked *at her*. He was confident, clearly perfectly comfortable being the smartest guy in the room, and completely at ease with who he was, knowing that he could give her exactly what she needed and wanted. Even while wearing glasses.

Those damned things should not be hot.

"If it means that you're going to be sneaking up on me, yes, you need to tell me where you're at," she said, trying to sound huffy.

"You needed time to get ready for me, Kennedy?"

His voice got that deeper rumble in it and she worked on not reacting. He had this way of talking to her sometimes that made her react as if he'd stroked his finger up and down her spine—setting off goose bumps and tingles.

"Yeah, I needed to dust this place and put on the tea," she said dryly. Even as her brain spun images of "getting ready" by waxing from head to toe, putting on her favorite tiger print thong, and making sure the bottle of cinnamon-flavored body oil in her nightstand was full.

"Would love to see you bending over to dust those bottom shelves," he said. "Don't let me keep you from it."

"You wish."

In any other situation that could be called sexual harassment, but she knew that he'd never do or say anything like that if he thought she was truly uncomfortable with it. She dished stuff right back to him. It was their thing and their employee-boss relationship was...weird at best. He owned part of the company she worked for, but he had no power to fire her. Her grandfather would make heads roll if anyone tried to get rid of her. For one thing. For another, her oldest brother, Sawyer, was actually the majority partner and got to make all big, final decisions.

"Doesn't look like anyone's dusted in a while," he commented, glancing around.

"That's because we're not stupid."

The front office for the company was a wooden building that sat smack dab in between all of the boat docks and had people tramping in and out all day long. They were either coming off the dirt path that led down from the road or were coming up the wooden ramp from the docks. The door opened and closed a million times a day. They swept the floor maybe every third day or when it got noticeable, but there was a constant layer of sand and dirt here. That would just always be true. There was no way she'd waste her time trying to keep it spotless, that was for sure.

She washed the windows every once in a while, if she noticed the view was getting hazy. Every so often, she ran a dusting cloth over the shelves that held the various supplies they offered the tourists—sunscreen, bug repellent, and snacks like granola bars and candy along with cookies shaped like alligators and turtles. They also had a cooler with sports drinks, water, and soda for sale.

On the other side of the room were shelves that held the aquariums full of fish, frogs, and smaller turtles that the kids could look at and ooh and ahh over while they waited for their tours. She wasn't going to dust a turtle aquarium, either. That was dumb.

The connected room was the gift shop full of the Boys of the Bayou merchandise they had for sale—T-shirts, travel mugs, tote bags, stuffed alligators, hats, kid-sized tackle boxes, swamp flashlights and more, along with fishing supplies for adults and Louisiana history books, books with swamp ghost stories, and Cajun cookbooks. Kennedy did actually keep that room well stocked, cleaned up, and yes, dusted. But she wasn't going to admit that.

"Well, sorry to surprise you," Bennett said, clearly not sorry at all. "But I decided to come straight over to get my payment from you before I got distracted by anything else."

Oh, he thought he might get distracted from whatever it was he wanted from her? Not bloody likely. She leaned onto the counter. "I'm short on cash," she said. "You willing to take something in trade?"

Did she mean that to sound flirtatious and a little dirty? She sure did.

She and Bennett teased and danced around this you-want-me-and-I-know-it thing, but she really did want to know how serious it was. She wasn't sweet, she wasn't shy, and she wasn't naïve. She'd grown up surrounded by men in a place where every other critter she came across could poison or maim her. She was tough and she knew how men thought. With their dicks.

Bennett Baxter was something new, she'd admit that. But she'd figured out very young that the easiest way to find out if something would bite was to poke it.

She really wanted to know if Bennett would bite.

"I'm very willing to take something in trade," he told her. "In fact, I'm going to insist on it. I did something for you. Now you're going to do something for me."

Kennedy lifted a brow. "I have lots of talents, Baxter. You're gonna have to be specific." Her heart was racing though. She was in for whatever this was.

The truth was, Bennett had made the Boys of the Bayou way more fun. He was different. New. She worked with people that she was not only related to, but who she spent *all* of her time with. She lived on the second floor of her grandmother's house. She ate at least two meals a day at her grandmother's restaurant. Where her brothers, parents, cousins, and other relatives also ate most of their meals. She worked with her two brothers, two cousins, and her grandfather.

Bennett was...just different. She liked it. Even if he did wear a tie.

And she trusted him. Whatever this was, it was nothing to worry about. He was a good guy who loved her family and who wanted to keep all of his body parts intact and who knew that her family would separate him from those body parts if he messed with her.

"I want you to go to Savannah with me this weekend."

She blinked at him. Oh yeah, he'd said something like that before. "Savannah? Seriously?"

He was from Savannah. That's where he lived and worked. In some stupid apartment that had been newly remodeled in the most modern style and that she hated just from the photos of the building she'd found online—not that she'd ever admit to anyone that she'd looked it up—and his fancy downtown office that was, at least, in an old—though huge and gorgeous—brick building.

"Yes, seriously. It's my father's retirement party this

weekend and my mom is throwing an enormous, ostentatious bash for it, and I want you to come with me."

Kennedy's heart thumped. Go to Savannah with him to meet his family? What? She did not want to do that.

Except, she kind of wanted to do that.

She narrowed her eyes at him. "You know, I start thinking about sleeping with you and then you throw out a word like ostentatious and the urge completely disappears."

Bennett gave her a slow, you're-full-of-shit smile and leaned in, resting his forearms on the countertop and bringing his face within inches of hers. "Completely, huh?"

"Totally."

He reached out and ran the pad of his finger over the backs of her knuckles. "Ostentatious."

She suppressed her shiver. "Nothin'."

He turned his hand, slipping his finger under her hand to run his finger over her palm, making tingles dance up her arm. "Ostentatious."

Kennedy swallowed. "Nope."

He leaned in until she could feel his breath on her lips. "Ostentatious."

She couldn't remember ever wanting to kiss a guy as much as she wanted to kiss Bennett Baxter. Which was messing with her head. He got his shoes shined, for fuck's sake. She knew for a fact because she'd asked him. He was wearing a pair of those shoes right now. She hung out with guys who wore work boots and tennis shoes. Dirty ones. Old ones.

But she wanted to kiss Bennett even when he was wearing shiny shoes and glasses. Maybe especially when he was wearing glasses.

He smelled good, too.

It wasn't hard to smell good on the bayou. At least compared *to* the bayou. But he smelled good in that expensive-fabric-and-cologne way that, again, she wasn't used to.

"Not doing anything for me," she lied.

She knew that he knew that she was lying. She was glad. Because he leaned in one more inch, putting his jaw against hers and rubbing slightly, his slight five-o-clock shadow scuffing her skin.

"Ostentatious," he said gruffly near her ear.

Her nipples tightened and her breath caught. She had to take a second that time before she could say, "Just not a good word, Baxter."

He chuckled, low and deep. The sound rumbled over her skin and made her squeeze her thighs together. She barely resisted reaching up to grab his tie to hold him in place while she finally kissed him the way she'd wanted to ever since he'd first walked into the Boys of the Bayou. When she'd realized that he wasn't the pompous old man she'd envisioned from the few phone conversations they'd had.

Oh, he was a little pompous. But he wasn't old.

And for the first time in her life, she'd been tempted to answer someone with, "Yes, sir."

"I can make you like that word, Kennedy," he said, still with his mouth against her ear.

That was just fine. It was like when they talked on the phone. He had a great voice. But this was better because there was body heat, and her nose had a first-row seat for how great his neck smelled.

"You think?" she asked.

"For sure."

"You are free to give it your best shot," she told him.

"I would love to put you up on this counter, hike up that cute little black skirt, pull your thong to the side, and *ostentatiously* lick your pussy until you scream."

Her world tilted.

That was the only way to describe what happened to

Kennedy as Bennett Baxter said the dirtiest thing any man had ever said to her. While wearing glasses. And shiny shoes.

Her world had wobbled when the guy had first showed up, it had rocked when he'd said they were going to Savannah, but when he said the phrase "lick your pussy" to her while also using the word ostentatiously, her world freaking *tipped over*.

She was into Bennett Baxter.

Completely. Fully. Unabashedly.

Ostentatiously.

She pulled back to look into his eyes. She stared at him for five long, quiet seconds. Then she asked, "You really think my skirt is cute?"

For one brief moment, something flickered in his eyes. But before she could put a name to it, he leaned back and smiled a knowing smile that she wanted to hate but that she couldn't quite.

"We're leaving in the morning. Bright and early. Be ready."

Oh, she was ready. They were going to Savannah for the weekend. To his father's retirement party. Her family was so going to tease her about this. And she so didn't care.

Bennett shook his head as he headed up the path toward Ellie's, the bar that sat across the dirt road from the Boys of the Bayou docks.

He was never sure who had actually won the battle of the wills between him and Kennedy.

But he was feeling pretty confident this time, to be honest. Her nipples had been hard and she'd been breathing fast when he'd pulled back. Not that he hadn't seen physical reactions from her in the past, but this time had been...more. Bennett shoved a hand through his hair. Damn. He'd said the word pussy to Kennedy today. He'd said "lick your pussy until you scream," to be specific. He wasn't worried about shocking or embarrassing her. Shocking and embarrassing Kennedy Landry was nearly impossible. He was just surprised that *his* self-control had snapped so easily. He'd been bottling up similar things for a while now. Today, it had taken just a little needling and a whiff of her shampoo, and his control had crumbled.

Taking her to Savannah might be a really big mistake.

It also might be the best thing he'd ever done.

He needed his family to see he was serious about the bayou. About his new life. About Kennedy.

Marie and Preston Baxter were not going to come to the bayou. No matter how much he loved it, no matter how many times he told them that this was his new life plan. So he was going to take some of the bayou to them. The most hard-to-ignore, impossible-to-resist part.

Kennedy was going to make his point.

Ostentatiously.

Grinning, he pulled the door to Ellie's open and stepped inside the gathering place for the entire Landry family and most of the town of Autre. Sure, it looked like a shed on the outside—and on the inside—but on the inside, at least the walls were covered with New Orleans Saints posters, a slow pitch soft ball tournament champions banner, a mishmash of photos, and a variety of drawings done in crayons of alligators, turtles, and airboats. It was also full of amazing smells, awesome people, and strong alcohol.

Talk about ostentatious. He wondered if Kennedy realized that the word applied to her own family and their lifestyle and get-togethers as well. It didn't always mean lavish. It also meant brazen and flamboyant. Two words that definitely described the Landrys.

Then he grinned. Yeah, she knew.

"Bennett!"

He was greeted by a friendly voice that immediately made him smile. Ellie Landry, Kennedy's grandmother, owned the place and manned the bar, greeting regulars and tourists alike.

"Hey, Ellie."

"Leo said you were headin' our direction today," she said.

Leo was perched on "his" stool in the middle of the bar. The stool had a bright yellow seat and each leg was painted a different color. It was where he could always be found if he wasn't driving a Boys of the Bayou bus to and from New Orleans, gathering and delivering tourists. He gave Bennett a wave in greeting.

It was midafternoon, so there weren't nearly as many people as would be filling the place after work. Even so, half of the barstools were occupied. As Bennett approached the bar, a stool next to Leo was suddenly empty. Bennett settled in across the scarred wooden top from the smiling face of the Landry family matriarch.

"Hello, darlin'," Ellie greeted, sliding him a sweet tea. "So happy to see you."

He leaned over for the kiss on the cheek she always gave him, then settled onto his stool with a familiar warmth in his chest. He loved these people so much. They'd welcomed him—as they did everyone—with open arms, even though he'd come in as a stranger, an outsider, to buy into the company that had been in the Landry family since Ellie's husband, Leo, had started it with his best friend Kenny.

The current owners—Leo's grandsons, Sawyer, Owen and Josh—hadn't been as sure of Bennett. But Maddie, who had inherited her share of the business after her brother, Tommy, had died, had brought Bennett in to help them turn the business around.

"Why were you so quick to be my friend?" Bennett asked Ellie. "You were never suspicious of me?"

She wiped up a wet spot on the bar then leaned for Cora,

her business partner and best friend, to set a basket of fried pickles in front of him. One of his favorite things. He'd never had them until he'd come to Autre, and now his mouth would sometimes water even when he was in Savannah just thinking about them. He gave Cora a smile and she gave him a wink.

"Well, honey," Ellie said. "Every single person who's important to me started out as a stranger. Figure I might as well start off nice with new people. There's always time to think they're assholes later."

Bennett smiled at that and dipped a pickle into the Cajun sauce on the side. Ellie always had something like that to say.

"How am I doing so far in the asshole department?" he asked.

Kennedy wasn't exactly the kind of woman who needed her family's blessing to date a guy. Or to go to Savannah with him for the weekend. Bennett wasn't exactly the kind of guy to worry about things like other people's blessings when it came to getting what he wanted, either. But the Landry family was a family that you wanted to be blessed by.

That was the only way he could describe it. He wanted them to want him and Kennedy together.

"So far, you're an eleven on a ten scale," Ellie told him.

He cocked an eyebrow. "Is the ten a really great guy or a roaring asshole?"

She laughed. "A really great guy." She reached out and patted his hand. "But don't worry. If you wanted to be a roaring asshole, I know you would do it well."

He chuckled. "Thanks. I think."

"Heard you saved me from having to have conjugal visits with Leo down at the jail," Ellie said, pulling two bottles of beer from under the counter and flipping the tops off before passing them down the bar to two of the older guys who had been perched at the end of the bar every time Bennett had been in here.

Bennett cast a glance at Leo. "Well, that might be exaggerating a little. He, Tori, and Kennedy were messing with the gal from Wildlife and Fisheries, but I don't think she really had any intention of taking anyone to jail."

Ellie snorted. "Exaggerating *a little*? The guy who once told me that he almost got hit by a meteor when he was out night fishin'?"

Bennett turned his stool slightly toward Leo. "A meteor?"

Leo lifted a shoulder, a small smile on his lips. "Thought so."

"What was it really?"

"Some stupid kids throwing rocks from a dock at one of the fishing cabins."

"Rocks the size of meteors?" Bennett asked.

It didn't take long to figure out that Ellie, Leo, Cora, and most of their friends were a little crazy. But they were funny and loving and always there for their friends and family, and a little crazy just kept it all more interesting.

"Well, it *seemed* like the size of a meteor," Leo said. "At the time."

"You mean, when you were two jars of moonshine in," Ellie said. "When you and Kenny went out night fishin', there was very little fishin' going on."

"Yeah, well, at least we baited hooks and dropped them in the water," Leo said. "When *you* and me went out night fishin', we didn't even unpack the poles."

"Not the *fishing* poles, no," Ellie said with a sly smile.

Leo chuckled. "I guess you could say that we—"

"Nope," Bennett cut in, interrupting whatever the older man was about to say. "That's enough of that."

It also didn't take long around Ellie and Leo to know that there were no off-limits topics, and that included their own sex life. They were crazy about each other, even fifty-some years later, and they had no filter when it came to inappropriate humor and sexual innuendo. Or up-front sexual conversation. Like flat out admitting they had make-out sessions in the restaurant's kitchen or why the bottle of chocolate syrup Kennedy had up at the house for her ice cream was suddenly empty.

"Anyway, the risk of anyone getting arrested today was pretty small," Bennett told them.

"Was still a great reason for Kennedy to call you," Leo said.

"She doesn't need a reason to call him," Ellie said. She gave Bennett a side-eye. "Does she?"

"Of course not." Bennett lifted his glass to try to obscure his expression. Ellie's ability to read people was well-known.

He and Kennedy were still at a place where they made up reasons to call one another. He'd say he didn't get a report she had already sent. She'd say that she thought he should know that the order of stuffed alligators for the gift shop was going to be delayed three days. She didn't always send the reports on time, but she always sent them eventually and he definitely didn't need to know about the stuffed alligators, but they both liked to flirt on the phone and they weren't to the point of admitting that they just wanted to talk yet.

"That girl really was givin' us a hard time about the wolf and her pups though," Leo said.

"You had it handled," Bennett told him. "Hell, Bailey left thinkin' *she* was the one in the wrong after ten minutes with you all."

Leo chuckled. "What we lack in actual know-how, we make up for with pure, very believable, heartfelt bullshit."

"Amen," Ellie said, lifting her own glass of sweet tea.

Bennett dipped another fried pickle and glanced around the bar. It was early enough in the afternoon that none of the other Landrys were in yet. Kennedy's brothers and cousins were still out on the bayou with tours and her parents were still at work.

"So, I'm taking Kennedy to Savannah for the weekend," he said to Ellie and Leo once he saw the coast was clear.

He wanted to get a read on the family reaction to him and Kennedy spending more time together, and Ellie and Leo were the best ones to start with. For one, they had no filter and would tell him exactly what they thought. For another, they liked him.

He knew that the guys—Sawyer, Josh, and Owen—liked him, too. Mostly. But that was, at least in part, because he'd helped save their business and was willing to come down and lend some muscle to whatever project was going on. He wasn't sure how they'd feel about him dating their little sister-slash-cousin.

"You're going to introduce her to your family?" Ellie asked. She wasn't wearing quite as big a smile as Bennett might have hoped for. Or expected.

He nodded. "Yeah. It's my dad's retirement party. I'll be there for the weekend and thought it would be fun to take her along."

"Why do you want her to meet your family?" Leo asked, frowning slightly.

Yeah, definitely not the bright smiling faces he'd been wanting. Bennett shifted on his stool. "Because I talk about the bayou and all of you a lot. Thought it would be good for my family to get to know one of you. To see what has me so... charmed down here."

Leo shrugged. "I'm free this weekend. I could go with you."

Ellie nodded. "Me, too. I haven't been to Savannah in years."

Bennett's eyebrows lifted. "Um. You two want to go to my dad's retirement party with me?"

Leo and Ellie shared a look. Ellie nodded. "We could. I mean if you want your family to meet some people from down here, we're a great choice. We've been here the longest."

"We're the fucking backbone of this community," Leo

agreed. "We know all the stories, the whole history. You want your family to have a taste of the bayou, you can't go wrong with us."

"I can whip up some food to bring along. Leo can bring his fiddle." Ellie gave them both a grin. "We can even take some bayou whiskey with us. Really give 'em a party bayou style."

"And hell, we charm people every fuckin' day, don't we, darlin'?" Leo asked his wife. Who had been his ex-wife for a while. Then was his secret girlfriend for a while. Then just his girlfriend. And was now his wife again since they'd "eloped" to New Orleans a couple of weeks ago.

Ellie gave him a smile. "We sure do. Leo drives the tourists around on the bus all day every day and I feed and water 'em. Nobody more charmin' than the two of us down here."

Bennett nodded slowly. He could imagine Ellie and Leo showing up at his parent's estate with crawfish pie, bayou whiskey—aka moonshine made in the backyard—and a fiddle, and entertaining the guests with the colorful stories from the bayou, including, of course, plenty of legends and myths mixed in with the hard-to-believe-but-mostly-true stories of real people living here. Not to mention some of the crazy tourist stories.

The governor and the millionaires and the local celebrities would all be very...entertained...by it all. Or something. It would be entertaining for Bennett at least.

His mother would hate it.

Of course, once her family showed up—the crazy Cajun side of his family—Ellie and Leo would fit right in. Someone would probably set something on fire. Someone—or more than one someone—would end up naked in the swimming pool. And his mother would end up in bed with a migraine for the rest of the weekend.

"Is there a reason that you think Kennedy would be a *bad* choice to go along with me?" he asked, attempting to turn the tables a bit. A near impossible feat with these two but worth trying.

Ellie narrowed her eyes. "Why don't you tell us why you're *really* wanting to take her to Savannah."

Leo leaned in closer.

Bennett swallowed hard. "I do want my mom and dad to meet her."

"Because?"

"I...like her."

Leo chuckled. "'Course you do. Everyone likes Kennedy. But not everyone wants to spend three days straight with her."

Bennett couldn't help but smile. He wasn't going to tell them it was going to be five days.

"Do you want her to go to Savannah with you because of *her* or because she's a single woman you know that you're attracted to who might be willing to spend the weekend with you at a fancy party?" Ellie asked.

Bennett swallowed. That was a fair question. "Because of her," he said honestly. "Not to sound like an asshole, but there are a lot of beautiful, single women I could have asked."

Ellie nodded. "I figured. Just wanted to be sure."

"But if you take her to Savannah with you, you can't leave her there and you can't send her home early and you can't pawn her off on someone else," Leo said.

Bennett shook his head. "I'd never do any of those."

"Ha," Leo said. "You can't actually say that. You've only spent a few hours at a time with her. Most of your talkin' has been on the phone."

"And you've already asked how high when she said jump," Ellie pointed out.

Bennett frowned. "How so?"

"She called you today, told you she was being arrested, she clearly wasn't, but you still backed her up."

"You wanted me to *not* take her call? Not help her out?" Bennett asked.

Ellie shook her head. "I want you to help her, if she needs it. I want her to be able to call you, if she needs to. But I want you to also know when she needs it and when she's just messing with you."

"She was messing with me today." Of course she was.

Why had she called him? Suddenly Bennett realized that there'd been no reason for that. Between her, Tori, Leo, and Owen, the plan to completely confuse and overwhelm Bailey—probably while someone else in the family was hiding the wolf and her pups and cleaning up any evidence they'd ever been there at all—had been right on track. Bennett hadn't done a thing. That was right up there with telling him about the stuffed alligators.

"She was messing with you today," Ellie confirmed. "I mean, she used you as a distraction with Bailey, too, I suppose. But mostly she wanted to see what you'd do."

"And what you did was try to fix something she didn't need fixed and then jump in the car and head down here to ask her to a big fancy, weekend-long party," Leo said.

"Trying to help her out and then ask her out was the wrong thing to do?" Bennett asked slowly, trying to process it all. His head was starting to hurt.

"Listen, I like you," Leo said. "So I'm gonna let you in on some insider information."

"That would be...great." Bennett was ninety percent sure that Leo's insider information would be useful.

Unless Leo was messing with him, too.

Okay, he was seventy percent sure that Leo's insider information would be useful.

"The guy she settles down with..." Leo trailed off and narrowed his eyes at Bennett. "You *are* thinking about the settling down part, right?"

These people definitely got right to the point. Bennett knew he shouldn't have been surprised. "I am," he admitted. "You're the first ones I've told though."

"We're often the first ones people tell stuff," Ellie said with a wink.

"We're very good listeners," Leo agreed.

"And we're very wise," Ellie said.

They both nodded. Then burst out laughing.

"You're not actually wise?" Bennett asked, with a shake of his head. He grinned at them. "Damn, I've been bamboozled."

"Let's put it this way," Ellie said. "We pay attention and we love everyone who hangs out around here. You put those together and you notice a lot. When you notice a lot, you can come off as pretty insightful."

"Fair enough," Bennett said.

"So here's what you need to know about the guys in Kennedy's life," Leo said.

Bennett actually felt anticipation tighten his spine. He wanted to know this. He wanted to know what it would take to be a part of Kennedy's life. He wanted to know how to win her over.

Damn, that had happened fast.

But again, that was the Landrys. He'd sat around a couple of crawfish boils now, drank some beer and moonshine with them, gone out fishing. That meant he'd heard the stories. The big, over-the-top, love-at-first-sight, burn-the-world-down-for-the-one-they-loved stories that made up the history of this family. They laughed and fought and worked and loved hard. Big. Loud.

He had very little experience with any of that. But he wanted it.

"There are four types of guys," Leo said. "First, there are the ones who come through, see how gorgeous and different she is, who like her sass, and like to flirt. The tourists, the delivery guys, the ones just passing through. She's not interested in them and usually puts up with them for just a few minutes at a time."

Bennett had actually seen that in action himself. She was friendly, but simply polite, not giving them much encouragement at all.

"Second, there are the guys who actually ask her out," Leo went on.

Bennett definitely liked those guys less. He hadn't seen Kennedy with any actual boyfriends, but of course she had them. A woman like Kennedy probably got asked out all the time.

"She goes out with them, checks them out, and if she's even a little interested, she calls them to come over to fix something," Leo said. "But, inevitably, when they come over, they bring their town tools, fix it all by themselves, and then offer to take her out for dinner."

"Okay," Bennett said, not sure where Leo was going, but more than a little fascinated by all of this.

"Then there's the guys like her dad and brothers. When she calls *them* over to fix something, they come, insist that she help, give her shit while they do it, and then clean out all the cookies they know she baked that morning."

"Okay."

"Finally, there's me," Leo said. "When she calls me over to fix something, I sit my ass in a chair, hand her tools, talk to her the entire time, and then tell her what I want her to make me for dinner."

Bennett looked at the older man. "So those are the categories?"

"Yep."

"I can just flirt and nothing more. I can do everything for her. I can *help* her do stuff. Or I can make her do everything while I watch."

"Yep."

"Okay." It wasn't okay. Bennett wasn't sure what to do with that at all. But he'd fallen into that second category today, clearly. He'd fixed the problem she'd called him about—or tried to anyway—and had then asked her to go to Savannah for the weekend.

"You want to know which of those guys she calls the most often?" Leo asked after a moment.

"Yeah."

"Me."

It was no secret that Kennedy had a huge soft spot for her grandpa. They were very close. They also gave each other the most shit.

"Because you're so charming and insightful?" Bennett asked.

Leo laughed. "It will come as no surprise to you that Kennedy doesn't consider me either of those things."

Bennett grinned.

"It's because when I'm there, we *talk*," Leo said. "Not about the project or the business or whatever. And I don't let her just feed me cookies."

Bennett turned his stool fully toward the other man. "What do you talk about?"

"The Saints. LSU. The sociology of small towns. The eroding of the Louisiana coastline. Climate change. Why Becky Gardner can't seem to choose a good man no matter how hard she tries."

Bennett blinked at him. Sociology? The eroding of the coastline? Climate change? Gossip and sports? "That's...a lot."

Leo nodded and took a draw of his beer. "We're both very interesting people."

Bennett couldn't help but chuckle at that. They were also very humble. Clearly. "But her cookies suck?"

Leo swallowed and shook his head. "Her cookies are amazing."

"But you don't let her make you cookies."

"Right. Because she's able to do so much more. I'm not going to settle for cookies from someone who can make a crab and shrimp souffle or crème brûlée that's so good it will make you wanna cry."

Bennett felt his eyebrows rise. He'd heard them all say that Kennedy was amazing in the kitchen, but she refused to help out at Ellie's because Ellie and Cora squabbled all the time. "No kidding."

"If you're in the mood for snickerdoodles, she's your girl," Leo said. "And if you're in the mood for more, she's your girl."

He was in the mood for...everything Kennedy had to offer.

"So, you make her do more, but she likes you best," Bennett said. "You think that's just because you're her grandpa?"

"It's because I know what she's capable of and I don't let her half-ass stuff," Leo said. "And I'm funnier than all those other guys," he added.

Bennett grinned as he thought about that. "This works out well," he said, dryly. "Rewiring kitchens and overhauling transmissions are the things she gives me shit for not knowing."

"Yeah, because it's easier for her to convince herself that she doesn't need you down the road when she doesn't, you know, need you," Leo said with a shrug.

Ellie nodded. "You gotta give her something to need you for. Something real."

"Like Leo does?"

Ellie smiled at her husband. "Like Leo does. Like the whole family does. People to be there when she calls but to understand what she *really* needs."

"What should I have done when she called me to legally defend her against an arrest that wasn't actually happening?" he asked.

"You should have told her to handle it and that you wanted her lemon orzo shrimp for dinner," Ellie said.

"Better yet," Leo piped up. "Tell her that you're craving something with rosemary in it and what can she do about that."

"Just give her a challenge," Bennett said.

"Exactly. Along with the assumption that she'll rise to it," Ellie said.

That was interesting. He was going to keep that in mind.

"I did more or less tell her that I was taking her to Savannah. Didn't really ask. Just assumed she'd be the perfect one to come along," Bennett said.

Ellie nodded. "That's not bad."

Thank God. He'd been feeling like he'd failed every Kennedy test so far.

"Now, just don't be too sweet or romantic, don't get wrapped around her little finger," Leo said.

"Oh, he's already wrapped around her finger," Ellie said. "I mean, he's in here talkin' to her grandparents about how to be the right guy."

"Good point," Leo agreed with a nod.

Bennett sighed. He was definitely getting a headache. "I just want her," he finally said. Blunt. That was what this family understood. "Just how she is. And this place. This town. The business. All of this."

Ellie and Leo shared a glance.

"What?" Bennett asked.

"That's a good start," Ellie told him.

A good *start*? Dammit. He was kind of thinking of that as the finish line.

But he should have known better than to think that any Landry, especially Kennedy, would be easy.

He looked at Leo. "So, crème brûlée, huh?"

"You keep your hands off my crème brûlée," Leo said. "You

can have her Bananas Foster though. That's pretty amazing, too."

Sure. That would be great.

Except that he was allergic to bananas.

Of course, he was.

3

"IT'S EXTORTION."

Maddie snorted. "No. It's really not."

Kennedy tossed a skirt—black, of course—into her suitcase the next morning. Of course it wasn't extortion. "How is it not?"

"He *threatened you*?" Juliet asked. "If you didn't go to Savannah with him, something bad would happen?"

Yeah, she might not get an orgasm from him for several more weeks.

Bennett was hardly forcing her to go. But she had to play this as if she wasn't completely eager. She'd made a big deal of Bennett *not* being the best thing since they'd invented peanut butter flavored whipped cream in a can, and she couldn't let down her cool façade now. She had a reputation to uphold.

Truthfully though, the last time she'd been this excited had been when Gus, the river otter that lived near their docks, had showed up with a girlfriend. Seriously, being *that* excited about an otter really meant Kennedy needed more in her life. A sexy trip to Savannah was a good start.

Kennedy shrugged. "He's my boss. When your boss tells you that you have to do something, you have to do it, right?"

Maddie outright laughed at that. "You've never in your life done something one of your 'bosses'"—she lifted her fingers in air quotes—"told you to do just because they said it."

"Which means...you *want* to go to Savannah with Bennett?" Juliet asked, looking between Maddie and Kennedy.

Juliet was the newer of the group of girlfriends and hadn't been there when Bennett had first walked into the Boys of the Bayou office and knocked Kennedy's world off-kilter. She also hadn't known Kennedy long and didn't know that she preferred blue-collar guys who got their hands dirty for a living.

Or that she insisted that was the case anyway.

Truth was, until Bennett, she'd basically believed it.

The bayou was her home. She didn't know anything else. She didn't really need to know anything else. Not everyone was made to live and work on the bayou, but this was where karma or God or the universe had put her down. Seemed like as good a reason as any to stay put. She loved it here. The heat and humidity and bugs and leftover dinosaurs they called alligators were all a pain in the ass, but at the same time, she couldn't imagine leaving. She intended to grow old here alongside her crazy family. The guy who was next to her through it all would have to not only put up with said family, he'd also have to deal with the wildness of living here. All that considered, being able to fix the AC and ceiling fans, kill the bugs, and deal with those gators were definitely must-dos.

Then Bennett had walked in with his stupid tie and shiny shoes and expensive cologne and the smile that said I-can-make-your-panties-wet-and-never-lift-a-wrench, and she hadn't known what the hell to think.

Kennedy tossed a pair of black boots into her suitcase and then crossed to her dresser. She opened her panty drawer and grinned. "Yeah, I want to go with him," she told her friends.

"I knew it," Maddie said. "He's gotten to you."

"Well, yeah," Kennedy admitted, turning with a handful of

panties and thongs in a variety of colors and prints. "He's hot and funny and smart. And he seems to think that there's something between us." She tossed her panties into the suitcase in a silky pile and turned for her bra drawer.

"And you agree and want to pursue it?" Juliet asked. Her tone suggested she didn't think that's what Kennedy was saying.

She was right. That was not what Kennedy was saying. "I'm not *pursuing* anything except orgasms. It's chemistry and a couple of people with enough sense of humor to find it entertaining that we're attracted to one another when we have zero in common." Kennedy turned back with her bras and tossed them in, too. They probably all matched up with some of the panties already in the suitcase, but she didn't dress that way. She'd had more than her fill of matching things up and making everything perfect when she'd been doing beauty pageants as a kid. Now she just wore whatever she fucking felt like.

"Your senses of humor are what this is all about?" Juliet asked.

Kennedy nodded. "Sure. We like needling each other, seeing if we can make the other one blink—or get tongue-tied. It's fun. But that's really all it is."

Maddie didn't look convinced. "You sure you're on the same page there? Bennett's been spending more and more time down here."

"Because he likes the fishing and the bromances he has going with Josh and Owen, plus Ellie's cooking and Leo's tall tales," Kennedy said, waving that off. "I'm just a part of this bayou fantasy vacation package he's got going on over the weekends."

Maddie laughed and Juliet grinned.

Kennedy grinned, too. "Seriously though. It's like the city boys who go to the dude ranches. He's got some stupid fascination with all of this. The crawfish boils and the alligator hunts are so different from..." She searched her mind for something she knew about what rich people did, "...playing croquet on the front lawn of their mansion that he gets all excited and into it."

"Do people actually play croquet anymore?" Maddie asked.

Hell if Kennedy knew. She barely knew what croquet was. "Well, they play something stupid and boring, I'm sure."

"I get it," Juliet said. "You're the Jack and he's the Rose."

Maddie and Kennedy both looked at her.

"*Titanic*?" Juliet asked when they just blinked at her without saying anything. "You're Jack. The everyday, normal one. Bennett's Rose, the rich, high-society one. And when Bennett comes down here to the bayou, it's like when Rose meets Jack on the lower decks for the party and dancing."

Maddie and Kennedy looked at one another. Then shrugged.

"Yeah, it's like that," Kennedy agreed.

Juliet grinned.

"Anyway, he's enamored with the whole thing," Kennedy said. "Which is fine. We're cool. We're fun. And he and I do have some definite sparks."

"And what happens after this weekend?" Maddie asked.

Kennedy flipped the top of her suitcase shut and zipped the zipper. Then she tugged it off the bed and let it thunk to the floor. "We'll have a great time until it burns out and then..." She shrugged. "It will burn out." She looked at Juliet. "Fortunately, the chance of either of us freezing to death in the water while the other floats on a door are pretty slim down here."

"You'll keep...doing this...even after Savannah?" Maddie pressed.

Kennedy shrugged. "Maybe. For a little while."

Hell, she hadn't even been able to keep a guy she *did* have things in common with going for more than six months. No way were she and Bennett going to keep this up for longer than that. But in the meantime, it could be fun.

"But he owns part of the business," Juliet pointed out. "He'll *keep* coming down."

"After he's eaten his fill of crawfish and gumbo and gotten liquored up on moonshine and done the airboat thing enough, he'll get tired of it," Kennedy said. "That's not really his thing. It's just fun because it's different right now. I'm guessing in a few months we start seeing less and less of him."

"He'll still be an owner though," Juliet pressed. "He'll be here once in a while, right?"

Kennedy shrugged. "Sure. Probably."

"It won't be awkward that you had a fling and then broke up when he shows up from time to time?"

Kennedy laughed as she rolled her suitcase into the hallway. "Oh, honey, this town is full of guys I've dated and broken up with and run into at the gas station and bar on a regular basis. Just because you've seen each other naked is no reason that you can't talk about the weather while standing in the grocery store line."

Thank goodness. Or she'd never be able to go anywhere in Autre outside of her family's businesses. She hadn't slept with all of the guys she'd dated over the years. But she'd been hung up on a couple, had a couple pretty hung up on her, dated a couple at the same time—without them knowing that, at least for a month or so—and even had a pregnancy scare with one. She had a history in this town. What could she say? She'd spent twenty-five years here and she liked men. But she also realized that stuff happened. People got together and they broke up and, in a small town, you had to keep living beside each other without a whole lot of drama. When they ran into one another around town, they had to all try to be grown-ups. Some of them were better at that than others, of course.

And speaking of grown-ups...

"Besides," Kennedy said, hoisting her suitcase up and starting down the stairs with Maddie and Juliet behind her. "A definite perk to having a fling with a mature, well-educated, sophisticated guy like Bennett Baxter is that I'm sure the breakup will also be mature. We'll agree on all the reasons it won't work and that it's best for the business if we get along. He'll still want to hang out with my family. I'll still want to tease him. We'll both still like and respect each other, we'll just be able to acknowledge that great sex doesn't mean the whole relationship will work out." She stopped at the bottom of the steps and looked up. "I definitely want a little taste, but I'm not looking for seven courses here."

Maddie rolled her eyes. "You're already thinking about the hors d'oeuvres at the party, aren't you?"

Kennedy waggled her eyebrows. "Maybe."

"Hors d'oeuvres?" Juliet asked.

Maddie laughed. "Kennedy loves hors d'oeuvres. I guarantee that the first thing she thought of when Bennett asked her to go to this party was cocktail wieners wrapped in croissant dough."

Kennedy shook her head. "Not true." She grinned at Juliet. "Stuffed mushrooms first. *Then* mini pigs in a blanket."

"You're really into hors d'oeuvres?" Juliet asked.

Kennedy grabbed her purse off the table by the door and pulled the front door open, rolling her suitcase out onto the porch. "Love them. Love everything about them," she confessed.

"Really?" Juliet seemed puzzled.

Kennedy propped a hand on her hip. "Do you know how many different tastes and combinations and textures you can get before you ever get even close to full with hors d'oeuvres?" Kennedy asked. "Dozens. Tons. You can have crunchy, soft, salty, sweet, exotic, basic, saucy..." She sighed. "And then there are the dips. Oh my God, I could eat dip all night."

Juliet laughed. "I forget that you're a cook. You definitely know good food being from here."

Kennedy straightened and frowned. "Yeah, well, around here, no one would consider that food. It's too small, doesn't all have seafood in it, and isn't covered in cayenne."

Juliet studied her and Kennedy shifted her weight. Juliet was surprisingly insightful. Kennedy loved how the other woman had brought Sawyer out of his shell over the past couple of weeks, but it made Kennedy jumpy.

"I like them because you get little tastes of lots of different things without getting too full," she said.

"Or having to commit to one big thing," Maddie said.

Kennedy lifted an eyebrow. Maddie thought she knew Kennedy. And maybe she did. A little. But Kennedy wasn't a commitment-phobe. Good lord, she came from a family of people who fell in love hard and fast and definitely forever. Even her grandparents had tried splitting up and it hadn't stuck. "Well, it's a lot easier to spit out a small mouthful of something you don't like than dump an entire plate, you know?"

Maddie laughed. "Got it."

Kennedy turned to Juliet. "And if you tell my grandma or Cora that I said not all food has to have Cajun spice, I'll deny it...and I'll make sure another bat gets caught up in your mosquito netting."

Juliet's eyes widened. "You heard about that?"

Kennedy narrowed her eyes. "We all hear about everything eventually."

"Your secret's safe with me."

Maddie laughed. "Enjoy the time you've got until Juliet figures out you're a big softie and stops being afraid of you," she told Kennedy.

Kennedy stuck her tongue out. She *was* a big softie and she had a suspicion that Juliet already had an inkling.

Kennedy got that from her grandpa. Along with her foul language, her sense of humor, her no-bullshit attitude, and her fear of missing out. Leo always wanted to be in the thick of everything and Kennedy had definitely inherited that.

Which was why she figured that she got her sense of relationships from him.

Leo had a tendency to stick and stick hard to the things and people in his life. From his business to his family, Leo was all in, all the time. Even with the food he ate. He loved huge helpings of the same food he'd been eating for fifty years in the same restaurant from the same barstool. He didn't sample. He didn't try different tastes. He didn't mix things up. He'd never spit anything out because he'd never try anything new. It was always the same thing. He'd found what he loved and he didn't waver from it. Ever. If he gave you his allegiance, there wasn't anything that was going to shake it. Even if you tried to push him away and didn't treat him so good.

Kennedy could just look at her grandmother and see that. She loved Ellie. She did. So much. But she'd hated everything about Ellie and Leo breaking up, and she'd *hated* when Ellie had dated Trevor—a much younger guy from New Orleans—for a while. Trevor had been great. Had fit right in. Everyone had loved him. Even Leo. Trevor had treated Ellie well. She'd been happy. In fact, she and Leo had both seemed happier when they hadn't been living together. Jerry, their son and Kennedy's dad, had explained to Kennedy that Ellie and Leo had met when they were very young and had gotten married within four months of knowing each other. That was par for the course with the Landry family—fall fast and do something over-the-top about it. But it seemed that Ellie and Leo had needed some time apart eventually.

They were back together now and happier than ever, and Kennedy really tried to focus on that. But damn...she just couldn't quite get past the idea that Leo had never faltered. What if Ellie hadn't come back to him? He would have sat on that stool at her bar and been her friend and loved her in spite of her going on with her life without him.

Kennedy was very afraid of falling too fast and hard and then not being able to un-stick.

That's why she liked hors d'oeuvres. You could sample a lot of things and toss the ones you didn't like without guilt.

And yeah, also the part about them not all having crawfish and cayenne in them.

She loved her Cajun roots and the food and everything else that went along with it, but there was a whole big world out there full of...other stuff. Other food, other tastes, other music, other history and traditions. There was nothing wrong with sampling a little bit of all of that, too.

Just then, a shiny silver BMW pulled up at the curb. Driven by a hot guy with a little stubble, wearing a T-shirt and jeans. And glasses.

Kennedy sighed and looked at the girls. "Is it just me, or does he send very mixed messages?"

"You mean smart and rich along with downhome and country?" Maddie asked.

"Yeah, that."

"Is it the blue jeans and the BMW?" Juliet asked.

"I think it's just the whole attitude," Maddie said.

Bennett came to stand at the bottom of the porch steps. He looked up at the three women looking down at him. He looked apprehensive. That made sense.

"Good morning, ladies." Then he tucked a hand in the front pocket of his jeans.

Kennedy grinned. Formal, polite greeting. He didn't even drop his "g." But when he put his hand in his pocket like that, he looked more small town. She had to remember that he was just playing dress-up when he was down here. He liked hanging out on the bayou, but he wasn't a true bayou boy.

"Hey, Bennett," Maddie greeted, propping her shoulder against the porch column.

"Hi, Bennett," Juliet said.

Kennedy started down the porch steps with her suitcase, trying to hide the way her heart was suddenly thumping. She was going away for the weekend with this guy. This guy who she hadn't quite figured out. Yes, he was enamored with her because she came with a bunch of crazy Cajuns he really liked and pots full of amazing food he probably didn't get in Savannah, but she was more fascinated with him than she had been by a guy in...ever. She hadn't thought that through. Why was *he* so damned intriguing to *her*? He didn't have a charming bunch of characters that were always around when he was, making things more colorful and entertaining. He'd never shown up with any kind of food, amazing or otherwise.

He'd shown up with a checkbook and a head full of legal knowledge that had helped save her family's business. He'd helped smooth over some online reviews that had been a little problematic for the business, too. That wasn't nothing.

She could only chalk her fascination up to him being different than what she was used to, and her having a curious streak that was almost as wide as her mischievous streak. He was a new taste that she wanted to sample. It was that simple.

Bennett met her halfway up the steps to grab her bag from her. He gave her a big grin and took the bag the rest of the way down the steps and to the trunk of the car.

He seemed happy to see her and excited about the trip. That was trouble. She wasn't getting stuck to Bennett Baxter and she needed to be sure he didn't get stuck on her, either.

Bennett started for the passenger side of the car and Kennedy realized that he intended to open the door for her. Oh no. He wasn't going to be chivalrous and boyfriend-like. She took the few steps hurriedly and reached for the handle at the same time he did. With their hands both on the car door, they looked at each other. He only had about two inches on her when she wore her boots, and she realized that put their lips on the perfect level for kissing.

They hadn't kissed.

Why did she feel like they had? That was weird. She swore that she felt like she and Bennett had made out prior to this. It was all the banter. All the blatant acknowledgement of their attraction. All of the at-night-in-bed-alone fantasies, too. She hadn't thought of another man while using her favorite vibrator since meeting Bennett Baxter. That was also trouble.

She definitely needed to get this all out of her system.

On impulse—which was one of her favorite ways to do things—she dropped her purse, ran her hand over his shoulder and into his hair, and put her lips to his.

To his credit, and her delight, Bennett didn't hesitate a second. He shifted, put both hands on her hips, and leaned into the kiss. In fact, he basically took it over.

He opened his mouth, deepening the contact, and brought her up against him more fully. She'd seen him without his shirt on when he'd been helping her brothers get the new dock into the water, so she'd had an inkling he was hard in all the right places. But feeling it was something altogether different.

Kennedy felt herself lift onto tiptoe and fist the front of his shirt, in an attempt to get even closer.

Bennett, being the gentlemanly type of guy who would carry her bags and open doors for her, decided to help her out with that, too, and he turned her, putting her back against the car. Then he pressed close. All of his hardness against her was exactly what she wanted. She gave a little moan that she realized she might be embarrassed about...later...and met his tongue with hers, kissing him deeply, relishing the heat that rose quickly between them.

If she could just keep him doing this kind of stuff for the

next two days, then there was very little risk of either of them mistaking this for anything but a hot affair.

She wasn't going to have two brain cells to rub together.

He *better* feel the same way. If he thought chivalrous thoughts about her after Kennedy had rubbed against him like Tori's pet piglet rubbed against the barn door, then she was really doing something wrong.

"Ahem."

Maddie clearing her throat was the only thing that caused Kennedy to pull back and open her eyes.

Bennett didn't pull back. He didn't let her get too far, either. He stood with one hand on her hip, one braced on the top of the car behind her, looking at her like he'd just figured a whole bunch of stuff out.

How to spend most of the weekend in bed with her better be what he'd just puzzled out. Kennedy let her gaze drop to his mouth, then go back to his eyes.

He gave her a slow smile that seemed almost knowing. Which made her itchy. "I'm excited about the trip, too," he finally said, his voice a little gruff.

"Just making sure you still want me along after I tell you that I don't play croquet or golf and that I tried, but I can't think of a single joke that's not dirty."

Bennett lifted a hand and ran this thumb over her bottom lip. "I still want you along, Kennedy."

She swallowed hard. She was going to enjoy this chemistry. That was the only option, really. Because she wasn't going to be able to say no to it.

"I do know the salad fork from the dinner fork, but beyond that, I might be a little lost." That wasn't entirely true. She knew the forks. Salad, dinner, oyster, dessert. But she didn't really care what Bennett's family thought of her, and this was her way of warning him that she wasn't going to be the perfect lady that his hoity-toity mother might be expecting him to bring home.

"I don't care if you eat with your hands," he told her.

She narrowed her eyes. "You shouldn't tell a girl who eats French fries six meals a week something like that."

His smile was slow. And cocky. "I know who I'm talking to, Kennedy."

For some reason that made a little tingle go down her spine.

But he didn't know her. Not really. He knew what she'd showed him, dammit. She had control of that. She'd gotten to be a master at that early on in her life. Dressing up, performing, smiling even when her head was pounding from all the bobby pins stuck into her updo, dancing even when her feet were killing her in the shoes that were a size too small but matched her dress perfectly. That was the other thing about sticking close to Autre. She could be herself here. She could say and do whatever she wanted. They might roll their eyes, but they weren't giving her a grade. They weren't lining her up against other girls and deciding who was the best.

Bennett thought he knew her because he'd observed her in her own habitat. Maybe there was something to that. She hadn't put on any airs with him. But they'd spent a total of, what, twelve hours together if she added all the phone conversations and short visits together?

He probably thought he was really good at reading people or something.

In actuality, he was just seeing what he wanted to see. Or what she wanted him to see. He seemed to like her tattoos and her piercings and the black shorts and skirts she wore, her combat boots, her sassy mouth and the sexual innuendo and banter she turned on for him. Lord knew, she didn't do that with every guy who walked in.

"Then I guess you know what you're getting into," she said, watching his face carefully.

"I really do."

He really thought he did.

And she was going to let him think that. For now.

Kennedy guessed she was pretty different from the girls he usually brought home. She just might shock his mother...

Oh.

Suddenly it made a lot more sense. She was a little bit of a rebellion.

Or a lot of a rebellion.

Now she got it.

"Okay, I think this is going to be...fun." She pushed him back and opened the car door—her own door—and got into the car.

Bennett looked like he maybe had something more to say, but instead he nodded and rounded the front of the car.

Kennedy waved at Maddie and Juliet who were still standing on the porch. Juliet looked a little confused. Maddie looked like she was disappointed she wasn't going to have to have a front row seat to whatever was going to happen this weekend.

That was because Maddie knew Kennedy far better than Juliet did.

4

"So, tell me about your dad."

Bennett looked over. They hadn't even pulled onto the highway out of Autre yet and Kennedy already had her boots up on the dash of his rented BMW, her black and blue striped skirt riding high on her thighs. It revealed the creamy smooth skin along with the flowers that trailed up her left leg. The intricate tattoo started with a tiny vine that wrapped around her ankle, then climbed her leg, getting bigger, with flowers in various stages of bloom along the way. It dove under the hem of her skirt, reappearing at her waist above the top edge of her skirt, then continued up her side, slipping under the fitted black top that left her midriff bare. He could see it again where it reappeared from the short sleeve of the shirt and then trailed down her arm to her wrist and then grew narrow, the vine continuing down to wrap around her pinky finger. He wanted badly to trace the entire length. With his eyes. His fingers. His tongue. He wanted to see it in its entirety. He wanted to know the meaning behind it.

She also had piercings that sparkled along the edge of her ears, one at the corner of her right eyebrow and one single tiny stud in her nose. She wore heavy black eye makeup and black nail polish and always had black in her clothing and shoes. Or boots. Today, her long, dark hair was pulled up into a high ponytail, the deep red tips hanging against her shoulder. And she was grinning at him with a grin that said she knew she frustrated him and entertained him at that same time.

He wanted her more every single time he looked at her.

And now she'd kissed him. So he was basically fucked.

He didn't remember a time when he'd been so into a woman before even kissing her.

Now he was going to do anything she wanted him to do and she probably knew it.

That was dangerous with a woman like Kennedy. Hell, her own grandparents had basically told him not to give everything she asked for.

"My dad is..." Bennett trailed off, trying to decide how to describe his father. "I mean, he's pretty much everything you already know about him. He supports entrepreneurs and is a strong advocate for education and business."

Kennedy didn't say anything and he looked over. She was looking at him with a puzzled frown.

"What?" he asked.

"What are you talking about?"

"You asked what my dad is like."

"And I meant, is he funny? Does he like to do jigsaw puzzles or golf? Is he a Beatles fan? Does he read spy novels or biographies? What the hell are you talking about being a strong advocate for education and business? You make him sound like a politician."

Bennett chuckled. "He *is* a politician. And that's about all he is." He glanced at her again. "Do you really not know who my dad is?"

"Should I?"

He supposed not necessarily. She was from Louisiana and

his father had represented Georgia. "He was the governor of Georgia until he ran for Senate. He's been a senator for...almost as long as I can remember," Bennett said.

"A senator?" Kennedy asked. "Like a real senator? Like a Washington D.C. senator?"

He nodded. "Yep."

"No way." She shook her head. "I thought you were just rich. Like he was in business or something. Investing. Stuff like Juliet's dad."

Bennett nodded. "Well, I mean, there's money. He inherited most of his share though. The rest is mostly from my mom."

"So your mom's the rich one?" Kennedy dropped her feet from the dash and turned to face him.

"Well, no. I mean, he came from money, too. Old Georgia money that goes way back. But then Mom came into money when I was about five. He took that and invested it and...it grew like crazy." Bennett shrugged. "I guess they're rich together."

He knew what question was coming next and knew that he had to fill Kennedy in on the next part. She was going to find out soon enough.

"How did your mom come into money? Did someone die or something?" Kennedy asked.

"Actually..." He glanced over. "It's a pretty interesting story."

"Spill it."

"My mom's parents won the lottery."

Kennedy's eyes widened. "What? Like the lottery lottery? That they draw for every week?"

"Yep. They went into a gas station, bought some beer and chips, and grabbed a Mega Millions ticket on a whim. Ended up winning big." He paused. "Really big. They divided the money up between them and their two kids. My dad decided to play with it, since it was extra money they hadn't planned on, and so he put it into some really aggressive things, new businesses, tech, that kind of stuff. And it took off."

Kennedy was grinning. "That's pretty cool. How much did they win? Can I ask that? You said really big. Like a million dollars?"

Bennett blew out a breath. "Really big. Like eight million. After taxes."

There was a pause. Then Kennedy said, "Fuuuuuck."

He nodded but couldn't help but grin. "Yep. Eight million. So my mom got two million. Just like that."

"Holy. Shit. So your parents are crazy rich."

He laughed. "Told you it was interesting."

"And your dad invested it," Kennedy said. "And made a killing."

"Yep."

"Okay, that's great. But please tell me *someone* in the family bought *something* completely stupid and excessive and ridiculous."

Oh, he could most definitely do that. "My uncle now owns a drive-in movie theater in the little town where they all grew up. And all he shows are the movies from the seventies and eighties that *he* loves. Basically, it's like his own big living room that he lets other people park in."

Kennedy laughed. "Okay, that's actually kind of great."

"They also only serve snacks he likes. So there's no popcorn because he doesn't like it. But you can get Corn Nuts in every single flavor. And Jelly Bellies."

"That's. Amazing."

"And his wife bought a castle. For their cats. That's about half the size of your grandma's house. And it's purple and sparkles. And they then, of course, had to get more cats."

Kennedy's eyes were wide. "They rescued the cats, I hope."

"Of course. They're good-hearted. If extravagant."

She nodded. "I love it. And you know that I know about having family like that." She grinned at him. "You've been holding out. You have a crazy family, too. Here I thought it was just me."

He shook his head. "Oh no. And it gets better."

"How so?"

"They're Cajun."

"No!"

"Yep. My mom grew up in Louisiana."

"So *that's* why you like the bayou."

He pulled up to a stoplight and looked over at her. "That's not why I like the bayou."

"But you—" She met his gaze and stopped. Then shook her head. "Damn, you're good at that."

"At what?"

"Throwing me off."

He grinned. "I take that as a huge compliment."

"I do not mean that as a compliment."

He lifted a shoulder. "I still take it as one."

Kennedy blew out a breath. "But you have Cajun blood. I mean, they're crazy rich Cajuns, but still Cajuns. So your affinity to the bayou makes sense."

"Maybe." He eased onto the gas again as the light turned green. "That's probably why I was curious about it in the beginning. But that's not why I like it now."

"You can just stop that right there, Mr. Baxter," she said.

"Stop what?"

"All the sweet crap about how I'm the biggest draw to the bayou now."

"Maybe I was going to say I kept coming around because of the crawfish."

"You like the andouille sausage better than the crawfish."

"How do you know that?" Damn, he wished they weren't driving. He'd love to be looking at her and seeing her expressions while they had this conversation.

"I..." She glanced over, clearly realizing she'd given something away that she hadn't meant to.

"You've been paying attention to me, Ms. Landry?" Bennett teased. "I'm touched."

"Yeah, well, don't go reading anything into it. I'm not a sucker for romance like the rest of my family."

"Aren't you?" He shot her a glance. Maybe not romance. She seemed too...practical—or maybe cynical—for that. But she was a sucker for their chemistry. She liked the idea that he was drawn to her and thought of her when he wasn't in Autre and that she was part of the reason he liked it there.

"I'm not," she told him. "It would be nearly impossible for you, or any guy, to top the Landrys in the romance department. I've seen or heard it all."

"Sounds like a challenge."

"Do *not* take it as a challenge." She pointed a finger at him sternly. "Romance makes people stupid. Super stupid. And they end up making decisions that they're then stuck with for the rest of their life."

Bennett couldn't help looking over again after that. She was scowling at the dashboard of his car, though clearly wasn't thinking about the smooth gray leather. "Sounds like you have a reason for that very firm belief."

She looked at him. "I do. And I'm very stubborn, so don't try to talk me out of it."

"I'm aware," he said dryly. He really wanted to know what had turned Kennedy off of romance so fully. And she'd noticed his preference for the sausage. That was something; he didn't care what she said. "I don't think I'm completely dissuaded here. You really are a big part of what I love about the bayou."

She looked at him and her eyes slowly narrowed. "I'll tell you what, Baxter. I'm going to *dissuade* you. Every time you say or do something sappy and romantic, I'm going to say or do something super hot and sexy."

Bennett felt his eyebrows fly toward his hairline. "How is *that* going to dissuade me?"

"Well..." She slid across the seat, closer to him. She put her hand on his thigh just above his knee and then slowly ran it up toward his fly. "Walking around with an erection at various inopportune times could make for a long weekend."

Bennett put his hand down on top of hers, stopping the movement. Yeah, she had a point.

"Maybe I'll make sure that I'm only romantic and sweet when we're alone and in a private place."

She grinned up at him. She was right there. Kissing distance.

And he was driving.

He forced his attention back on the road.

"That's fine," she said, leaning back and sliding back to her side.

He both appreciated and hated that at the same time.

"But I didn't say I'd be pulling out the sexy stuff at the same exact time you were romantic." She returned her boots to the dashboard.

Bennett swallowed as her skirt pulled up her thighs again.

"You do all the romantic stuff you want," she said. "I'll be keeping track. And paying you back for every one of them. When it best suits me."

Damn, this woman was a handful. But he couldn't help his grin.

He hadn't even told her yet that they were going to be in Savannah for five days, not just for the weekend.

ONE OF THE MANY PERKS TO FLYING VIA PRIVATE PLANE WAS THAT there was very little wait time at the airport.

They were the only ones on the plane, and the main cabin

on the plane looked very much like a well-decorated living room in someone's penthouse apartment. Bennett chose one of the high-backed leather chairs, but after she'd paused in the doorway and gave a breathy, "Holy shit," Kennedy had chosen the long couch that took up the length of one wall, complete with throw pillows.

She lounged on the plush cushions, tucking a gold satin pillow under her head and stretching her long, bare legs out against the cream-colored upholstery. She looked like a cat settling in for a nap. "Wow, you left out two really important words when you talked about this trip, Bennett," she told him.

"Hot sex?" he asked.

She gave him a grin. "You don't have to say *those* words. Those are a given. Like hors d'oeuvres and champagne." She paused and gave him a tiny frown. "This is where you assure me there will be hors d'oeuvres and champagne."

"Lots of both," he said with a nod.

She sighed in relief. "No, the words you left out were *private plane*. I would have jumped at this chance to go with you."

He chuckled, settling in to appreciate the view. And he didn't mean out the window. The tiny top she wore pulled up to expose more of her smooth stomach, and the stretchy fabric of her skirt hugged her curves and moved with her as she wiggled against the ridiculously expensive fabric covering the couch. He felt his cock stirring and decided that he should probably just get used to that for the next few days.

Kennedy oozed confidence and sex appeal. She was clearly completely comfortable in her skin. No doubt that came in part from spending time on a pageant stage from a young age. She'd gotten used to parading around in front of people. That had to make someone less self-conscious when they were offstage, didn't it? Or maybe it was just her. Lord knew, her family had very little concern about what other people thought of them.

"You didn't exactly fight me on the idea of coming to Savannah," he commented. "You almost seemed excited about it."

"I love stuffed mushrooms," she said, of course not giving him an inch. "I'll eat my weight in stuffed mushrooms. You might want to notify the catering staff." She rolled to her back and tucked her hands under the pillow behind her head.

Lying with her left side toward him, he could again study her tattoo and he wondered if she had others. She wore lots of tank tops and shorts and skirts. He would have noticed, he was sure. He'd certainly studied her body every chance he'd had. So what was the significance of this tattoo?

"Tell me about your tattoo."

Kennedy was a straight-shooter. Her whole family was very upfront and honest. Bennett also wanted to get used to being like that. He'd spent far too much time with lawyers and politicians who measured everything they said. Not to mention his mother. She'd worked hard to leave her Cajun roots behind, and she had to really concentrate when she got frustrated or angry or even overly excited. It seemed when she felt strong emotions was when her accent and the slang she'd grown up with would slip out. So she'd trained herself to be even-keeled and always in control of her emotions. As a kid, Bennett and his brother would sometimes poke at her just to hear her call them *couyon*.

She looked down at her arm. "What about it?"

"What's it mean? Why'd you pick that particular one?" He let his eyes roam over her from head to toe, making sure she noticed. "Why only that one?"

She arched a brow but rolled to her side and propped her head on her hand. "It represents a path that's like life. Twists and turns, a few thorns mixed in with lots of areas of beauty along the way. It's all tied together along my strongest side, which also happens to be the side where my heart is."

Bennett wasn't sure why he was surprised by her serious,

insightful, lovely answer. It was probably because she was usually a smart-ass with him. But yet, even then she was clever and witty and intelligent.

He nodded. "It's beautiful."

She smiled. "Thanks. And, as you'll see, the biggest flowers are near my pussy, beside my breast, and over my heart."

Bennett knew she was trying to rattle him. And it worked. Whether it was the "as you'll see," which sounded like a promise he was, by God, going to hold her to, or it was hearing her say "pussy," he wasn't sure, but he had to swallow hard.

"Ask me why, Bennett," she said. Her voice was a little husky.

It was clear from the way she was looking at him that she knew the effect she was having.

"Why?"

"Because those are the parts of me that make me the most feminine and the most powerful. The biggest blooms are there because it reminds me that even if those parts are the most hidden, private parts, they are also the parts that make me most beautiful and that I don't have to show those parts, or any parts, to anyone to be judged worthy."

He stared at her for a few long moments. He didn't need to reassure her. He didn't need to tell her she was right. She knew. She didn't need him to tell her anything at all.

"That's pretty fucking hot," he finally said. He didn't mean the roses inked where they were. He meant the reason they were where they were. And he knew she knew what he meant.

She gave him a slow smile.

"And is this sexy payback for some romantic thing I did without realizing it?" he asked. "Because it's working."

She rolled back to her back and crossed one long leg over the other, getting comfortable on the couch. "Whisking me off to a fancy weekend party on a private plane? That's some *Pretty Woman* stuff there, Baxter."

"I didn't mean it to be romantic. It's efficient."

"Well, you're screwed if the romantic stuff just happens without you even intending it."

She stretched. He gave a little groan. She grinned.

But so did he. He loved that she was comfortable here with him, with their sexual chemistry, and the inevitable result of that chemistry once they had a bed and a long night at their disposal. And because making Kennedy smile had become one of his favorite hobbies about five minutes after meeting her.

The rest of the flight was spent with casual conversation on a variety of ordinary topics. She'd paged through a magazine. He'd looked over some work papers. She'd curled up with her phone and headphones to watch a movie. He'd pretended to read a book while trying not to watch her the entire time like a creepy stalker.

"Do you have any ink besides that tattoo on your shoulder?" she asked as they pulled out of the airport parking garage in the back of the huge black SUV that had been sent by their car service to pick them up.

"Oh, you noticed that?" he asked her.

She'd seen him without his shirt when he'd been down in Autre to help put the new dock in the water. She'd pretended to be annoyed with him because he'd ended up needing first aid on his arm, but she'd fussed over what was nothing more than a small cut as if he'd almost lost the limb, and he had to wonder if she'd been just a tiny bit worried about him for a few minutes there.

"If you're asking if I checked you out from the office window while you were stripping down and parading around in nothing but your boxers, then yes. Yes, I did," she said. "And I gotta say, I'm in *favor* of you keeping up that gym membership and listening to your trainer."

"You think I have a trainer? That I don't just take care of myself?" he asked.

She gave him a look and he laughed.

"His name is Greg," Bennett confessed with a grin.

"Yeah, tell Greg I'm making him cookies as thanks," Kennedy said. "Oh, wait, he probably doesn't eat cookies. I'll make him..." She frowned. "Fuck, I don't really make anything that you could call *health food*. I guess I'll buy him a new gym bag or something."

Bennett laughed. "You just stay away from Greg. I'll tell him that you're appreciative."

"I can't meet Greg?" she asked. "Why's that?"

"Because you're hot and into guys with big muscles who can lift cars over their heads and shit. No way am I introducing you."

"First off, he can lift a *car* over his head? I mean, I'm not sure how useful that really is. Then again, if he can lift a car, he can lift an airboat and *that* could be handy," she said, clearly teasing him. "Second...are you jealous of the idea of me with another guy?" She braced her hand on the seat between them and leaned in a little.

Bennett knew she was setting him up for trouble. She had that little glint in her eye.

But the bigger problem than her being trouble was him liking that about her. A lot.

"Nah. I know what you really want."

"Stuffed mushrooms," she said with a nod. "And pigs in a blanket. If you've got mustard. But not honey mustard." She mimed gagging. "I want *hot* mustard."

She also wanted a guy who wasn't easy. Who she couldn't figure out with only a half-assed effort. Someone who made her think a little bit. That's why she was attracted to Bennett. He was different. She couldn't quite put her finger on him. The bayou boys were good old chocolate chip cookies. Solid. Enjoyable. A staple in her life. But he was crème brûlée. Or, he supposed, Bananas Foster, if Leo insisted. He'd just have to warn her about the itching and hives that went with that.

"Hot mustard and a guy who can make you forget that his hands ever do anything other than make your pussy throb with need, then drip with sweetness, and stretch you out for his cock to fuck you into the hardest orgasms of your life."

Her mouth literally fell open. He fought his smug smile. Maybe she would eventually realize that she was not going to keep the upper hand with him, even if she did get it once in a while.

But he kind of hoped she wouldn't realize that.

He leaned in, took her chin between his thumb and forefinger and brought her ear to his mouth. "And that's not even including what he's going to be able to do with his tongue."

She blew out a long slow breath. Then asked, "Have you ever had a blow job in the back of one of these cars on the way to your parents' house?"

He sat back and let her go. "No."

"Awesome. I love firsts."

She reached for his pants, but he caught her wrists. "What are you doing?"

"Dirty stuff every time you get romantic, remember?"

"*I* was just dirty."

"Talking about all that foreplay? Making sure I'm throbbing and dripping and stretched out—" She said each word slowly and huskily, "—before you take me hard and give me the best orgasms of my *life*? Dude, *that* is romantic. You realize most guys are just about getting off themselves, right?"

She sat back on her side with a self-satisfied smile he wanted to kiss off of her lips. Badly.

Bennett shook his head. He was hard and aching listening to her. Even though he'd started it. And she knew it. "You're trouble."

"Yep. And you're stuck with me for the whole weekend." She looked very pleased with herself.

"Well, 'til Tuesday." Bennett looked down at his phone, fighting his smile as he pretended to check for texts.

"Tuesday?"

"I mean, yes, it will be the whole weekend. Too. But also Monday and Tuesday."

"We're staying until Tuesday?"

He glanced over. "I didn't mention that?"

She lifted both brows. "No, no you didn't."

"Huh." He looked back down at his phone. It might be a long five days, but he was already having more fun than he'd had in the five months before he'd met Kennedy.

"Well, I didn't pack for two extra days. Guess I'll be going without panties for a couple of days," she said, settling back in her seat.

There she was getting the last word again. And making him hard again.

And there he was not minding it a bit. Again.

"Okay, so Dad's side of the family bought this house," Kennedy said, as they pulled through the iron gates and started over the cobblestones that led to the "house" that Bennett Baxter called home.

It was a small castle. She'd fight anyone who tried to tell her otherwise.

"That's right." Bennett sounded amused. "This house has been in the family for a hundred years."

"Woo-boy, I'll bet there are some ghosts with good stories in there," she said. "My grandma would love that."

"No hauntings. Sorry."

Kennedy looked over at him. "Oh, that's not true. They're

just not showing themselves to you. That doesn't mean they're not there."

He lifted a brow. "That house is *not* haunted."

"It is. It's gotta be. There are definitely spirits that wanted to hang around this place."

The car pulled up in front of the huge doors. She started to reach for the door, but he grabbed her elbow.

"The house is *not* haunted, Kennedy."

She pressed her lips together and nodded.

"Seriously. Never heard of a single ghost sighting."

"Okay."

"Really."

"*Okay*."

He narrowed his eyes. "You've seen a ghost?"

She shrugged. "Sure. Of course, I live on the bayou."

"Come on."

"You come on. There are spirits all over. Good and bad."

Good and bad. Right. Was she messing with him? It was about fifty-fifty, he figured. "You don't worry about the bad ones?"

"Well, not when I've got the gris-gris bag my grandma made me. But that's back home in Autre."

Bennett sighed. He didn't know if the Landrys actually dabbled in voodoo or not. He knew they went to the local church so it wasn't their primary religion or anything, but voodoo seeped into many of the Louisiana traditions and legends. It wouldn't surprise him a bit if there were talismans or charms to be found around the homes and businesses. He had no doubt that Kennedy had a gris-gris bag—a traditional voodoo charm that consisted of a small cloth bag filled with herbs, stones and personal items that would ward off evil spirits—that Ellie had made for her. "Of course."

"But if you get scared tonight, I'll be happy to come sleep in your room."

"You'd scare the ghosts off?"

She snorted. "How would I do that?"

"Then how are you going to protect me?" he asked, his grip gentled and he ran his thumb over the sensitive skin of her inner elbow.

"If I'm with you in your room tonight, you'll be too distracted to notice anything else going on."

That wasn't a bad point. "We'll talk about the sleeping arrangements later," he told her as the huge front door swung open and his mother stepped out onto the porch.

"Oh, let's not. Let's sneak around," Kennedy said. "That's way more fun."

He gave her an eye-roll. "Stay right there. I'll come around and open the door for you." He started to get out.

"I can open my own door."

"I know."

"So that's stupid."

"Humor me."

"I might consider it romantic," she warned. "Which means I'm totally going to feel your ass as we walk up those steps to greet your mother."

He ducked his head back into the car. "Well, the joke's on you," he told her. "You're trying to give me a constant hard-on with that stuff? Thing is, I'm already hard for you just seeing you smile and hearing you talk about gris-gris bags."

"That's pathetic," she told him, but she was clearly fighting a smile.

"I know."

"And kind of romantic."

"Yeah."

"So I'm definitely not wearing panties to dinner tonight and I'm hoping that you'll pull me into a dark corner and finger me."

Bennett dropped his head and blew out a breath. "You're going to kill me."

"That's a nice change," she said. "Usually, people want to kill *me*."

Bennett opened the car door for her, which wasn't really that romantic—it was more a stupid patriarchal tradition that she really wished would die—and then threaded his fingers with hers as they climbed the wide stone steps to the porch.

She suspected the hand holding was to keep her from pinching his ass. But it was also nice—and yeah, a little romantic—and she liked it more than she should.

When they got to the top, though, she was fully focused on Bennett's mom.

She was a Cajun. Kennedy hadn't been expecting that. She felt more comfortable instantly just knowing that.

"Hi, Mom," Bennett greeted, leaning in to kiss his mother's cheek.

"Hello, Bennett." His mom gave him a little smile then turned her attention to Kennedy. "Hello."

"Mom, this is Kennedy Landry. Kennedy, this is my mother, Maria," Bennett said.

"Kennedy," Maria Baxter said with a smile as her eyes traveled from the top of Kennedy's head to the toes of her combat boots. "I've heard a lot about you and your family."

"Hi, Mrs. Baxter! Thank you for inviting me." Kennedy stepped close and put her arms around the other woman's shoulders, giving her a quick hug.

When she stepped back, she realized that Maria looked stunned. Okay, not a hugger. Kennedy made note. She wasn't really, either, but it seemed *everyone* else was, so she'd decided to make a good impression with Bennett's mom.

Might have miscalculated that.

"Okay, then. Please come on in." Maria turned and preceded them into the gigantic house. She wore wide-legged white pants with a baby blue sleeveless tunic, all in a silky material that moved in a flowy way that made Maria seem to glide over the stone porch and through the door.

Kennedy felt Bennett's hand on her lower back. "Oops," she said quietly to him.

"Don't worry about her," he said. "She's just surprised to see you."

Kennedy glanced up at him, then realized what he'd just said. She stopped short and elbowed him in the side. "What?" she hissed. "She didn't know I was coming?"

"No."

"Ben—"

"Is everything okay?" Maria asked, turning back in the middle of an enormous foyer.

Kennedy was not pleased with Bennett and she *was* going to let him know all about it, but she wasn't going to add any tension to this moment. For some reason, she didn't want Maria to think there were any problems between them. There was something about how Maria looked at her that made Kennedy feel like she was back up on the pageant stage and something inside her clicked into place. That something that reminded her that at any point she had the option to walk out. She could have walked off that stage and left the whole thing behind her. When *she* decided to. Which she'd eventually done.

She had been there by choice, and *she* got to decide how far she went with everything.

And the same applied here. Maria Baxter didn't control how long Kennedy was going to be standing next to Bennett. No matter how many times she looked at Kennedy's tattoos with a mix of curiosity and dismay.

"Everything is fine," she told Maria with her best pageant smile. Then she looked up at Bennett with that same smile.

He also wasn't in charge here. He might like to think he was, or that they were partners in deciding how this relationship went or some stupid shit like that, but it wasn't true. Kennedy got to decide what she did, when she did it, and how she did it. She wasn't going to become a Leo, hanging onto someone even long after she should let go just because of some crazy idea about romance and love.

"Right, honey?" she added, snuggling closer to Bennett's side.

Bennett was a smart guy though. Wisely, a flicker of apprehension crossed his face before he nodded. "Right. Totally fine."

Yeah, he knew that wasn't true. Which was perfect.

5

BENNETT'S HAND SLIPPED FROM KENNEDY'S BACK TO HER ASS.

Kennedy gritted her teeth. She supposed that in his mind she should appreciate the obvious signal that they were *together*. If his mother hadn't already realized what all of this was about. But this all seemed a little on-the-nose.

Maria sighed. "Your grandmother is also staying here. Just so you know that you and Kennedy will not be sharing a room. At least not...obviously."

"I'm thirty years old," Bennett said mildly. "I don't think Grandmother would believe that I was a virgin even if we had Father Brad tell her so."

"Father Brad would never say that," Maria said, rubbing the middle of her forehead with one perfectly manicured finger. "He's been hearing your confessions since you were a little boy."

Bennett grinned.

Kennedy shook her head slightly. This had hints of Landry craziness to it. They were *almost* teasing about sex. She couldn't quite tell if Maria was actually teasing or was trying to bite back the urge to tell Bennett that he was grounded for the next two weeks. It was as if him being a grown man and immune to her scolding was giving her the beginnings of a migraine.

"And unless you're going to propose to Kennedy and have the wedding ceremony in the backyard this evening, then you will not be sharing a room as far as your grandmother knows," Maria said. She dropped her hand. Then she narrowed her eyes. "And so help me, Bennett, if you propose to her and tell me to throw together a wedding in the backyard tonight, I will disown you."

"You already have the tents set up and caterers and music coming," Bennett said.

Kennedy elbowed him for that. This was getting unfunny.

"For the friends and family cocktail party for your father's retirement," Maria said.

"I'm happy to share. Dad can make his speech first and all of his friends can do their toasts. I'll hit my knee after everyone's gone through the buffet, how's that?"

"Oh, please do that," Kennedy said. "I'd love to say hell no to marrying you in front of a big crowd." She turned to Maria. "Will the party tomorrow night be even bigger? Can we wait until then? I'll sleep on the couch tonight."

Bennett laughed. "There will be a *ton* of stuffed mushrooms tonight though," he said. "By the time I ask you, you'll be well fed and happy."

"Not even stuffed mushrooms can make me *that* happy," Kennedy said.

"How about the champagne?" he asked.

"Nope."

"How about a chocolate fountain?"

"N—" She stopped and frowned. "There will be a chocolate fountain?"

"Yep. With strawberries to dip in it. And marshmallows."

"What about shortbread cookies?" She'd been to a wedding

in New Orleans that had had a chocolate fountain at the reception. She'd wanted to take a bath in it.

"I will personally guarantee shortbread cookies if needed," Bennett said, looking into her eyes.

Kennedy took a deep breath. "Dammit," she said softly. She also made a quick note that this whole thing was a little romantic. He'd pay for that. She looked over at Maria. "Sorry. I'm going to be powerless at that point. It will be a definite yes."

Maria rolled her eyes. "Wonderful. You found a smart-ass just like you," she said to Bennett.

Kennedy considered that a compliment. She grinned up at him as she felt him squeeze her butt.

"Oh no," he told his mother. "She's a *way* bigger smart-ass than I am."

Maria sighed. "I suppose Kennedy can take the room next to yours."

Damn right she could. Kennedy felt stupidly triumphant at that.

"That's probably the best choice," Bennett said with a nod.

"And, of course, exactly how you expected this to turn out," Maria said.

"Pretty much."

"I'll, of course, have some gowns sent over for you," Maria said, looking at Kennedy.

"Oh, that's not necessary," Bennett said. "Kennedy is fine."

Kennedy frowned up at him. She most certainly was not fine.

"You never once said the word 'gown' to me, Baxter," Kennedy told him. "I'm not fine."

"You don't have to wear a gown," Bennett said. "For God's sake, the party is in the garden."

"Well, tonight's gown is more of a dress," Maria conceded. "But tomorrow the party is in the ballroom."

There was a ballroom here. Awesome.

"I could definitely use some help with wardrobe," Kennedy told her. "Bennett kind of sprung this trip on me, too."

Maria gave her son a look that said clearly his plan had been stupid, and he wasn't getting points with *any* of the women involved. "I'm happy to."

"Kennedy, how you usually dress...your dresses and things...are *fine*," Bennett told her.

Oh, she was sure they were. If Bennett was trying to make a point to his mother that he was...going in a different direction with his sex life. But she wasn't here to play games with his family and their friends, and she wasn't here to be a pawn in *his* games. "I trust that you'll let your mother put the new *gowns* on *your* credit card?" she asked him.

He sighed. "Of course."

Kennedy nodded. "Yeah, I'm going to *Pretty Woman* the hell out of this. Prepare yourself."

"I should probably see that movie sometime."

"It's probably too late to do you any good," Kennedy told him honestly.

Bennett gave her butt a little pinch. "I'll just skip to the end."

The very romantic, grand gesture ending of the Cinderella-esque story where the guy overcame his fears to climb the fire escape to rescue the prostitute-turned-love-of-his-life? Yeah, no. The last thing she needed was him getting any ideas about the happily ever after stuff. Chocolate fountain or not. "I'll summarize it for you," Kennedy said.

"Okay." He looked vastly amused.

"He gives her anything she wants. And she gives him..."

One eyebrow went up and the corner of his mouth curled.

"...some really great advice that makes him a better person."

Bennett chuckled. "Can't wait to have all your...advice."

Maria cleared her throat. "Do you need Chester to help with the bags?"

She also gave a little stink eye to Kennedy's suitcase and Kennedy rolled the bag closer to her leg. "Oh, I don't trust anyone but myself and Bennett to carry this," she said.

Maria arched a brow. "Oh?"

"Well, this—" Kennedy swept her hand down her body. "Doesn't happen accidentally or easily, you know."

"Yes, well..." Maria clearly didn't know how to finish that sentence.

Bennett grabbed Kennedy's bag and his own and then tipped his head toward the staircase to the left. Kennedy headed up in front of him.

"Take a right," he said at the top.

She did and started across the space that overlooked the foyer below then became a hallway that led to what appeared to be six rooms. "Good lord."

Bennett chuckled. "Our rooms are the last two."

"Where's the bathroom?" she asked as she headed in that direction. The ceiling in the hallway was a good twelve feet high, and the walls were decorated with gorgeous art pieces and painted a soft green.

"We'll have a bathroom to share that joins our rooms."

She looked back at him. "Is that right?"

He nodded. "Doors lock from both sides. You'll only have company if you want it."

"Big shower?"

"Huge."

"What's the showerhead situation?"

"What do you mean?"

"Is it detachable or what?" she asked.

He gave her a wink. "No. But there are like six, maybe eight, different ones mounted all around."

"Oh yeah," she said. "I'm not gonna need your company with that setup."

He laughed. "Well, at least let me watch."

She sent him a sly smile. "Maybe as torture for not telling your mother that I was even going to be here. And not telling me that she didn't know."

"Uh, yeah. Sorry about that. But it's kind of a...thing with her and I."

"You showing up with girls she's not expecting to see?"

He stopped in front of one of the doors. He set the bags down and opened the door. "This one's yours."

Kennedy stepped through the doorway and into the room that looked exactly as she'd been expecting it to look. The room was done in a soft blue and cream with deep navy accents. There was a four-poster bed, a thick duvet, a cream-colored armchair with an ottoman that had a throw blanket draped over it and a reading lamp beside it. There was also a huge fireplace and an honest-to-god armoire. Which was really cool. The wood matched the rest of the woodwork in the room from the moldings to the fireplace mantel, and the front had an elaborate painted design that used the blue and cream of the room. But the best part of the room, the part that made Kennedy almost forget that Bennett had brought her here as a surprise, to both her and his mother, was the dressing table.

She actually gasped when she saw it.

It took up nearly the entire portion of the wall across from the bed and just to the left of the door.

It was painted cream as well and had gorgeous spindle legs, a huge middle surface with other shelves at varying heights, a multitude of drawers, and a gigantic round mirror hanging over the center.

"I'm never leaving this room," she said, turning to face Bennett.

"I can sneak some stuffed mushrooms up here, but I'm not sure about the chocolate fountain."

"Hey, that reminds me," she said, stepping close to him, tipping her head back to look up at him. "You're in trouble."

"I am?"

"You brought me here to shock your mother."

"I don't—"

"That's not cool, Bennett."

"That's not why I brought you, Kennedy."

"You brought me here to prove a point to your mother."

He took a deep breath. "Yes."

"You love your mother."

"I do. But I don't want to live a high society life in Savannah, rubbing elbows with millionaires and politicians and CEOs. I want to live with real people and do real things. Work every day doing something that matters."

"You want to live in Autre and work with Boys of the Bayou," Kennedy summarized.

"Yes," Bennett confessed. "I don't know if I'm tour guide material, but expanding the business and working on conservation efforts and finding ways to keep the coastline from eroding and fighting the big companies that are encroaching on the natural habitats are all things I'm passionate about."

She looked up at him and sighed. *He can't rotate your tires, Ken,* she told herself. But the thing was, he could learn. It wasn't brain surgery. And hell, she could do that herself while he was off saving the swamp frogs or whatever the hell he wanted to do. He just had to be hot and love the bayou, didn't he?

But did he really belong on the bayou long-term? She did not want to be stuck madly in love with him and unable to let go when he decided to leave.

And she did *not* want to live in Savannah.

"Well, if you have a problem with your mother, you need to tell her. I don't want to be this little pawn in your game of you-can't-tell-me-what-to-do."

"That's not why I brought you here," he repeated. "I wanted my mother to meet you because I knew that she'd take my feelings about you and the bayou more seriously if I brought you to this party. But," he continued before she could speak. "That's certainly not the whole reason I wanted you here."

"Oh?"

"I like being with you."

"You don't know me very well."

"I want to get to know you better."

"I've warned you about the romance stuff," she said.

"And I brought you here because of this." He put his hand at the back of her neck and brought her forward.

He kissed her, his lips meeting hers firmly but gently. At first.

When she gave a little moan, he moved in, splayed a hand on her lower back to press her into him, and opened his mouth. He tipped her head to the side and deepened the kiss and Kennedy let him. In fact, she gripped his belt with both hands and arched closer. Next to the chocolate fountain and stuffed mushrooms, this was also a huge part of what she'd been hoping for this weekend.

Okay, this was most of it. Even without the hors d'oeuvres. She'd expected to have a fun, sexy time with this guy. And to get him, *this*, out of her system.

Bennett turned her and backed her up against the wall next to the door. He kicked the door shut and as it thudded closed, he pressed into her. She could feel how hard he was and she was suddenly hot and aching.

Kennedy let her head tip back, thunking against the wall, and Bennett dragged his mouth down the side of her neck, making heat lick down her arm and into her belly. She swallowed. "Now if we could combine *this* with that chocolate fountain, I'd probably forgive you for anything."

He chuckled against her collarbone. "You say that as if you think I don't have the means or motivation." He ran his hand up her side to cup a breast, running his thumb over her nipple.

She sucked in a quick breath.

"And I believe you said something about someone getting fingered?"

She would have sucked in another breath, but that first one was still lodged in her chest. "That—" She coughed. "That was after I ran around panty-less all night because you'd been too sweet."

"Take them off."

Kennedy felt her stomach flip. Bennett Baxter had this thing where he could be laid-back and friendly with her family and the people in Ellie's bar, even a little goofy when it came to playing around with fishing tackle. But then he'd turn his attention on her and he'd get this deep voice, this I'm-in-charge tone, and her panties would just say, "well, we're clearly not needed here."

"I think that you—"

He took her nipple between his thumb and finger and squeezed. "Take them off, Kennedy."

Fuck, yes.

Nearly panting, she reached up under her skirt and caught the top of her panties with her thumb.

"Pull your skirt up."

She made the mistake of looking up at him. His eyes were swirling with heat that made her wobble slightly and she had to grab onto his belt to keep herself up. "Damn, you think you're going to get to be bossy like that?" she asked him.

"Push me away," he challenged.

Yeah, she wasn't going to do that.

"I'll let go if you really want me to," he told her.

She knew that. Even if he didn't know that her brothers could easily feed him to the alligators deep in the bayou and no one would ever find a trace—and hell, that her grandfather, grand*mother*, and everyone else in her family could, too—Bennett wouldn't mess with her if he wasn't certain she wasn't fully on board.

"I know you will," she told him honestly, wanting him to know she understood that. There was a time for flippant and sassy and a time for him to know that they were absolutely on the same page.

This page. They were absolutely on this page together.

"Do you want me to let go?"

She wet her lips. "If you do, I will fill your bed with fire ants."

See? That was a moment where sassy was better than being totally sincere. Because sincere would have sounded like, *If you don't touch me right now, I'm going to cry and beg and maybe tell my grandma on you.*

"I definitely don't want that to happen."

"Good."

"So pull your skirt up and lose the panties."

She took a deep breath and did both. She tossed the bright purple thong to the side, her skin tingly as Bennett's eyes tracked from her ankles, up her legs, and right to the spot that ached for him. His gaze lingered on the rose bloom that did, indeed, spread its petals toward her pussy.

"Damn, you're gorgeous," he said gruffly. He reached out and ran the pads of his first three fingers over the ink. "Bet this rose smells pretty fucking sweet."

How did this suit-wearing, science-loving rich kid make her want to do such naughty things to him? *For* him? That was the weirdest thing. She wasn't really the "yes, sir" kind of girl. But for Bennett? She was starting to think she could be.

"I'm flexible, but maybe not quite *that* flexible," she said, moving her feet apart slightly. The move hiked the skirt a little higher, baring her completely. "Why don't you tell me?"

Bennett's jaw tightened for just a moment, then the hand holding her head tightened in her hair and he brought her forward for a deep kiss. He stroked his tongue along hers, firmly, possessively, and Kennedy's clit begged for the same attention.

"Put your hands on the wall behind you. And don't move them," he said, tearing his mouth away.

She did. Without even thinking. Damn, the guy was good. Don't move them? Seriously? But then he went to his knees and put his nose against the rose tattoo, breathing in deeply, and Kennedy not only planted her palms flat on the wall behind her, she wished she could dig into it and hang on.

"Ben—"

He dragged his tongue over the rose as he lifted her leg and propped her knee over his shoulder. The position opened her thighs fully, right in front of his face.

And her clit didn't go without attention for long. He ran his tongue over every swirl of the tattoo, making Kennedy whimper and lean hard into the wall to stay upright. But he worked his way toward the crease of her hip, over to her mound, then down to the nub that was aching and throbbing. He licked, then sucked. Her hips bucked, pressing closer and her eyes slid shut.

"Watch me," he growled, barely lifting his mouth away from her.

Heat washing through her, Kennedy looked down, watching as he tongued her, feeling and seeing the licks, the sucks, even the nips of his teeth as her climax tightened, deep in her pelvis. A spot so deep she didn't think she'd ever felt it before began to pulse. Her whole body tingled. She lifted a hand to her breast, squeezing one of her nipples.

"Fuck yes," Bennett encouraged, looking up, his eyes heavy with lust. "Pull your top up."

"I moved my hands."

"Pull your fucking top up and play with your nipples."

She shivered. Oh, she *loved* this dominant Bennett. Damn. Too much, maybe.

She did without any more teasing. She *needed* to be bare. To be exposed. She wanted him to see her, she wanted to touch herself, she wanted every bit of stimulation she could get.

As she pulled the fitted top up and the cups of her bra down, her breasts and nearly painfully hard nipples now fully on display for him, he slid a finger into her.

She hissed out a breath, pinching her nipple, as he moved the finger in and out.

This was so good. Why was this so good? She'd figure it out later. For now, she *really* wanted that orgasm that was right there, nearly within her grasp.

She arched her back, pressing closer to him and he took her clit in his mouth, thankfully not taking the chance to tease or even talk dirty. He just sucked on her, exactly as she needed him to, while sliding a second finger deep into her pussy.

Yes, right there. That was almost exactly what she needed.

She tugged on her nipple. "Harder," she begged.

He complied. He sucked harder and picked up the pace of his fingers. He kept pushing her closer and closer to the crest. Then he said, "When I lean in to kiss another woman on the cheek tonight, she'll be able to smell you on my skin."

That sent Kennedy crashing over the edge. She cried out his name and clamped down around his fingers as she came. The orgasm hitting hard.

She slumped back against the wall, pulling in air, her hands once again flat against the sturdy surface.

Holy crap. What was that? How had *that* been what sent her over the edge? She wasn't possessive. And certainly not about Bennett. But the very dirty thought that she would have somehow marked Bennett, that another woman might be able to *smell* Kennedy on him later on...that had definitely worked. That was definitely dirty and gave her a very stupid, pretty frightening, sense of satisfaction.

And he knew that it had worked.

Dammit.

If he knew that dirty and possessive worked, he'd use it again. And she, clearly, wasn't going to be able to fight it.

She felt him moving, her leg lowered to the floor, and a big, hot, hard man pressed into her, kissing her deeply.

Kennedy wrapped her arms around his neck and opened her mouth. She tasted herself on him and found that also dirty and very satisfying.

She was in big trouble here. Yet she felt herself already embracing the idea. If they were here for the next few days and he would keep putting his mouth right where it had just been, then Kennedy figured she might as well enjoy all of this for the time it would last.

"*This* is also why I wanted to bring you along," he said, lifting his head and brushing back a few strands of hair that had escaped her ponytail.

"I would have let you do *that* back in Autre. And pretty much anywhere else you wanted to do it," she said, still a little breathless.

"But here you're not going to be distracted by work or your family. Here, you're all mine," he said, kissing her again.

That possessive note in *his* voice made her already happy inner muscles ripple a little. There was something to that theory, too. The Landrys were very entwined in everything every one of them did. All the time. If Bennett wanted her full attention for any stretch of time, getting her away from Autre had been a smart idea.

"But you keep saying that's where you want to be long-term," she reminded him, rubbing against him, unable to help herself. She wanted more of him. Of him touching her, but she hadn't even gotten her hands on his bare chest yet. "They will always be there." Why was she even teasing with conversation about "long-term" and how Bennett and she would handle being together with the family always around?

"That's why this trip seemed like the perfect way to get things established between us before we start dating back there."

"We're going to start dating back there?" she repeated, then laughed lightly. "Thanks for letting me know."

He gave her a slow smile that was completely confident and very sexy. "See, if we were dating in Autre, you might not even realize it. It would just seem like we were hanging out at crawfish boils and on the pontoon boats on the weekends or at Ellie's after hours. Even if I pushed you up against a wall and went down on you, making you come in my mouth like you'd never had your pussy eaten so well in your life—"

Kennedy actually had to squeeze her thighs together as her pussy wholeheartedly agreed with every cocky word he said.

"—you'd still be able to chalk it up to just a hot moment or having too many beers or letting curiosity win for one night."

She just pressed her lips together. Those all sounded like things she might have tried to use as an excuse.

"And you'd be able to immerse yourself back into your regular life and normal routine and not think about it anymore afterward."

He ran the pad of his thumb over her bottom lip.

"But here, there's none of that. Here, you are not just on *my* schedule and on my turf, but when I push you up against the wall, or fuck you from behind in the shower, or tell you to suck my cock behind the gazebo, or eat chocolate from the chocolate fountain off your gorgeous tits, it will all be because you want it, from me, and you won't be able to run away from it and all the things it makes you feel afterward."

Kennedy stared up at him. Crap. Right now was when she really should say something sassy and sarcastic and glib. But not one thing came to mind except *this guy knows me and I'm screwed.*

Bennett moved his hand, kissed her again, then stepped

back. "My room is right through there," he said, pointing in the direction of the door to her left. "I'm going to go freshen up. I'm guessing Mom has dresses on the way for you. Don't let her pressure you into anything. I like you exactly as you are."

He ran a hand down her hip, smoothing her skirt down. Kennedy hadn't even realized it had still been hiked up.

"And by the way…you taste as good as you smell."

Then he stepped back and grabbed his suitcase and headed for the door that led to the bathroom between the rooms.

She watched him saunter out of the room, cocky and clearly very pleased with himself even if he was walking away with a massive erection.

As the door closed behind him, Kennedy sucked in a deep breath and blew it out.

The guy shines his shoes, for God's sake, she reminded herself.

But now that she knew what he could do with his tongue, he could have a shoe polish *collection* and a set of books about the history of shoe-shining and she wouldn't care.

———

BENNETT STEPPED INTO HIS ROOM WITH A FULL-OF-HIMSELF, LIFE-is-really-good, halfway-in-love grin on his face, he was sure.

That fact was confirmed by the, "Damn, I haven't seen you look that happy since you talked Poppy Parsons into going to prom with you."

Bennett realized that he should have been expecting Duke Chastain to be waiting for him. "Not true," Bennett said, setting his suitcase to the side. "I've *never* been this happy."

Duke laughed, from where he was slumped in the armchair near the window. "I'd shake your hand, but I have a feeling I know where your hands have been."

Bennett grinned and propped himself against the headboard of his bed, kicking his shoes off and stretching his legs out on the mattress. "You'd be right."

"So I was right not to interrupt you and the lovely Kennedy to introduce myself?"

Duke gave him a sly grin that told Bennett that his friend had a pretty good idea what he and Kennedy had been up to next door.

"*Very* good call," Bennett agreed.

"Then you're also welcome for keeping my mother and wife from coming to say hello."

"My mom told *you* that Kennedy was here but not them? I suppose she was hoping they'd walk in and interrupt us."

Duke chuckled. "Oh no, she told all of us about Kennedy. My mother's reaction was 'Oh, well, I can't wait to meet her' and she immediately started for the stairs."

"Which means, my mother texted your mother ahead and told her she needed some reinforcements."

"You've got it." Duke grinned. "Good thing Jo was with me," he said of his wife, Jolene. "She went rushing in with gossip about Delilah Bedford."

"Oh yeah? What was the gossip?"

"No idea. There's always a lot to choose from with Delilah," Duke said. "Or she could have been making something up. Anyway, Jo's got you. For now. Of course, you can't keep Kennedy from my mother and Jo forever. She's dying of curiosity."

Bennett gave him a grin. "Why's that?"

"She thinks she has a really good idea about the type of woman you'd eventually fall for. We have a little bet on it, actually. She wants to see which of us has to pay up."

"What's in the pot?"

"Romantic weekend of the winner's choosing."

Bennett laughed. "So you both win."

"I might get sex out of it, but if you think spending the

weekend at Broadway shows and *shopping* in New York City is winning for me, in any way, you're crazy," Duke said.

"Your wife, who's known me for about eight years, thinks she knows more about the type of woman I'd fall for than you would? The guy who's known me my whole life?" Bennett asked, curious suddenly about what Jo thought was his perfect type. And if she'd gotten it right. Because he wasn't sure *he'd* known Kennedy was his perfect type until he'd met her.

"She thinks she pays more attention to that stuff," Duke said with a shrug.

"She probably does."

Duke nodded. "But if someone wanted to know the kind of Scotch to get you or what kind of sporting tickets to buy you, I'd nail that for sure."

Bennett nodded with a grin. "No doubt about it."

"So, tell me about this woman who has you thinking about giving up all your plans and exchanging Armani for...what's a brand of work boots?"

Bennett wasn't surprised that Duke had no idea who made work boots. Why would he know that? But it hit Bennett just how far removed from Sawyer, Josh, and Owen his friends in Georgia were. "DeWalt, Timberland. There are a few."

"Right. Trading Armani for DeWalt," Duke said. "Tell me about her."

"Kennedy is..." How to describe her? It seemed that describing her physical features—her colored hair, her tattoos, her piercings, her affinity for the color black—would give Duke a picture. But that was all just not enough. There was so much more there.

Duke lifted a brow. "Wow. Hard to describe, huh? That's something."

Bennett nodded. "She's something. Something unexpected and unique and fun and sexy and challenging and...she makes me want to be more real, more honest, more *raw*, more hands-on."

"I'll bet," Duke quipped.

But Bennett shot him a frown. "I mean it. She makes me want to *do* things...with my life. Things that produce something. Things that I can point to and say, 'I did that and it matters.'"

Duke's smile faded. "Okay. That's..."

Bennett knew what Duke meant. It was...hard to explain. They'd grown up in a world where people made things happen more than actually *doing* things. They influenced people and policy. They worked in the law and in government. They had meetings and came up with ideas. They invested money and time. They helped make it possible for *other* people to do things. But it was a little removed from the actual work. It was as if Bennett knew a bunch of puppet masters who pulled all the strings but didn't actually *do* anything.

He wanted to *do* stuff.

"She's very different from any of the women I've been with before," Bennett finally said. That was true. It didn't seem like a full enough description, but it was a start. "I can't wait for you to meet her."

He wasn't worried about whether Duke would like her or not. That didn't matter. He was more curious what Kennedy would think of his friends.

"Well, sounds like it's going to be an interesting weekend," Duke said. "But I should warn you, you're not sitting with her at dinner."

Bennett frowned. "Yes, I am."

Duke shook his head. "The seating arrangement is already set."

Bennett swung his legs over the edge of the mattress. "Why do I hate the way you said that?"

"Because you're going to hate the reason."

Bennett blew out a breath. "What reason?"

"Governor Ray is here tonight. And sitting right next to you."

Bennett shoved a hand through his hair. "I don't want to talk to the governor. I'm here for my father's retirement party. This isn't about me."

"Come on, man," Duke said. "It's always about you."

That was true. His mother's life revolved around his father and him. Now that his father's career was coming to a close, she had shifted full gear to Bennett's. She'd always been concerned about what he was doing, especially after he'd shifted his focus his senior year of college, but he knew that she'd been confident he'd come around and follow in his father's footsteps. Now that his father was officially retiring and Bennett was not just interested in the bayou but had invested in a business there and was spending more and more time there—and had a woman he was interested in there as well—Maria was getting nervous. Now she was going to really start pulling on the reins hard.

"I don't need a dinner party to get me close to Governor Ray," Bennett said. "If I wanted to talk to him, I'd just call him up."

"Yeah, this isn't about getting you close to *him*," Duke said. "*He* requested being put next to you."

"What?"

Duke nodded. "He always figured you'd be in elected office by now. But you're not. So he wants to talk to you."

Bennett sighed.

"Your parents aren't the only ones who think you should run," Duke said. "It's not just because they're biased and think their little boy can do no wrong."

Bennett looked up at his friend.

"Don't make me say it," Duke told him.

Bennett cocked a brow. "Oh, I think I'm going to need you to say it."

Duke sighed. "You already know it."

"Maybe. But I don't know if I care anymore."

"You do. Somewhere down deep. Where the moonshine and hot bayou girl haven't quite gotten yet."

Bennett frowned. "It's not like Kennedy has talked me *out* of anything. She doesn't even know any of this is a possibility."

"So you're not running away?"

"I'm *choosing* something else."

"Why?"

"Because it feels like something else can matter more."

"Yeah, well, I think that's where you're wrong."

The two men sat looking at one another for a long moment.

Finally, Bennett said, "I think you have to say it."

Duke muttered something that sounded like, "Asshole," under his breath, but then said, "You were born for elected office. You would be a fantastic public servant, Bennett Baxter."

Bennett took a deep breath. His oldest friend might not have given a lot of thought to the perfect woman for Bennett, but Duke knew exactly what words to use when he was trying to make a point. Public servant. Duke had specifically used those words instead of "you would be a fantastic governor", or "you'd make a great state senator." Public servant meant more. Sounded better.

And dammit, it did make Bennett listen.

6

A SOFT KNOCK AT THE DOOR MADE KENNEDY JUMP. HER HEART leapt into her throat. It wasn't Bennett. He wouldn't knock. He'd walk right in. And he wouldn't be coming from the hallway. They had an adjoining bathroom.

From which she could hear the shower running. She'd been sitting on the bed imagining Bennett in there, wet and soapy, only a few feet away. Wondering what he'd do if she walked in and joined him. Definitely wondering about that multi-jet system in there.

Please just be someone delivering the dresses. Please just be someone delivering the dresses. Please don't be—

"Hi, Mrs. Baxter," Kennedy greeted Bennett's mother, who was standing on the other side of the door with two garment bags.

"These just came for you."

"Thank you so much. I appreciate it. I'm so sorry that Bennett didn't tell me more about this weekend so I could have been more prepared."

Maria Baxter didn't hold the bags out for Kennedy. She was clearly keeping them. For now. "Perhaps he thought that you would just assume what kind of dress code this would require."

Kennedy couldn't help but laugh at that. "I don't think that was it."

"No? Why is that?"

Maria stepped forward and Kennedy didn't have a lot of choice but to step back and let her into the room. It was her house after all. She also didn't strike Kennedy as the type of woman to take no for an answer.

"Because where I'm from, when someone says party at their parents' house, that means shorts and T-shirts, and beer and barbecue in the backyard."

Maria laid the bags on the bed and unzipped them. "Maybe Bennett didn't realize *that*."

"Oh, he knows that," Kennedy said, still standing by the door, but not sure if it was because she was hoping that Maria would be on her way right back out or because Kennedy wanted to have a clear escape path. For some reason. "He's been to a few of those parties in Autre."

Maria pulled one of the dresses out and held it up.

It was beautiful. The color was a dusty rose, the material a light and filmy fabric, overlaid with lace. The sleeves would come to her wrists, but they were blousy and loose and would move almost like wings if she gestured too exuberantly. The waist was cinched, and the skirt flowed to a high-low hem that would show her ankles, but would cover most of her legs.

It didn't take a PhD from whatever schools people around here went to to realize that Maria had chosen a style that would cover most of Kennedy's tattoo. People might catch a glimpse at the ankle if her skirt swirled just right. They'd see the one on her hand, wrist, and forearm, but the ink was less prominent there anyway, and damned if the dress color didn't also go with the pale pink hue of the roses in the tattoo.

Maria was good. And not incredibly subtle.

"Honestly, there's not a single event in Autre that I'd show up to in that dress."

"How about a wedding?"

Kennedy realized she'd come forward when she reached out to touch the silky, soft material of the dress. She shook her head. "Nope."

"That's too bad. Dressing up can be fun," Maria said.

That's what Kennedy had thought as a little girl, dressing up for pageants. She met the other woman's eyes. "We're just pretty down-to-earth, what-you-see-is-what-you-get people, I guess."

Maria nodded. "Try it on." She held the dress out.

Kennedy realized she didn't have much choice. Maria had clearly picked this dress out specifically. Kennedy was on her turf. This was her house, her party. Kennedy wasn't going to give her a hard time. At least, not if she could control it. Sometimes things came out of her mouth, or showed in her expressions, before she got them tamped down. But she'd try.

She took the dress and headed for the bathroom.

"Oh, you can change right over there."

Kennedy looked back. Maria was pointing to the corner of the room. There was a three-paneled screen near the wardrobe. Of course. Changing clothes in the same room with her...what was Bennett? Her boyfriend? Not really. Her boss. Yes. Her friend? Okay, maybe. Her weekend fling. She definitely hoped so... *Anyway,* changing in the same room with his mom was awkward. But whatever.

Kennedy slipped behind the screen and started unlacing her boots. There was a little part of her that wanted to try the dress on. What could she say? She liked girlie stuff. She loved her makeup and jewelry and clothes. Now she used them to make a statement about how she didn't really care what people thought and approved of. But that was part of what she loved about it all—the ability to express things that were easier seen than heard sometimes, to make an impression, to make people take a second look.

"I hope you understand about the seating arrangement at dinner tonight."

"The seating arrangement?" Kennedy asked, pulling her second boot off.

"I have you seated with my family. They live in Florida now but they're from Louisiana originally. I thought you might be more comfortable."

Kennedy frowned, but said, "Yeah, Bennett told me about the whole lottery thing and all. Cool that y'all have Cajun roots."

"He did?" Maria didn't sound particularly thrilled that Kennedy knew about her family's money. "Well, yes, it's been a while since they lived there, but I..."

She trailed off and Kennedy frowned as she slipped out of her skirt and pulled her shirt over her head.

"I need Bennett focused tonight. I hope you're not upset about sitting apart. But it's important that Governor Ray has a chance to speak with Bennett tonight."

"We're not sitting together," Kennedy clarified.

"For dinner," Maria said. "If Bennett would return the governor's phone calls, then maybe that wouldn't be necessary. But I don't want him to be distracted."

Kennedy slipped the dress over her head. It fit perfectly. Like it had been custom-made for her. The front plunged low. Very low. Not everyone would be able to pull that off, but it looked fantastic on her. She turned and looked over her shoulder at the back. It left her back bare almost to her waist. She was going to need some tape to keep everything where it should be, but yeah, she liked this dress. The skirt actually had three filmy layers and fell to the perfect length to brush her ankle bones, the higher hem in the front giving just teasing hints at her legs. She twirled once, loving the way the skirt lifted, then floated back down. This would look amazing with some strappy sandals.

She hadn't worn sandals in forever. She went barefoot or wore Converse or her boots. She'd need a pedicure if she was going to do sandals. But there was no way her boots were appropriate for this dress. Dammit. And now she actually cared about what she was wearing. What was Bennett doing to her?

She stepped out from behind the screen.

Maria gave her an approving look. "That's perfect." She held out a pair of shoes.

Strappy sandals. The perfect strappy sandals for this dress.

"I might need—"

"I have a woman coming to do a manicure and pedicure for you in about thirty minutes."

Okay. Maria Baxter was good.

"Why won't Bennett return the mayor's phone calls?"

"The governor," Maria corrected.

"Right. Sorry." Shit, she needed to pay more attention. She didn't want Maria to think she was a flake. "Why doesn't Bennett want to talk to him?"

"Because Governor Ray wants to talk to Bennett about running for state legislature."

Kennedy frowned. "Oh."

"Of course, he's not the only one. Or the first one. But he's gotten closer than anyone else in getting Bennett's attention with the environmental legislation William—Governor Ray—has been working on. Bennett wants to ignore it all, but he can't. He's far too passionate and knowledgeable about it all. And he has all the right contacts. I think he fights with himself nearly every day about picking up the phone and putting his two cents in."

"Why does he fight it?" Kennedy asked.

"Because he doesn't think that he wants to be a politician."

Kennedy studied Maria's face. "You don't believe that?"

"Bennett is perfect for that role in every way."

"Unless he doesn't *want* that role." Kennedy knew a little about doing things other people wanted her to do or expected rather than because she wanted to do them. Not on the same level as this, maybe, but she did know that it was damned hard to do well at something you didn't like or feel proud of.

"He wants to make things better. He wants to influence decisions. He wants to *make* important decisions. He wants to educate people about issues that matter to him," Maria said.

"Okay."

"All of that means he *does* want this role. He's just resisting it."

"Why would he do that?" Kennedy asked.

"He hasn't talked to you about this?" Maria asked.

That was a fair question. If Kennedy and Bennett were actually a couple. "We haven't. We actually don't...talk much...about that kind of stuff."

That sounded fishy. And Maria's expression in response said she thought so, too. "You don't talk much," she said.

"We talk about Boys of the Bayou," Kennedy amended. Otherwise it sounded like they spent their time together doing things other than talking. And they didn't. Not yet, anyway. "We talk about the business. And just kind of give each other a hard time. He knows a lot about my family and stuff."

"Oh, I know all about your family," Maria said. "It's just... interesting...that you don't know much about ours."

Interesting? Was it? "He talks about us?"

"Of course. The Boys of the Bayou and the Landrys are the main reasons he gives for not being interested in Georgia politics."

Kennedy lifted her chin. "And you don't believe those things are important to him?"

Maria gave her a smile, but it lacked warmth. "Oh, honey."

God, Kennedy really hated when people she didn't know

well called her honey. Especially in that condescending way Maria Baxter was doing it.

"He thinks you all are important. But you're...summer camp."

Kennedy felt a twist in her gut. She also had been telling herself that the bayou and everything down there was just playtime for Bennett. A break from his real world. And that his interest in her was just the connection she had to all the rest of it. But hearing Maria say this was making her stomach hurt. She swallowed hard. "Summer camp?"

"When he was ten, he went to summer camp for two weeks. He came home completely energized about everything that he'd seen and learned there. Boys of the Bayou is his new summer camp. Your grandparents are the camp counselors, keeping everything in check and teaching him how things work. Your brothers and cousin are his buddies that he shares all the activities with. And you're the cute girl that he develops a crush on because you're new and different."

Kennedy crossed her arms as emotions swirled through her, then realizing it was a very obvious defensive posture, dropped them. "You think we're just a diversion then?"

"Yes. An excuse for him to not do what he should do here. A way for him to punish his father."

Kennedy frowned. "Why does he want to punish his father?"

"That's not important," Maria said. "But it's tiresome. Bennett has made his point. Now he needs to grow up and do the right thing. This juvenile need to rebel is getting in the way of Bennett being successful, and their personal quarrel shouldn't keep the people of Georgia having Bennett's leadership."

Kennedy strongly disagreed that the story about what was going on with Bennett and his dad wasn't important. But she wanted to get that story from Bennett.

"And I'm sure you would feel terrible thinking that you somehow played a part in continuing the divide in our family, not to mention holding Bennett back from great things."

Yeah, Kennedy was already tired of being in the middle of whatever this was. "The only thing I intend to hold Bennett back from is role-playing any camp counselor thing in the bedroom that he might have in mind. Because that's weird." She looked down at her dress. "Of course, rich bitch debutante and the serving boy passing out champagne at the hoity-toity party downstairs is totally on the table."

Maria's eyes narrowed slightly, but she simply said, "The other dress is for tomorrow. It looks like we got the size and style right. You can try that on later."

Kennedy had to admit she was impressed with Maria not taking the bait Kennedy had thrown out there. Her family never would have let a comment about role-playing sex go by. Then again, the Landrys would have never tried to warn someone off the way Maria was. The Landrys didn't always make the best decisions and they flat-out screwed up sometimes, but they all believed that making mistakes was one of the best ways to learn and grow. No one got in the way of relationships, even the crazy ones that seemed like a bad idea. Hell, some of the best ones in the family tree were the crazy ones.

"The woman from my spa should be here soon. I hope you don't mind, but I also asked her to do your makeup." She crossed to the door and then looked back at Kennedy. "I think you'll enjoy the conversation with my family tonight. And I trust that you understand how important it is for Bennett to have time with Governor Ray and some of our other guests."

Kennedy nodded. "I'll make the blow job in the gazebo a quickie."

Maria lifted both brows, clearly refusing to be cowed. "I appreciate that. And you won't end up pregnant that way."

Kennedy's mouth dropped open as Maria swept through

the door and shut it behind her. Had she just insinuated that Kennedy might get pregnant on purpose? To trap Bennett? Wow. What a bitch.

Strangely, it made her want to sleep with Bennett even more. She wasn't going to let Maria scare her off. When she and Bennett broke up—if they could even call ending whatever this was an actual breakup—it was not going to be because his mom had showed her claws.

Kennedy decided who she dated and for how long and how that relationship went. Kennedy got her birth control shot right on time, thank you very much, and she'd make damned sure he used a condom. Maybe two now.

If Kennedy wanted Bennett wrapped around her finger, she'd get him there without needing a baby to do it.

Not that she wanted him there.

Not only did they clearly have nothing in common in all the areas she'd known about, but now she knew that their families were nothing alike. Thank God.

She did *not* want to live in Savannah. She did *not* want to be a politician's wife.

And she did *not* want Maria Baxter as a mother-in-law.

DUKE HAD JUST TAKEN A DRINK OF HIS SCOTCH WHEN HE LOOKED over Bennett's shoulder and started coughing as if he'd swallowed it wrong.

Concerned, Bennett stepped forward and whacked him on the back. "You okay?"

Duke coughed again, then cleared his throat. "Holy shit, Bennett."

"What?"

"That." He pointed at something behind Bennett.

Bennett turned. And was grateful he hadn't just taken a drink of anything.

Kennedy had just appeared on the back patio and was looking around. She spotted him and her face relaxed into a big smile as she started for the steps that would lead her down onto the grass.

"From the way you described her, *that* is not what I was expecting," Duke said.

Yeah, this wasn't the Kennedy Bennett had been expecting, either. At all.

For one, she was wearing a dress. That was *pink*. And had lace on it.

He'd seen her in sundresses and skirts, but this was a *dress*. Like a dress she could wear to any of his mother's gatherings. Or any cocktail party he'd ever want to take her to with the upper crust of Georgia society and politics. He narrowed his eyes. Of course it was. His mother had picked it out.

He would have never thought Kennedy would go along with it though.

It was *pink*.

The only time he'd seen her in lace was the time she'd worn thigh-high stockings with one of her skirts. The stockings had had lace at the top. The entire ensemble had been completely inappropriate for a crawfish boil in front of her grandma's bar. But she'd worn it like she was a fucking princess and that was her coronation outfit.

He'd wanted to pull those stockings down. With his teeth.

This was not that kind of lace.

But the dress was only part of it. As she approached him across the expanse of perfectly manicured lawn, he noticed that her tattoo played peek-a-boo, at least, with the sleeve and skirt of the dress. Her hair was also down and softly curled.

Freaking *curled*. He'd only seen it straight, in ponytails, in a braid a couple of times, and once in pigtails. Curls were way too...soft...for Kennedy.

Then she got close enough for him to notice that she was also lacking her usual dramatic eye makeup and lipstick. Her makeup was subtle and tasteful.

She had also taken out all of her earrings, including the ones in her nose and eyebrows, except for a pair of subdued pearls.

"Hi."

He grasped her upper arm and turned her away from Duke without making an introduction. "We need to talk."

She looked over her shoulder at his friend. "Nice to meet you."

Bennett heard Duke's chuckle. "Oh, you, too, Kennedy."

She let Bennett hustle her across the grass toward the back door that would lead them into the kitchen. At the last minute, he realized that the kitchen would be full of caterers and he changed direction, heading instead for the fountain that was surrounded by a stone path with a couple of benches and a ton of flowers and bushes. It was a great place for people to hang out and mingle during his mother's parties, but at the moment, the guests were all staying in the tent, closer to the tables of hors d' oeuvres and the bar. After dinner, some might drift out here, but for now they had it to themselves. He stopped and turned to face her.

"What the hell?" he asked.

"Shouldn't I be asking that question? You're the one who dragged me away from the party after ten seconds of being there."

"What's this?" He looked her up and down.

She looked amazing. Beautiful. Soft. Sweet.

Not at all like Kennedy.

She always looked gorgeous. Kickass. Feisty.

"This is how the girlfriend of a future state senator from

Georgia should dress," she said, spreading her arms wide. "Apparently."

He should have fucking known. "My mother told you that I'm running for office and that tonight the governor is here to talk to me about starting a campaign."

"More or less," Kennedy said, dropping her arms.

Frustration gnawed at the back of his neck, but it was frustration toward his parents. His mother was well-known for getting her way. She pushed things. Always. But she was really forcing this. And not listening to him at all. He knew it was about more than just getting him into politics. Maria did believe in him and that he could do good and be fulfilled in public office. But she also wanted him and his father to mend their rift and the only way to prove that had happened, to his father, was for him to declare a candidacy. At this point, it could be a candidacy for nearly anything. But it would be a signal that he was getting started, and it would be the first step toward...everything. The governor's mansion. An office in D.C. alongside the other senators. Maybe something even more. This was supposed to be his legacy. And it would have been. If his father wasn't a corrupt enabler of criminals.

"And you're going along with it?" Bennett asked.

She stepped close, narrowing her eyes. "What I'm doing is not allowing you to use me," she said.

Bennett scowled. "What's that mean?"

"It means, I won't be your excuse, Bennett. I won't be a distraction that you can blame for not doing whatever this is that your family and everyone thinks you should do. I won't be the reason that you're *not* doing it. As far as everyone here is going to know, I'm on board. I'm behind you. I think you'll make the best president this country's ever seen."

His scowl deepened and he moved closer. "You're on board?"

"I don't even know what it all is," she said. "But if you have issues with your family, you need to deal with that straight on. I'm not going to help you run away from your problems. You brought me here to shock your mother and make a point. I'm your big rebellion. Well, I'm not doing that. As far as everyone here knows, including your father, I'm a sweet southern girl who just wants whatever is best for you."

Bennett couldn't describe the emotions going through him. He wanted to laugh and he wanted to yell. It occurred to him that if he wanted to be with this woman long-term, that mix of emotions might become the norm rather than the exception.

This was Kennedy. He should have known this wouldn't be easy. Had he envisioned her coming here and being...*her*... flashing her tattoos and her black nail polish and making it obvious that he wanted something different and was going a new direction? Yeah.

He blew out a breath. That wasn't the entire reason he'd wanted to bring her along. She just made him smile. She turned him on. He wanted her undivided attention, just as he'd told her. He'd wanted to get her naked. He'd wanted to get to know her better.

But was she supposed to be the flesh-and-blood proof of his new direction and that he clearly wasn't going to be following in his father's footsteps?

Yeah. That, too.

Which wasn't fair.

"I didn't realize that would all upset you," he said, reaching for her hair. He took a strand between his thumb and finger, running down the length of the hair that curled at the end. "You do look beautiful. You always do. Guess you can pull anything off."

"I was a pageant queen," she said. "Changing clothes and makeup to affect people's impression of me is a piece of cake."

"I don't want them to have a different impression of you," he said. "I really do want my family and friends to know *you*."

"Because it will make them let up on *you*?" she said. "I don't want them to blame me for you rejecting everything here." Her annoyance wavered. For a second she looked almost hurt. "That's your choice and it's not fair to let them think it's me."

Bennett nodded. "You're right." He bent a little to look her in the eyes. "You okay? You can go back upstairs and change. Honestly, Ken, you don't have to go along with my mom."

She shook her head. "It's not your mom."

"Then what?"

She took a breath and then met his eyes, lifting her chin slightly. "You talk about the bayou as if it's truly your new passion. I told myself that you were just playing around and having fun with something new—including me. But I didn't realize until your mom said that it's all just your way of punishing your father, that I really wanted to believe that you liked it, I guess." She shrugged. "I wanted your enthusiasm for Autre and Boys of the Bayou...to be real."

She'd hesitated after *Boys of the Bayou*, and Bennett could have sworn she was going to add on to that thought right there. His heart was suddenly pounding. He lifted her chin with his finger, realizing she was now looking at the collar of his button-down shirt. "And you?" he asked, his voice a little gruff.

"And me what?"

"You wanted my enthusiasm for you to be real, too?"

She pressed her lips together. She didn't answer. But she didn't have to.

He gave a half groan, half laugh. "God, Kennedy, I'm so *enthusiastic* about you I don't even know what to do."

"I know we have chemistry. I'm enthusiastic about that, too," she said. "But—"

"It's more than that."

"How can it be? We don't even really know each other that well."

"I know you," he said. "I know your family. I see how much

Sawyer getting back to normal has meant to you. I know how much you love Tori for loving Josh. I see your relationship with Leo. I see your affection for and annoyance with Cora and Ellie. I see how you treat the customers. You don't let anyone get away with anything, but you're also kind and patient and you want everyone who comes to the bayou to leave loving it at least a little. The business matters to you, your family matters to you, the town matters to you. Because you value roots and loyalty and being true and honest."

There was a flicker of emotion in her eyes, almost a wariness.

"But I didn't know any of this about you," she said, quietly.

"I know. I guess maybe that was part of bringing you here, too. I wanted you to know." He sighed. "Though I really didn't expect my mother to jump right in on campaigning and pushing. I probably should have."

Kennedy was chewing her bottom lip now.

"What is it?" There was something going on with her and it was making him feel edgy.

"I just..." She swallowed and shook her head. "I take after my grandpa. I become attached to people and then I'm just done. I'll defend them no matter what they do. I'll stick by them no matter what. I'll hang on, caring about them, even if they treat me like crap."

"Okay," Bennett said slowly.

"So I can't get attached to you," she said with a shrug. "There's a lot of stuff really uncertain in your life. You have a lot of issues to work out, things to figure out. And I can't get attached because once I'm there, I won't let go. Even if that means I have to change everything up to move to Savannah and"—She looked down at her dress, flipping the skirt—"wearing pink, lacey dresses." She looked up at him. "I would do it. Even if it wasn't what I really wanted. And I just think it would be better if we...don't go there."

His heart thunked and his gut clenched.

He was already there.

"I don't want Savannah and I don't want you in pink, lacey dresses," he told her.

"I believe you at this exact moment," she said. "But your mom basically said you were born to be a politician. You're resisting that for whatever reason. But that might not hold. Not if that's really what you should be doing."

"It's not."

"Why not?" she asked. "I was thinking about it while I was getting my pedicure. Why don't you want to be a politician? Make a change? Do some good?"

He scoffed. "Is that what you think politicians do?"

"Don't they?"

"It's sweet that you think so." He'd once thought so, too.

She frowned. "Well, then even more reason to get in there and change things."

"It's too far gone." God, he really wished he didn't feel that way. But he knew too much.

Her eyes widened. "Wow."

"What?"

"You think I look different wearing pink lace, you really look different wearing cynicism and bitterness."

He blew out a breath. "Sorry. I just know how it works. I don't know if I've got what it takes to make a difference."

She nodded. "Okay. Well, good then."

"Good?"

"Sure. You're way less sexy when you're negative and jaded. And if you definitely want nothing to do with it, then I guess we can keep messing around."

It was stupid, but for just a second, her words gave him pause. Did he *definitely* want *nothing* to do with it?

But he shook his head. *Of course* he was sure that he didn't want to get involved in politics. He knew better. He'd made that decision. He was going to be a bayou boy now.

He put his hands on her hips and pulled her against him. "There might be *one* way I'd like pink lace on you."

"Gee, I have no idea what you mean," she said, teasing in her tone.

As she slid her arms around his neck, Bennett felt some of the tension leave his shoulders. He understood, completely, where she was coming from not wanting to be his excuse for how things were with him and his dad. It wasn't fair of him to make it look that way. But the fact that she still let him hold her made him feel like it would be okay.

He leaned in, rubbing his chin along the sensitive skin of her neck behind her ear. "I'm thinking a barely-there thong, with some pretty pink lace that I can rip with my teeth when I'm on my way to making your sweet pussy drip for me, would be okay."

She shivered and Bennett grinned. There was no denying the chemistry, and if he had to use that to keep her close, for now, he would. Without apology.

"Well, I did mention that I might take you behind the gazebo a little later," she said.

"You did? To who?"

"Your mom."

Bennett pulled back. "Oh really?"

"We had a...nice...talk," Kennedy said. "At least, I think we both know where the other stands."

Now see, *this* was what he'd expect from Kennedy. Even without black nail polish on, she wasn't a pushover. Not even with Maria Baxter.

"Did you exert yourself with my mom, Kennedy?" he asked with a little smile.

"What do you think?"

He thought that Kennedy would always be honest and true to herself. And it made him want her even more.

"Should we get back over there for dinner?" she asked.

He sighed.

"You have to face this, Bennett. Make a decision and stand by it. Make them listen."

That was the problem. In the past, he hadn't been as firm as he should have been. Because he'd been wavering in his own mind. Saying absolutely no to all future opportunities was difficult, for some reason.

But, whether she wanted to be his excuse or not, Kennedy was making it a lot easier for him to look in this new direction with more confidence. Enthusiasm had never been a problem. He'd wanted the bayou since the first time he'd set foot on that dock. Confidence about it being the right decision had been harder to come by.

The woman in his arms was making him more and more sure.

"Okay, dinner," he said, slipping her hand into his. "And I should tell you about the seating arrangement."

"Oh, your mom already did."

"Of course she did," Bennett said with a sigh.

"I'm fine," she said. "Honestly. It will be okay. I can talk to your aunt and uncle on the far end of the table while you let the governor kiss up to you before disappointing him."

Bennett lifted her hand to his lips and gave it a quick kiss.

"But your mom did ask me for one thing I'm not sure I can do," she said.

"What's that?"

"To not be a distraction," she said.

"You're going to *try* to be a distraction?" he asked. 'That's not gonna be hard."

She gave him a mischievous grin. "I totally want you to be distracted thinking about how to get enough chocolate out of that fountain and into a container that we can take behind the gazebo for the blow job that's going to be sticky and sweet and that will make you definitely take me upstairs and straight into that shower with all the nozzles."

Bennett sucked breath in through his nose. "You're a cruel and wonderful woman."

"I'm comfortable with that assessment," she told him.

He took her back to the party, proud of himself for not taking the detour around behind the gazebo on the way. Though the reason was less his self-control and more that he didn't have that container of chocolate yet.

7

"You don't know about the buried treasure?" Kennedy looked back and forth between the little girl and the little boy seated across from her at the dinner table. They were the grandkids of Maria Baxter's brother. She looked at Teddy Benoit. "You haven't passed down the stories?"

Teddy shrugged. "I'll admit we've gotten away from it a bit. Bein' away from the bayou means this stuff doesn't come up as much."

Kennedy shook her head, looking at the kids, Jaxon and Adeline. "Well, I'm gonna fix some of that right here and now. You wanna know about the pirates?"

"Yes!" Adeline gushed.

Jaxon nodded enthusiastically.

Kennedy set her fork down and leaned in.

They were through the salad course and halfway through the entrée. No one seemed overly excited about the chicken cordon bleu and roasted asparagus. Fortunately, Bennett was a gentleman—and a good listener—and he'd nabbed her an entire tray of hors d'oeuvres when they'd returned to the party. The stuffed mushrooms had been divine as had the mini quiches and the crab puffs. There had been no pigs in a blanket but she'd dipped two strawberries in chocolate. And had very much enjoyed licking the chocolate off while Bennett watched.

The kids also put their forks down and leaned in. Adeline tucked her knees under her butt so she was taller on her chair. Kennedy grinned at Teddy, who gave her a wink.

So far the dinner conversation had been easy and friendly. Teddy and Bonnie Benoit were down-to-earth people. Their kids—two sons and their wives—were a little louder, laughed more, talked more, and had more of the borderline-inappropriate sense of humor that she was used to with the Landrys. But everyone was laughing and eating and drinking and seemed relatively comfortable even in the suit jackets and dresses they wore. Still, Kennedy sensed that they would be completely at ease down on the bayou gathered around her grandma's crawfish boil pot, too, and she'd already invited them to town for swamp tours and a party.

"Okay, so the biggest pirate, the one you have to know about if you're gonna call yourself Cajuns, was Jean Lafitte. He was a French pirate and worked the Gulf. He also loved to party. There's stuff all over New Orleans named after him." She grinned at the kids. "Legend has it that he and his brother buried bits of their treasure all over the Gulf Coast to keep anyone from finding it all, and people claim that there's a lot of it still lost. People keep looking anyway. But he was pretty wily. I totally believe there's still treasure out there, but I don't know if anyone will ever find it."

As the servers cleaned up their plates and started serving dessert, Kennedy went on to tell them more stories about Jean Lafitte along with the wealthy plantation owners who buried their treasures and money when they fled their homes in the Civil War. There were tons of stories around buried treasure and, even more fun, stories about the ghosts and spirits that protected the treasure.

"So if you find treasure and want to dig it up, there are some rules you have to follow to keep the spirits happy," she said, cutting into the amazing looking strawberry cake.

"The spirits?" Adeline asked, ignoring her own cake.

Kennedy chewed and swallowed, realizing that all of the adults were also listening, as well as a few from further up the table. She didn't know who those people were, but she suspected they were lawyers or politicians that were in Preston Baxter's inner circle.

"Yep. According to some of the biggest treasure hunters around, there are spirits protecting all of the hidden treasures. They will only let people who are worthy get close to it. If someone who's greedy or cruel comes to nab the treasure, the spirits scare them off."

Jaxon's eyes were wide.

"There's a story that a little girl was walking in the woods one day on her way home. She got lost and wandered into an old mine shaft. Said she saw *piles* of gold and jewels. She ran out and straight home to get a grown-up, but she was never able to find her way back to that mine shaft and even though they combed the area for weeks, no one else could ever find even where an old mine had ever been, not to mention any treasure."

"So the ghosts hid it after she accidentally found it?" Adeline asked.

"Or the ghosts decided that the people she brought back with her weren't worthy of the treasure. At least, that's what people say," Kennedy told her with a nod.

Honestly, that's what Kennedy thought, too. She completely believed that there were spirits roaming the bayous and woods where she grew up, and she also believed that if you were a good person with good intentions who didn't mess around with them or their space for any nefarious purposes, then they'd pretty much leave you alone. She even thought some of them protected people who lived there, keeping them safe from the storms and other things that made southern Louisiana a tough place to call home sometimes.

"But sometimes people do find treasure and dig it up?" Jaxon asked.

"Oh yeah. There's a guy not too far from where I grew up who was out digging in his garden one day—now, keep in mind, this guy was in his sixties and had been living there for a long time. He'd been planting that garden every year for *years*. Just like he was doing that day—and all of a sudden his shovel hits something hard."

She paused, enjoying the rapt attention from the kids but also aware that her audience had grown. Most of the lower half of the table was now listening. And she thought she'd seen Bennett glancing her way.

Kennedy had restricted her looks at Bennett to quick glances only, but he was definitely into the conversation—whatever it was about. He might say that he didn't want this life and wasn't interested in what the governor was saying, but Kennedy wasn't buying it. He was a natural.

"What was it?" Jaxon asked, his eyes wide.

"What do you think?" Kennedy asked the little boy, turning her full attention back to the story. She could do this all night. She might not be able to talk politics and policy, but she could tell all the legends and myths from the bayou. And she didn't even have to exaggerate them. Much.

"It was a treasure chest!" Adeline exclaimed.

Kennedy laughed. "Yep. It sure was. It wasn't very big, but it was *heavy*. He had to call his son over to help him pull it out of the ground," she said, getting back into the story easily. She'd sat for hours listening to these stories from the old guys and gals who sat around her grandma's bar. "And when they finally got it out and pried it open, it was full of silver coins. It came up to about two hundred thousand dollars."

She glanced at the adults. There were several wide eyes. The kids wouldn't have an idea how much that was, but the adults were impressed. Kennedy looked back at the kids. "People say that the spirits gave him that treasure that day. His wife had just died and he was sick and needed the money so that he could stay in his house."

"So the ghosts sometimes *give* the treasure away?" Jaxon asked.

"That's what they say." Again, she also believed it. "But," she said. "Sometimes you do have to earn it. Some of the hunters who've found treasure have had to really work for a long time to figure out all the rules."

"What are the rules?" Jaxon had to know.

"Well, the most successful hunter says that you have to go at dusk—a lot of people think you have to hunt at night and that's not true. You also have to go with a pure heart, and everyone who comes with you has to be a good person, too. One time when he and some guys were out, they opened up this door that led down to the cellar of a house and they started down the stairs. All of a sudden, it started filling up with water and they heard a voice whispering 'murderer.'"

Kennedy paused for effect and she thought that Jaxon was probably holding his breath.

"Well, this guy knew *he'd* never killed anybody and he knew a couple of the other guys really well, but there were two he didn't know. No one ever confessed, of course, but he says he's positive now that one of those guys killed somebody sometime. The ghosts always know."

Kennedy grinned as she looked around, finding the same unblinking attention from several of the adults as well.

"He also takes a gift for the spirits. Usually really good liquor or tobacco."

Adeline gasped. "The ghosts can drink stuff and smoke?"

Kennedy laughed and shrugged. "I don't know. I guess so?

They're always friendlier when he brings those things. He's tried other gifts, but the digs don't go as well as they do when it's those."

"So he has found actual treasure?" This question came from one of the men sitting a couple spots down from Teddy.

Kennedy nodded. "Yep. I've met him personally. He's odd, but he's sincere. He's shown me a few of the coins and if they're fake, they're really good."

"No shit," the guy said, clearly interested. "That's cool."

Kennedy grinned. "It is. And the best part is that he never finds like a million dollars. Never enough to really be rich. It's always just enough. Enough to help make ends meet or to allow him to do something like buy a new truck when he needed it."

"That's all he does?" another man asked. "Hunts treasure?"

"He's a fisherman, too," Kennedy said. "The treasure hunting is just a passion or a hobby, I guess. But he gets rewarded for it every once in a while."

"You really think there are spirits who are punishing and rewarding people?" the first man asked.

Kennedy looked at the kids and gave them a wink. "Well, like my grandpa always says, 'why argue?' Bein' a good person is a good thing to do anyway, and if once in a while you find a few gold coins for it, that's not bad. And I sure don't want to have spiders coming out of my walls or hear voices saying 'turn back' every damned time I drive down a certain road."

"Those things have happened to people, too?" Adeline asked.

"Yep. There's a guy who was treasure hunting with some others. He went along to help out but didn't actually touch the treasure. He was being paid cash money by the hunter, but wasn't supposed to have any part of whatever they dug up. But after they actually found some stuff...gold bars, I think it was... he hit one of the men over the head and took off with part of the gold. Later that night, when he was in bed, spiders came out of his walls—hundreds, *thousands* of them—and bit him all over. He ended up in the hospital and was *begging* the cops to take the gold back to the men he stole it from."

"Whoa," Jaxon said.

Kennedy nodded. "I figure it's just safer down on the bayou to be a good person, you know?"

Jaxon and Adeline both nodded.

Kennedy grinned. "Or better, yet, we should all just be as good as we can be, no matter what."

The kids nodded again.

Spirits hanging around after death was a common legend in Louisiana. New Orleans was one of the most haunted places there was. But some of the stories about spirits punishing and rewarding people had probably been started by parents wanting to make their kids behave. Kind of like "Santa's always watching. You don't want to be on his bad list, do you?" In Kennedy's opinion, the idea of an old man watching her all the time and deciding if she was good or bad was also kind of creepy, so why not throw some ghosts in there, too?

"And having a gris-gris bag isn't a bad idea," she said.

"What's a gris-gris bag?" Adeline asked.

They were interrupted by the servers appearing to start clearing away the dessert plates and coffee cups.

"Well, gris-gris bags are little bags that contain—"

"Okay, time to get washed up," their mother interrupted, pushing her chair back from the table. "You have a little time to play and then we'll head to bed."

"But we want to hear more stories!" Jaxon protested, even as he set his napkin on his plate and shoved his chair back.

"Another time, maybe," his mother said. She glanced at Kennedy. "I think we'll save the voodoo stuff for now."

Oops. She probably shouldn't assume everyone was cool talking about all of that. "I've got lots of gator facts and stories, too," she told the kids. "Oh, and stories about river otters. And wolves."

Those were all thanks to her brother's girlfriend, Tori, really. Well, not the gators. Good lord, Kennedy had more gator and snake and bat and spider and fire ant stories than she ever wanted to recount. But kids did seem to love hearing about dangerous animals and creepy crawlies. She saw kids regularly on the swamp boat tours and interacted with them. But that was for short periods. She really didn't know that much about kids. She'd been the youngest in the family and none of her brothers or cousins had kids yet. But ghost stories and voodoo and pirates were maybe a bit much. Real pirates anyway. They were a lot less funny and charming and interesting than the films and kids' books made them out to be.

The other adults started getting up and drifting away from the tables as well.

It was well past dusk. The area was lit by twinkle lights strung overhead across the top of the tents, and the bugs were being kept at bay by tall torches lit at the edges of the party area. And probably some expensive bug spraying techniques. The air was a little cooler now, though there was still a touch of humidity—it was summer in Georgia, after all—but somehow it was pleasant out. Almost as if even the weather didn't dare mess with Maria Baxter's event.

"Hope I didn't screw up there," Kennedy said to Teddy. "Didn't mean to bring up voodoo if that's a bad subject. Was just kind of teasing."

"Oh, don't worry. Sarah is just a little touchy with the kids. She's from Florida, doesn't really know the Louisiana ways, either."

"Well, please tell her I'm sorry if I brought something up I shouldn't have. I can tell the kids some other crazy stories and get their minds off of gris-gris bags easily enough. Or I can make something up. Tell them gris-gris bags are something else. They probably won't remember what I said by the time they're old enough to fact check me, right?"

He chuckled and pushed his chair back, stretching to his feet. "Oh, don't worry about it. She'll come back out after putting them to bed and want you to tell *her* all about it."

Kennedy stood, too, as she laughed. "Really?"

"For sure. But I want you to promise me something."

"Okay."

"You make the stories you tell her *really* crazy."

Kennedy nodded. "I can do that."

"*You've* probably been listening to stories like that all your life, yeah?"

"Absolutely. Most of them are even true. Ish," she said with a grin. "My grandma owns a bar in Autre. She and my grandpa and all their friends love nothing more than a good story."

"Hey." Bennett came up behind her and wrapped his arms around her.

She hadn't even noticed where he was or what he'd been doing. It seemed that most of the party, except for Maria's side of the family, had moved indoors.

"Hey." She turned in his arms. "You got any chocolate sauce on you?"

His eyes darkened briefly as he looked down at her. Then a look of regret crossed his face. "I don't. And I've..." He glanced toward the house.

"You have more talking to do?" she guessed.

He sighed. "I know I told you I didn't want to do any of this, but he actually wants my ideas on some environmental policies and wants to talk about how my foundation can get involved. I have to hear him out."

"Your foundation?" Kennedy repeated.

He nodded. "I run a nonprofit foundation that funds scientific research into the impacts of industry and climate change on the environment." He gave her a half grin that was sheepish and adorable at the same time. "Very nerdy stuff."

"I thought you were a lawyer."

"I am. I mean, I have a law degree and I do some consulting work. Some pro bono cases, too, from time to time."

"But it's all environment based?" she asked.

"Mostly. Every once in a while, a hot girl calls me about harboring endangered wildlife in her grandpa's trailer." He grinned down at her.

She couldn't help but laugh. "Nice of you to help out like that."

"Well, *that's* not for free, remember," he said. "I'm getting paid back."

"I'm here at a dinner party, in a pink lacey dress and getting in trouble with your cousin's wife for talking about voodoo," she said. "I'm definitely paying my dues."

"Yeah, but you sucked down stuffed mushrooms like they were candy and have been charming every single man, and several women, here tonight. Don't think that you're not getting something out of this deal."

"What does charming all of these people get me?" she teased. "Last thing I need is a bunch of stuck-up Georgians showing up and wanting to take swamp boat tours."

He pulled her closer and dropped his voice for her ears only. Of course, most everyone else, including Teddy, had moved off away from the tables that the catering company was now working to clean up. Still, she loved the deep, gruff note in Bennett's voice when he said, "It makes me a little jealous and makes me even crazier about you and that means that when I get you upstairs later, you're going to get as many orgasms as I can wring out of your sweet body before the sun comes up."

She shivered. "Dammit. Guys wearing shiny shoes should *not* be able to talk like that."

He chuckled, the sound dancing down her arm in a tingle. "My shoes being shiny matters?"

"I'm just saying that if you wear some work boots and talk like that, my panties are toast."

He lifted his head and looked around. Then he pulled her a few feet away and around behind a tree. Without a word, he gathered her skirt up in one hand and dragged the other palm up her thigh and straight to the center of her panties. Her head fell back against the trunk as he slipped a finger under the lace edge and over her now throbbing clit.

"Seems like I can get you plenty wet even in shiny shoes," he said, staring directly into her eyes as he slid a thick middle finger into her.

He was totally right, of course. "Bennett," she moaned, gripping his wrist.

"Tell me again that you don't like my shiny shoes, Kennedy." It was almost a command.

She knew that he could feel the way her core clenched when he said it. "I don't like your shiny shoes," she said, breathlessly.

He slid his finger in and out. "Liar."

"No seriously. They're totally..."

He curled his finger to stroke over her G-spot and she lost her train of thought for a second.

"Dorky," she managed.

"Uh-huh." Again, he moved that finger. Slowly.

"I mean," she said, struggling for air. "Who even buys shoes that you have to shine in the first place?"

He added a second finger. "The guy who can get you dripping wet and losing your mind against a tree trunk in his mother's backyard."

"You don't just want to take me upstairs to your big old bed instead of going to talk to a bunch of stuffed shirts about pollution and stuff?" she asked.

"Oh, I definitely do."

He curled both fingers now and she felt her orgasm tightening already. He stroked his thumb over her clit.

"But I also want to make you think about this for a little while." He slipped his hand out of her panties and let her skirt drop back around her legs. "Now you can sit all hot and sticky and throbbing and wait for me to come and relieve it all. In my shiny fucking shoes."

She stared at him, sure that her cheeks were pink from lust. "I hate you."

"Yeah, I know. Just like you hate my shoes." He gave her a cocky grin.

She blew out a breath and pushed him back. "Okay, yeah, well, guess I'll see you upstairs later."

She started around the tree, but he caught her elbow. "Where are you going?"

"Upstairs. To that shower. To get the orgasm that you just denied me."

His grip tightened slightly as heat flared in his eyes. "No. You're not."

"Oh, pretty sure I am."

"You're going to take your pretty ass over to that firepit," he said, jutting his chin.

She looked and sure enough, Maria's family was gathering at the edge of the patio. She snorted. "That's a fireplace. An outdoor fireplace." The thing was huge. It had clearly been built as part of the patio, with the same stone and iron work. She looked up at Bennett. "You've been to real bonfires. Don't you dare call that thing a firepit."

"Well, whatever it is, you're going to take your butt over there and hang out with them while I get the rest of this discussion done. Then I'm going to come get you and we'll go up the back stairs so that you can start stripping on our way up."

"You realize that I could just excuse myself to use the

bathroom and get myself off quick, right?" she said. "I mean, I could be back down in front of that fireplace, telling tall tales and drinking beer with your family *and* feeling pretty damned good in my lady parts and you'd never even know."

He bent and put his mouth next to her ear. "If anyone gives you an orgasm other than me—and that includes *you*—I'm going to take you upstairs, tie you to my bed, and take you right to the edge of orgasm, but deny you, ten times before I let you come. You understand?"

That hot shiver went through her again. That all sounded great, actually. Except for the denying part. People didn't deny her things. "Those fucking shoes are really deceiving," she told him. "They are so not hot, but all of that...damn."

"God, you're thinking that being tied up might be okay, aren't you?" he said with a short laugh. "I really do have my hands full here, don't I?"

"You really have no idea."

"I think I know better than you think."

She was afraid he might be right.

"Teddy!" Bennett called. "Can Kennedy hang out with you all for a bit?"

"Of course!" his uncle called back.

She narrowed her eyes as she looked up at him. Now that Teddy was expecting her, she couldn't slip off upstairs and do anything. "Just for that, I'm going to get your family really drunk playing Flip Cup."

She saw the flicker of "oh shit" on his face. He'd played the drinking game with the Landrys once. He'd truly regretted everything about it the next morning. And well into the next afternoon.

"Not sure they know how," he hedged.

"It's not really rocket science."

He sighed. "So the longer I keep you waiting on the orgasm,

the drunker and louder and more obnoxious things are going to get out here?"

She shrugged. "Pretty much."

Bennett groaned. "Maybe I can put the governor off."

"Oh no" she said, shaking off his hand. "You made your choice."

If he was going to mess with her, she was going to give it back. Tenfold. That's how the Landrys did stuff.

"I've actually lost you for a while, haven't I?"

She did love Flip Cup. And she kind of wanted to get Maria's family drunk. She was just that petty. "You go fix the environment," she said, waving her hand toward the house. "That's your thing. This"—She pointed at the party that was just starting up on the other end of the patio—"is my thing."

He gave her a quick kiss and then headed for the house.

For just a second, Kennedy felt a twinge of *well, fuck*. She definitely knew how to tell ghost stories and play Flip Cup. And about a dozen other drinking games. She was also incredibly good at corn hole and pool. Not exactly stellar credentials to be bragging about though. Bennett was going off to talk to the governor of Georgia about environmental policies while she went to flip plastic cups upside down...and get drunk.

Well, everyone had their thing, she supposed. And she was going to try not to compare her thing to Bennett's. They were complete opposites. She'd always known that. That was obvious to every single person here tonight. Bennett's things were big and important and mattered. Whether he liked it or not, he had opinions and ideas that important people wanted to hear. Maybe even needed to hear.

Yeah, they just really didn't have a lot in common. No one *needed* to hear about the buried treasure of Louisiana.

As she headed for the patio, she realized that having an excuse to drink a lot just then was really perfect. Because that would maybe help her *not* think about how Flip Cup and buried treasure really wasn't a thing. Or that she really didn't have a thing at all.

"Okay," she said, as she stepped up onto the patio and kicked her shoes off. "I'm going to need eight solo cups, some vanilla vodka, a speaker to hook my phone to, and seven people who aren't afraid to have some fun."

"Vanilla vodka?" Teddy asked.

"Don't tell me they don't have it," she said. "I tasted it in the strawberry punch." And it had been delicious.

"Isn't that a little lightweight for a bayou girl?" Teddy teased.

"Yes," she admitted. "And if you tell anyone, I'll deny it and will do bourbon shots with you until you're lying under the table in a fetal position."

Teddy just laughed. "So the vanilla vodka is gonna be like you're drinking water. Isn't that an unfair advantage?"

She shrugged. "All's fair in love and Flip Cup."

Amazingly, within about three minutes, she had all of the things she'd asked for. Except for the seven people. There were only five others. Adeline and Jaxon's mom, Sarah, had gone inside to check on the kids and to head to bed herself. That meant teams of three for Flip Cup. That meant the game would go faster and that meant more drinking for the six people playing. Kennedy was okay with that.

The patio didn't just have a built-in fireplace, grill, and bar area. It also had a sound system with amazing speakers. Of course it did. Maria might seem a little stuffy, and she probably played Sinatra over those speakers, but the woman knew how to entertain.

Country music—Hank Williams Jr., to be exact—came over the speakers that were tucked in the landscaping, and Kennedy felt some of the tension in her shoulders unwind. This wasn't exactly like the parties in Autre, but it was going to be an okay stand-in for tonight.

Kennedy lined Teddy, his son Steve, his other son Brian's wife, Tawny, up on one side of the long, wrought iron patio table. She and Brian were across from them along with one of Teddy's friends, Charles. He was in his mid-to-late forties and claimed he was a lot happier outside with red Solo cups than he was inside with martini glasses. Kennedy liked him from that point on.

She put a cup in front of each person and filled it about a fourth of the way up with vodka. She eyed the bottle. If things went well, they were going to need another.

"Okay, so this is a relay-race drinking game," she told the group. "First we toast," she said to Teddy, who was straight across from her. She lifted her cup and tapped it on his. "Then we chug the vodka—" She did. She had to demonstrate, after all. The vodka was smooth and sweet and she felt the pleasant warmth spread through her chest and stomach. "Then you put the cup on the edge of the table, and with one finger"—She held up her index finger—"you try to flip the cup so it lands upside down."

She did it perfectly. She was the Flip Cup champion in her family. Though Ellie's best friend, Cora, always gave her a run for her money.

"You can only touch your cup with one hand," she told them. "You keep trying until you get it flipped over. As soon as it lands upside down, your next teammate grabs their cup, drinks, and then flips. They can't touch their cup until yours is upside down. And it just goes on down the table. Since there are only three of us on each side, I think we should go down the table twice in one round."

Everyone agreed, they cranked up the Hank Williams Jr., and started to play.

As per usual, the laughter and cussing and cheating and, of course, the liquor flowed freely after only one round. Kennedy's team kicked Teddy's team's ass. Charles, as it turned out, was pretty great at Flip Cup. He also knew all the words to all of the Hank Williams Jr. songs, all the Garth Brooks songs, and all of the Toby Keith songs.

Finally, after six total rounds and the equivalent of a bottle and a half of vodka, Tawny begged to end the game.

Steve and Brian mentioned they were hungry.

Kennedy perked up. "Should we raid the kitchen?"

They both looked at her. "Seriously? You want to raid Aunt Marie's kitchen?"

Kennedy glanced toward the house. This side of the house was made up almost entirely of huge windows. The formal living room was still full of people. She couldn't even see Maria. She nodded at the guys. "Of course. The caterers have probably cleaned up and put the leftovers in the fridge."

Steve wrinkled his nose. "I don't think I want any more of the chicken."

Kennedy chewed her bottom lip, thinking. Not about what she could do in the kitchen but about if she *should*.

Well, Marie already didn't like her and the chances of her getting invited back weren't great. And if Bennett didn't want her roaming free, getting into trouble, then he should have taken her straight upstairs. And tied her to his bed the way he'd threatened. She felt heat lick through her. Ugh. That guy was in so much trouble later.

"I can make sandwiches," she said. "The shrimp isn't fried, but with my special sauce, you won't care that they're missing the batter."

"Sandwiches?" Brian asked, looking very interested. "Like what?"

"Shrimp po' boys," she told him. They were simple and there was no way Marie didn't have the ingredients in the kitchen. Kennedy hadn't even seen the kitchen, but a house like this had to have a huge, well-stocked, amazing kitchen.

"Seriously?" Brian asked. "You can just whip those up?"

She laughed. "Of course. Now gumbo...that would be way better, but it would take me a lot longer. Can't do that for you tonight. But po' boys, absolutely."

They followed her into the kitchen where she threw the sandwiches together in less than twenty minutes. The shrimp was already cooked, it just needed a quick sauté on the stove-top. The batter she and Cora used in the restaurant was amazing, but these shrimp were seasoned nicely and were a fine substitution. The sauce was better if it sat for a while and let the cayenne really work its way through, but it was delicious even freshly mixed. Brian, Steve, Teddy, Charles, and even Tawny all exclaimed over the food. Which was funny. It was shrimp, sauce, lettuce, and tomato on rolls. It was so simple, especially compared to some of the stuff she did on a regular basis in Autre. Her seafood souffle was heavenly and her Bananas Foster was talked about all through the parish.

Still, the way they ate and appreciated even the simple sandwiches made her happy.

After they'd eaten and cleaned up the kitchen, they all made their way back to the patio. The party was still going inside and Kennedy could see Bennett standing nearly in the center of the room, surrounded by people, all of whom seemed to be hanging onto his every word.

She sighed and followed her little party toward the cushioned patio chairs that faced the fireplace. Brian, Steve, and Tawny took the chairs a little off to the side. Kennedy, Teddy, and Charles settled closer to the fireplace.

It was stupid to have a fire at all, of course. It was late summer in Georgia. There was no need for a fire in summer if there were no marshmallows to toast. Kennedy surveyed the area quickly. Were there marshmallows? She wouldn't have been surprised. But all she saw was a cooler full of bottled water sitting in ice. Well, that was a good idea. She grabbed one and unscrewed the top as she settled onto the chaise lounge chair to Teddy's left.

The chair was more comfortable than her grandmother's sofa, for fuck's sake. She sighed. Sure, some of it was the vodka coursing pleasantly through her veins, but it really was relaxing out here. Someone had turned the music down to a more background level versus a party level. The fireplace was gas and seemed set to give off more light than actual heat. She could hear the crickets and other night noises and, in the distance, outside of the circle of light thrown on the lawn from the house, she could see fireflies winking. Of course, bugs wouldn't dare come any closer to Maria Baxter's backyard. But it was reminiscent of the sights and sounds Kennedy would have from her own front porch, and she took a deep breath and sunk further into the cushions.

"So, you and Bennett."

Kennedy rolled her head to look over at Charles. "Bennett is my boss," she said, stretching her legs out and wiggling her bare toes. "There's no me and Bennett. We're not dating."

"Okay." Charles didn't sound convinced.

"Seriously," she said.

"I have a feeling Bennett doesn't boss you around much."

She laughed. "That obvious that I don't take direction well?"

"You just seem very sure of yourself," Charles said smoothly. "Purely a compliment."

"Bennett needs someone who knows herself," Teddy said. "He's got plenty of other people to be pushing and fighting with."

"Does he?" she asked. "Pushing and fighting, huh?"

Teddy nodded. "His whole job is convincing people to do things his way."

"At the foundation?"

"Right."

"He doesn't do that at the boat tour company?" Charles asked.

Kennedy laughed. "Bennett's the new kid. He's still learning."

"Huh."

She looked at Charles. "What?"

"Bennett is still learning about the bayou?"

"Yep." Kennedy watched her toes wiggle in the firelight. "It's my family's business. We've been there forever."

"Ah. Okay, that makes sense."

Kennedy glanced at the men. "What makes sense?"

"Why he's planning to move his foundation to Louisiana."

Kennedy frowned. "He's doing what?"

"Already has, mostly," Teddy said. "He's been in New Orleans all this past week."

So that was why he'd been in New Orleans when she'd called him. But he was moving his foundation there? The foundation she hadn't even known that he had?

"Why would he move all of that to Louisiana?" she asked.

Charles chuckled. "Guessing the gumbo has something to do with it. But thinkin' you might, too."

Kennedy shook her head. "We just kind of started...whatever. We're just messing around. He's not *moving* because of me." But there was a little voice in the back of her mind that said, *You sure about that?* Bennett *really* loved the bayou. And her family. And if she was now sleeping with him, he didn't have a lot of reason to think that he couldn't just move right in and have it all.

Except...his life was in Georgia. Sure, he said that he didn't want the politics and everything that his family was trying to push him into. But he was a lawyer here. He had a foundation. She didn't even really know what that meant exactly, but even the word *foundation* was a pretty big, solid, permanent-type word.

"Well, he's been interested in projects in Louisiana for a while," Charles said. "But he never said a word about moving there until he got involved with the swamp boat company."

"But he isn't really *involved*," Kennedy said. "I mean, he owns a percent—and not much really," she added. "It's like seventeen percent. And it completely runs without him. We've been doing it for years without him. He doesn't need to be any more involved. He comes down some weekends and plays around with my brothers, but it's not like we're having board meetings and shit." She winced. "Stuff."

"Exactly," Charles said, lifting a red Solo cup.

Huh, still drinking. She had to give the man points for that. It was vanilla vodka, but he showed signs of being able to hang with the Landrys at a crawfish boil.

"What do you mean by *exactly*?"

"I mean, he doesn't *need* to be there. He could be nothing more than an investor. He's done plenty of that. It's not like he moves to the town where all of his business interests lie. So there must be another reason he's thinking about getting closer to Autre," Charles said with a wink.

Kenney frowned at the fire. Okay, it was one thing for Bennett to think that they would date and she'd fly back and forth to Savannah for him and they'd sleep together on the weekends he was in Autre. Which, honestly, had been all but maybe one or two since he'd bought into the business. It was another for him to move his *life* to Louisiana.

"Isn't it a big deal to move his whole foundation?" she asked. "Uprooting a foundation and reestablishing it in a new state seems like a lot. I assume he has contacts and donors and stuff?" She didn't know what exactly it did, but foundations typically raised money and then gave it out to groups that needed funds. Wouldn't it be difficult to start that all over in Louisiana?

"He has a few donors," Teddy said. "But his foundation

mostly runs off of the investments he made with the money his grandfather passed down to him."

Oh. So his connections in Georgia weren't that critical.

"Of course, since most of his passion projects have to do with the environment, it helps that he knows a lot of people in public service here in Georgia," Charles said.

"Public service?" Kennedy repeated. "You mean politics."

Charles grinned and sipped again. "Yeah, politics."

"So *that* would make moving to Louisiana difficult, right? He might have all the same money, but he'd need connections to get things done with it?"

Teddy was the one to chuckle this time. "Bennett makes connections about as easily as you do, Kennedy. He's never met a man, woman, or child he can't make a friend."

"You think I make connections easily?" Kennedy asked. She did okay with the tourists who came to the bayou. But that was her job. Other than those people, she didn't really meet new people. She lived in the same town she'd been in all her life. With the same people. All. Her. Life. She sighed. Her world wasn't really all that big, honestly.

Teddy grinned at her though. "I've been with you most of this evening. My entire family thinks you're great. All of the people at dinner who were listening to your stories were enchanted. My sons may never eat a po' boy that you haven't made again in their lives. Hell, you have Charles here half-drunk and flipping plastic party cups instead of inside talking business. I think you make connections very easily."

That made her feel a little warm and she smiled. "Well, thanks."

"And you and Bennett have that in common. You have a way of making people feel comfortable. You're very genuine and people are drawn to that."

Kennedy sipped from her water bottle, thinking about that. So she and Bennett had something in common. Not just their love for Cora's bread pudding and the bayou—hell, her *family* —either. There might actually be something in their personalities that was similar. She liked that idea. Even as she realized that was a kind of weird thing to care about in a guy she was using just for sex and hors d'oeuvres.

You're not just using him for sex.

Yeah, well, she was going to ignore *that* thought.

Feeding her hors d'oeuvres addiction, though, was real. She couldn't eat that stuff at home without being majorly teased.

Don't be stupid. No one falls for a guy because of stuffed mushrooms.

Well, of course not. But she could want to spend weekends in Savannah with him because of those mini quiches. She wasn't sure she should even hint at what she'd do to him to get more of those.

It's not about the quiches!

Kennedy frowned and looked around for the bottle of vodka. Her subconscious was being a real bitch tonight. She was determined to ignore any niggle that her attraction to Bennett was more than physical. Because that complicated things and was risky.

He might be considering a move to Louisiana—maybe he was already in the midst of it, in fact—but it wasn't just about her. Bennett was the kind of guy, with the kind of resources, that made a move like that no big thing. He could spend a few months in Louisiana and then head right back to Georgia. Or hell, maybe he'd decide to try Colorado on for size. Or New York. He didn't have any real limitations. Bennett Baxter was meant to do big things.

And if Ellie can leave Leo, then a guy like Bennett can absolutely find something bigger and better than you.

Yeah, she really needed to find that vodka bottle.

8

"I GUESS KENNEDY AND THE BOYS OF THE BAYOU EXPLAIN WHY he's trying to fast track everything," Charles said, seemingly to Teddy.

Kennedy located the vodka bottle next to the leg of Charles' chair. It was empty. Dammit.

Teddy nodded. "When things get personal, the drive amps up."

"He's fast tracking his move?" Kennedy asked.

"He's fast tracking Sauveuse Island," Charles said. "Or trying to."

"Sauveuse Island? Where's that?" Kennedy found herself unable to relax fully into the chair now.

"It's how he's trying to protect you," Teddy said with a smile.

"Me? He's trying to protect me?" Kennedy felt her heart start beating faster. "What do you mean? From what?"

"Well, you and the rest of coastal Louisiana," Charles said.

"What are you talking about?" Kennedy turned on her cushion to face the men and folded her legs under her, tucking her skirt in around her.

"You know what the barrier islands are?" Teddy asked.

"Of course." The islands were naturally occurring strips of land that lay between the open waters of the Gulf of Mexico and the wetlands.

"You know what they do?" Charles asked.

"They protect the coast from the waves out of the gulf. They act as sponges and speedbumps with storms," Kennedy said. "They slow all of that stuff down so that storms and wind and waves lose some of their power by the time they get to the coast. Especially, the wetlands."

Charles nodded. "They also provide calm waters for fish, crabs, oysters, and shrimp to live and reproduce. Along with millions of birds who nest there or stop on their long migrations. They protect the bayou and the things that live there."

Including the people, Kennedy thought, but she didn't add it out loud.

Teddy nodded. "The towns and seaports would be slammed by storms without them. But they're eroding very quickly."

Kennedy nodded. "We know."

"Do you?" Charles asked.

"It's obvious," she said with a frown. "The people that live there know. The storms are stronger, we have a lot more water coming in now. And those who make a living off the fish and crabs and shrimp, all definitely know. Some of the fish that don't survive in saltwater have died off with the rising salt content in the water that washes in. We're even worried about the alligators eventually. They can live in saltwater for short periods, but they really need fresh water."

Charles nodded. He looked a little surprised. Or impressed. Or something. "Sea levels are rising and burying some of the islands," he said. "Hurricanes are getting stronger and more common. They're washing some of the islands away faster than they are replenished. If those islands disappear, people aren't going to be able to live right along the coast."

"It's not just nature, Charles," Kennedy said. He knew that, she was sure, but suddenly she wanted him to know that *she* knew about all of the forces that were changing Louisiana. "Sure, sea levels and storms are part of it, but so is the fact that the oil and gas companies have carved out some of the land for their ships. Not to mention that the Mississippi has been redirected. It's not bringing the sediment in to rebuild the islands and coast. Even New Orleans is sinking."

"You're right," Charles told her.

Of course, she was. "But what's all of that got to do with Bennett?"

"He's building an island."

Kennedy blinked at Teddy. "What?"

"There's a lot of negotiating and troubleshooting going on about what's happening above Louisiana with the river," he said. "But one big way of protecting the coast is by building up the barrier islands."

"Okay. But..." Kennedy shook her head. "He's just...making a whole island?"

"Well, he's working to help build up the others as well, but..." Teddy shrugged. "Yeah. Sauveuse Island will be a manmade barrier island."

"Sauveuse?" Kenney repeated. "That's French for 'savior.'"

Teddy nodded.

Wow.

Kennedy frowned. "So Bennett decided to just build an island himself."

"Pretty much," Teddy said with a shrug. "It's a huge project because he wants to use natural materials and he has to work with the state and federal government, but he's getting it done."

Kennedy opened her mouth to respond but...she had no idea what to say. Bennett was *building an island* that would help protect the Louisiana coast. With the shrinking barrier islands, the wetlands, the *bayou*, was at risk. The changes that they were already seeing would just continue and get worse. Kennedy's own grandchildren might not be able to live in Autre if there was no protection. The open waters of the Gulf would pummel Autre and the towns around it. Unless someone stepped in. Unless someone *did* something.

"That's amazing." She wasn't sure if she was more shocked that Bennett cared that much or that he had that much money.

The money thing, she realized only a second later. His affection for the bayou, the coast, and the people that lived and worked there was real. She'd seen it from the beginning. She'd teased him about it—what was an ivy league lawyer in shiny shoes doing down on the bayou anyway?—but she'd seen it.

"He's impatient," Charles said. "That's a blessing and a curse working with Bennett. He gets stuff done. But he pushes everyone else to do the same and, in spite of being around politics all his life, he gets frustrated with how long bureaucracy takes sometimes."

"What happens when he gets frustrated with it all?" she asked. He wouldn't give up. She knew that. She wasn't sure *how* she knew that, but she did. Bennett Baxter wasn't a quitter. That was something else he had in common with the Landrys. None of them had ever walked away from something just because it was hard.

Charles and Teddy both chuckled. "He goes ahead with it anyway. Figures getting forgiven is easier than getting permission."

"Really?" She'd seen the determined side of Bennett, but she'd never seen the rebellious side.

"He spent some time yelling at some people the other day and then moved some ships into place to start dumping sediment. They were stopped, of course, but he's got most of the Louisiana state government going 'round in circles trying to figure out what exactly he did wrong and how to stop him. Which is complicated by the fact that they don't really want to stop him. What he's doing is great. He's just not getting the right approvals first."

"Why can't whoever is supposed to approve it just approve it?" Kennedy asked. "That doesn't seem that hard. Surely there's *someone* in charge."

"Actually, there are lots of someones in charge," Teddy said, casting Charles a look. "Government isn't—can't be—run by just one person. It has to be done democratically."

"There are people who don't want Bennett to build this island that's going to protect fish and wildlife and jobs and homes?" Kennedy asked.

"There are people who want..." Charles trailed off and sighed. "There are people who want to build the island—islands—themselves."

"But they want to make money off of it somehow," Teddy said with a scowl. "So they're mucking things up to keep Bennett from being the first out there."

"And the first to do it for free," Kennedy guessed. "Because if he does it, then they won't be able to justify charging money for it."

"You've got it," Teddy said.

"Well, good for Bennett," Kennedy said, feeling something that felt a lot like affection for the shiny-shoed guy who'd denied her an orgasm just a little bit ago. Arrogantly. Without a hint of remorse. Yeah, they weren't done talking about *that*. But the idea of Bennett building a freaking *island* and just doing it, whether all the government red tape was taken care of or not, made her tingly in a new way. "When something you love is being threatened, of course you want to just get in there and fix it. If protecting my home and the people I love required an island and I had the money and resources to build it, I'd just build a freaking island, too, and deal with the consequences later."

"The consequences could be steep," Charles said.

"But are they going to *unbuild* the island that's protecting everything?" Kennedy volleyed back. "No. So he'll have accomplished his goal."

"He could face hefty fines. A ban on future building. Jail time," Charles said. "He needs to learn some patience. It will get done, but he needs to play by the rules."

Kennedy snorted at that. Then looked at the men. "Sorry. I just...I don't spend a lot of time with people who let rules get in the way of doing the right thing." She grimaced. Maybe she shouldn't be admitting that.

"Is that right?" Charles asked.

"I just mean, my family would be the first to...I don't know... take care of a hurt animal, for instance, and worry about it being an endangered animal that probably shouldn't be sleeping on a dog bed in the living room later." She looked back and forth between the men. "Just as an example."

Charles cleared his throat and Teddy said, "Theoretically, of course. Right?"

"Of course."

"You know," Charles said. "Some people think that some of the tourism on the coast needs to be curbed." Clearly, he was trying to change the subject a little.

Kennedy frowned. "But those people don't really know what they're talking about. Obviously."

"No?"

"No. Tourism on the coast is incredibly important."

"Some people think that having boatloads of people in and out of the bayou all day long just stirs things up a little, antagonizes some of the animals, tames some of the others—like the gators. They think it's unbalancing the system out there."

She thought she saw a little mischief around the edges of Charles' supposed nonchalant look. Maybe he was baiting her, but she couldn't help but reply.

"Yeah, well, I'm guessing you're talking about the politicians who are paid to look the other way when the gas and oil industries go in there and 'stir things up a little,'" she said, lifting her fingers in air quotes. "I'd say oil spills kind of antagonize the animals, wouldn't you? And, of course, there's all the people—engineers and scientists for the government, right?—who have been messing with the Mississippi up north. If anything, tourism, especially companies like ours, can *help* the coast."

"How so?" Charles asked.

She didn't really care at that point if he was being a smart-ass. She swung her feet to the ground and leaned in, bracing her hands on the edge of the lounge chair. "When *we* take people out hunting and fishing and camping, we teach them to respect the land and the ecosystem. We teach them about the animals and birds. We help them see the Cajun culture up close and personal. They meet the hardworking fishermen. They get to spend some time in our town and see how we live with the bayou. I promise you that they leave with a better understanding and a love for the place they didn't have before."

Charles was looking at her with a thoughtful look now. "And how does that help the environmental problems?"

"Well, for one thing, it keeps people coming back and telling their family and friends to come. That helps contribute to the nearly nineteen *billion* dollars that tourists and visitors spend in Louisiana each year," she said.

He looked surprised.

"Oh, you didn't know that? Yeah, besides coming to appreciate the state and things we've got that they can't get anywhere else, those fifty-two *million* visitors to our great state every year help generate almost two billion dollars in tax revenue. And they help employ two hundred and thirty-seven thousand people."

"I, um..." Charles cleared his throat. "Yes, I did know all of that, actually."

Teddy coughed. It almost sounded like he was covering a laugh. But Kennedy didn't look away from Charles.

"And, I can promise you that *our* visitors in Autre leave feeling connected to the place in a way that I think would make them agree that the coast needs to be saved and the bayou preserved."

Kennedy took a deep breath, frowning. She'd never gone on about that before. But it was all true. People had to care about a place before they would defend it. Maybe not every person from Wyoming or Kansas or Pennsylvania that had visited Boys of the Bayou would write a letter to the state government or the White House for them, but...some might.

Bennett didn't, apparently, need money to actually build the island, but it sure wouldn't hurt him to have more people supporting the idea and telling lawmakers to get behind it.

"You think that you could actually make a grassroots advocacy effort out of the Boys of the Bayou mailing list?" Charles asked. He didn't sound like he was being sarcastic.

Kennedy nodded. "I do. I mean, it can't hurt, right? If we make enough noise, we can get local people caring. Louisianans are proud people. If some guy in North Dakota can care about the bayou, then people in Baton Rouge sure can. And hell, at least we could flood the governor's office with letters that say 'Free Bennett' if he ends up in jail, right?"

Teddy cough-laughed again.

Kennedy nodded. "One thing I do have a lot of experience in is making noise."

Teddy grinned. "You're a Cajun. I wouldn't expect anything less."

"So you really think you can make people care about the bayou?" Charles asked.

"Hell yes, I've been doing that all my life," she said.

"It will take people with a lot of passion."

She nodded. "The Landrys are perfect for that."

Charles laughed. "Glad to hear it."

"So, what do you do, Charles?" Kennedy finally asked, realizing she didn't know much about the man.

"Oh, I'm—" He glanced at Teddy. "I'm in politics," he finally said.

Kennedy rolled her eyes. "Of course you are."

He laughed. "That obvious?"

"Just because you're at this party," she said. "I should have known. You a senator from Georgia or something?" Maybe he could introduce her to some influencers in Louisiana.

Kennedy frowned at that stray thought. Why did she want to meet politicians from Louisiana? That was Bennett's thing. Her thing could be baking him a cake with a file in it if he ended up in the slammer. And conjugal visits. Because as creepy as *that* whole idea was, the guy who was *building a freaking island* to protect her home deserved some hot, rowdy, jailhouse sex.

"I'm...not," Charles said.

"Just tell her," Teddy said, with a chuckle.

"Tell me what?" Kennedy asked.

"I didn't want to get into it. I wanted to hear your honest opinions without you knowing," Charles told her.

"Without me knowing *what*?" Kennedy insisted.

"What I do for a living."

"Jesus, Mary, and Joseph," Kennedy said with an eye-roll. "What the fuck, Charles? Just tell me."

"I'm the Governor of Louisiana."

Kennedy stared at him, letting those words roll around in her head. He was the what? Of what?

"You're the governor," she repeated.

"Yes."

"*My* governor."

"Yep."

Kennedy regarded the man who was seriously a really good Flip Cup player. "No shit," she finally said.

"Seriously."

"You're kind of far from home, aren't you?"

He nodded. "I've known Preston since I was in law school and attended a guest lecture he did. I'm here as a personal friend tonight. In part because Bennett is pissed at me and isn't speaking to me right now."

She frowned at him. "So you're the one who isn't approving Bennett building that island? *You're* the one that might put him in jail?"

Charles' eyes widened. "Well, um..." He cleared his throat. "I'm not going to put Bennett in jail. But I was hoping to talk him into slowing things down a little." He looked at her with a small smile. "I don't think that's going to happen, though, now that I've met you."

"You came out here to play a drinking game with me, hoping to bond with me and butter me up and get me to intervene with Bennett?" she asked. "That's not cool."

"I will admit the thought crossed my mind," Charles said. "But it became quickly clear that you were not going to be an ally for me."

"You've got that right," she told him. "I don't think I'm the right girl to talk to about slowing things down and making sure all the Ts are crossed."

"No," Charles agreed. "Definitely not an ally for me." He grinned at her. "Because you're very clearly the perfect ally for Bennett."

Kennedy felt a little squeeze in her chest. An ally for Bennett. She liked that.

Bennett Baxter was a *really* good guy. And now she knew that he was more than a nerdy, scientist-wannabe who couldn't even keep his footing in the bayou he was trying to save. She'd seen him fall in that beloved, dirty water more times than she could count. No, that wasn't true. Nine. She'd seen him fall in the bayou nine times. But she'd thought he was pretty cute even then. Hell, when he'd stripped his shirt off to help put the new dock in, she'd almost tripped over her own tongue.

And now she knew he wasn't just playing around on the airboats for fun. He was literally putting his knowledge and money and influence to work. He was willing to take personal and professional risks to save that bayou. Yeah, that was all really hot. She wasn't sure she'd ever truly been turned on by a man's mind and power before.

Bennett Baxter was definitely on a whole other level, and she was finally able to admit that she was a little intimidated by him and the things he knew and did that she had no clue about.

But it was also kind of exciting.

Bennett could get shit done. That was sexy as hell.

She and Bennett didn't know each other very well, but she was also realizing that this trip to Savannah was helping her get to know *herself* a little better. Maybe she did have a thing. Maybe that thing was what she'd been doing all her life—loving the bayou and helping other people discover they loved it, too. And that it was worth preserving.

Maybe she and Bennett also really did have more in common than she'd thought.

And maybe having him around more wasn't a completely terrible idea.

She sat back in the chaise and tucked her feet up under her skirt. She lay her cheek on the cushion and listened to Charles and Teddy talk. She wasn't even sure about what. They just fell into conversation like two old friends do.

This had to be one of the most interesting evenings she'd had in a long time.

And as long as Charles didn't ask her who she'd voted for in the last gubernatorial election, she'd be okay.

9

Bennett stepped back out onto the patio nearly three hours later than he'd expected to.

Fuck, the entire night had gotten away from him. That happened when he started talking to people who were into hearing what he had to say about his passions. And if Governor Ray had been faking his interest to butter Bennett up for future talks about campaigns and elected office...well, he'd done a great job. Bennett had really believed that the other man wanted to hear his ideas.

The issues in Georgia weren't quite the same as what he was working on and pushing in Louisiana, but he had a passion for environmental protection in his home state as well. He knew there were good people there who could make a difference. But the government had to let them.

Bennett shoved a hand through his hair and took a deep breath of the summer night air. He let it go, letting the mix of frustration and optimism leave his shoulders. Business was over for the night. He owed a certain sassy brunette an orgasm. Or three.

He started toward the fireplace at the far end of the patio.

He could see that some of the chairs in the area were still occupied. He hadn't seen Kennedy or Teddy head inside. The back of his mother's house was nearly all windows, and he'd been able to observe the game of Flip Cup as he stood talking to Governor Ray and assorted other stakeholders. He'd also heard the country party music every time someone opened the French doors going out or coming in from the backyard. He'd cast a few glances in his mother's direction. She hadn't looked pleased, but neither had she been shocked that her side of the family was getting a little loud.

He'd never been so grateful for his uncle Teddy and family. Kennedy had clearly fit right in with them, and it gave her a group to hang out with while he was with the governor. He really did intend to spend this weekend with *her*. This was about having time to really show her that they should give this thing between them a try. He knew that she didn't believe they had any business talking long-term, but he was going to change her mind.

Of course, he needed to be *with her* to do that.

She'd seemed fine with him spending dinner at the other end of the table. But that was Kennedy. She was easygoing. Almost to a fault. She was a challenge and a handful in many ways, but she was also hard to truly rile up. She put a good face on it sometimes. She ranted at her brothers and bitched about them not checking schedules and so on. She also loved to give her grandfather and his cronies shit. But none of it was very sincere. She loved her life and loved the people in it and handled everything with barely a hair out of place.

She would have made a great CEO, if that had been her calling. If she'd maybe been born somewhere else, into a different family. She could have run a company with one hand tied behind her back. Her sharp tongue, quick wit, sense of humor, and that look she could give that said, *My God, you're a dumbass* would have kept people in line and working hard.

But she was a bayou girl. Instead of running a company, she kept her family running. He knew that she didn't see it that way. She saw them as a bunch of people she had to put up with and the things she did as just stuff she had to do. From scheduling at the company, to ordering supplies, to protecting them from bad news when she could, to convincing the wildlife authorities that the gray wolf was hers, not Tori's, to helping in the big kitchen when everyone descended on Ellie's on the weekends to relax and kick back and enjoy some great food, drink, and company, she did it all for them. With them. Without a second thought.

That was why when *he* could get her riled up—actually annoyed or frustrated or hot—it felt like a victory. He could get under her skin. That had to mean something.

Bennett didn't see her right away as he approached the fireplace. Clearly, everyone was far more mellow now though. The later hour and the empty bottles of vodka probably had something to do with that.

"How's everything?" he asked his uncle.

"Good," Teddy answered with a smile. "Really good."

"Yeah?" He glanced around. His cousins were slumped in the chairs, feet up, a couple still with plastic cups in hand but sipping slowly now. Charles was in the chair to Teddy's right, his head tipped back, softly snoring.

"Charles had fun?" Bennett asked.

"Charles did. He kept right up with Kennedy. But he's a little drunk." Teddy gave a soft chuckle.

Bennett sighed. "Kennedy got the governor of Louisiana drunk?"

"She did," Teddy confirmed.

Bennett shook his head. "Did she know who he was?"

"Not until after Flip Cup and several drinks. He finally confessed."

"What was her reaction?"

"She was pissed that he might be sending you to jail." Teddy grinned up at him.

Bennett's eyebrows rose. "You told her about that?"

"Yep."

"*All* about it?" he asked. Had Teddy filled her in on all the reasons he might be doing jail time and how that had all started?

"Yep. Everything."

"Why?"

"She needed to know."

"Did she?" Bennett asked.

"It's who you are. If she's going to fall in love with you, she needs to know who you are."

Bennett felt like Teddy had just reached into his chest and squeezed his lungs. In love with him? He wanted Kennedy. He'd been thinking of long-term, hoping this weekend would turn into something more. But he hadn't really put the L word to it. And hearing it out loud from someone else made it very real and very...huge.

"She's over there." Teddy pointed to the chaise lounge chair that looked like it was covered in pillows and a blanket.

But the pillows were actually Kennedy.

Kennedy was lying curled up on the seat, covered in a light blanket. She had her hands up under her cheek and her feet were tucked underneath her and the blanket, her shoes lying on the stones below the chair.

His heart kicked against his ribs. He cleared his throat. "You wore her out?"

"Surprised?" Teddy asked.

"Shocked." Bennett leaned over and lifted her a little, sliding in behind her, letting her rest on him instead of the chair. She mumbled something but settled in against him without opening her eyes. He rested his hands on the curve of her hip and let the warmth of her body soak in.

"She's a partier, huh?" Teddy asked with a grin. He lifted a coffee cup now instead of a plastic cup or bottle.

"Her whole family knows how to have a good time," Bennett said with a nod. "She can outlast every one of them from what I've seen."

"Well, she definitely kept up when we were playing. She kicked the boys' asses," Teddy said, glancing at his sons.

Bennett chuckled. His sons were hardly big partiers now. Maybe at one time they would have been able to hang with the Landrys, but one was a college professor now and one was a novelist. They both had wives and kids and had probably never been to a crawfish boil. Which was too bad.

"So the game didn't last all that long really," Teddy said. "Then the guys were grumbling that they were hungry since they hadn't been too excited about the chicken. Kennedy headed into the kitchen and made us all po' boys."

Bennett was definitely surprised by that. "No kidding."

"Yep. Made herself at home in the kitchen and had us all fed in no time."

"How were they?" Bennett already knew that answer. Amazing.

"The boys swore they'd died and gone to heaven. Even Tawny ate two."

"That's...Kennedy," Bennett finally said.

Teddy nodded. "She's wonderful." He frowned slightly though.

"What?" Bennett asked. "Something wrong?"

Teddy shook his head. "Nah. She's sweet and friendly. Has a million stories. Loves to laugh and make others laugh."

That was all true. Bennett felt a warmth in his chest that could have almost been pride. He loved having everyone here know that she was with him. He put his lips against her hair and gave her a kiss that he knew she wouldn't feel but that he couldn't resist.

"But..." Teddy said.

Bennett looked up at his uncle. "But what?"

"Sounds like she's pretty wrapped up in the family business and what all's going on with all of them." He paused. "And you."

"What do you mean?"

"You were telling me about the tour business and all of the Landrys."

Bennett nodded. Teddy had always been a big supporter of his and he kept his uncle informed on what he was up to. Lately, that had involved a lot of the Landrys.

"Sounds to me like those girls are all on an adventure. Coming to the bayou. Making a new life. Figuring their stuff out. Growing and expanding their horizons."

"Okay," Bennett said slowly.

"And now you're planning the same thing. Uprooting things and going down there to pursue your passion. Doing something new and exciting."

"Right."

"And Kennedy's just doin' the same old stuff," Teddy said. "Just seems...unfair, you know. She's there for all of you to have fun and try new things. But she's not getting to do that."

"She *likes* the...usual stuff," Bennett said. She shifted in his arms, and Bennett realized his hold on her had tightened. He took a breath and relaxed his arms. "She's just already found her place," he said. "She knows who she is, what she wants, where she wants to be."

"And that's why you're drawn to her," Teddy said. "You want all of that. You want a place to settle, where people do what you expect them to do, where you can count on them."

Bennett was nodding even before his uncle stopped talking. "Yes. Definitely. Where people say what they mean and where you know they'll stand by the right thing even if it's hard."

Teddy nodded.

"Is that bad?" Bennett and his uncle had always been close. In spite of his mother's eye-rolling over this side of her family, she loved her brother and when she could relax and not worry about good or bad impressions made on her husband's colleagues and supporters, she'd been known to kick her shoes off and lounge by a fire, too.

Bennett, on the other hand, had enjoyed this side of the family's more relaxed approach to life. They laughed more, had more fun, seemed to worry less.

But the biggest thing was that when Bennett had disagreed with his father's politics, had broken ties with the law firm his father had founded with his best friend, and had started supporting his father's political opponents, Teddy had stood beside Bennett. Teddy loved his sister and he and Preston Baxter had always gotten along, but Teddy had immediately called Bennett with his support after his falling out with Preston. Furthermore, Teddy had been the first major donor to Bennett's foundation. Over the past couple of years, Teddy had continued his financial backing as well as his emotional support of his only nephew.

"It's not bad at all," Teddy said. "I know that you really want all of that. Just don't make Kennedy be something for you that she doesn't really want to be."

Bennett felt a stab of awareness in his chest. Was he doing that? Did he just want the Landrys and their lifestyle, to be a part of the family? Was he making Kennedy into something in his mind that she wasn't really so he had a way into the Landry family?

But no. He never knew what she was going to say or do *exactly*—in a fun way—but he knew she'd speak her mind and she'd be there for the people she cared about no matter what. That's what he wanted. Honesty, someone who knew who they were and what they believed, someone who believed the same things he did, and someone who would do what they promised they'd do every single time.

That shouldn't be a lot to ask, but in the world he'd grown up in, full of politicians and powerful men wanting to be even more powerful, it seemed those things were hard to come by.

"She's someone I know I can count on," he said, as Kennedy stirred a little in his arms.

"That's wonderful," his uncle said. "Just be someone *she* can count on, too. If you're serious about her, she can't just be the soft place where you land. She should have a chance to do some of the flying and landing, too."

Kennedy's hand flexed where it was resting on his chest, gripping his shirt gently. He looked down at her. Her eyes were still closed. She was so damned beautiful. He wanted her. Period.

At least, he was ninety-nine percent sure he did. He wanted this woman that he thought she was anyway. But was he missing something? Was he only looking at their relationship and what *he* needed?

Probably.

Because it really didn't seem that Kennedy Landry *needed* anything.

"Maybe we'll just—" Her hand started moving over his chest, making him forget what he was going to say. Was she still asleep?

"I think you can figure it out," Teddy said. "I'm not saying that you can't. Just wanted to make you aware that I think Miss Kennedy is kind of used to being in the background and maybe she needs a chance to be up front, too, you know?"

Kennedy's hand ran a little lower to his abs, moving back and forth across his shirt, and she turned her face, putting her mouth against his chest. He could feel the heat of her breath through the expensive fabric.

"She seems...loud and sassy and has this unique style,"

Bennett said. His stomach tensed as her hand moved even lower, her fingers skimming the waistband of his pants. He put a hand over hers to stop it. "But yeah, if I think about it, she does do a lot of the behind-the-scenes stuff—taking care of the business, helping her grandma, that kind of thing."

He hadn't realized that before. Or at least he hadn't really *thought* about it before. Did that make him an asshole?

Teddy chuckled as Kennedy seemed to move closer, wiggling against him and nuzzling his chest. "Maybe we can talk about this more later. After you think about it. I think you need to get that girl upstairs."

Yeah, he was going to end up embarrassing himself if he didn't. Her hand wasn't *that* far from a part of his body that was going to need reminding that she was drunk and half—or more—asleep and didn't really know what she was doing.

"I appreciate you caring about this," Bennett told his uncle.

Teddy looked at Kennedy and smiled. "Caring isn't hard. I can see why you fell hard and fast. She's something."

Bennett nodded. He hadn't always been the best judge of character in the people around him, but dammit, he'd gotten this right. Kennedy was special.

He shifted her in his arms, standing from the chair, and then lifting her. "We'll see you tomorrow," he said. "Are you golfing in the morning with us?"

His father loved to golf, so there was a big group going out first thing to his favorite course.

Teddy sighed. "I guess so. I hate hanging out with most of those guys, but if you and Steve are there, it will be tolerable."

Bennett smiled. "You just want to golf with us because you can beat us."

"I can beat nine out of ten of those fuckers," Teddy said.

He was right.

"'Night, Teddy."

"'Night, Bennett."

Bennett carried Kennedy across the patio to the back doors that would lead into the kitchen. He shifted her slightly to manage the door but she kept her head on his shoulder, barely stirring. Well, he wasn't going to get the chocolate sauce blow job or the multi-nozzle shower with her tonight, but that was his own damned fault. He again cursed his inability to walk away from someone saying "tell me more about that" when it came to the environmental issues he'd decided to dedicate his career to.

He was a scientist at heart. He'd gone to law school because that had seemed like the thing to do, and he knew he could use that knowledge to help further the issues that really mattered to him. He'd imagined that with his connections through his father and school, as well as his comfort in talking to people about donations to causes, he could better use his position and experience to work for the environment from an office with a foundation. He hadn't found one that did exactly what he wanted them to be doing, so he'd started his own. But he had to admit, the idea of being out in the dirt, water, and air was always there, tempting him. It made his trips to the bayou even more fun. He really had the best of both worlds at this point. His foundation was doing great things and he'd garnered a lot of support.

In Georgia.

The thought that had been nagging him since he'd first set foot on the Boys of the Bayou dock niggled just then. Could he replicate that support in Louisiana? Where the last name Baxter didn't mean anything? He knew, whether he liked it or not, he had Governor Ray's ear, initially, because of Preston. Bennett was confident that he'd convinced the governor that he knew what he was talking about and that his foundation was worthy of the government's attention, but initially, the man had sat down with him because of Bennett's last name.

He nudged his bedroom door open, then shut it softly

behind him. He glanced toward the door that led to Kennedy's room. He should maybe take her in there and put her to bed.

But he didn't want to. He wanted her in here with him. All night. Whether they had sex or not.

Just being with her, holding her, was making him feel less conflicted. His dad's circle of friends and colleagues always made Bennett feel tight. Like he had to be on guard and watch what he said and how he said it. With Kennedy it wasn't like that. He could be himself. He could say what he thought and act on his feelings.

He laid her down on the bed and stepped back, stripping off his shirt and shucking out of his pants, kicking his shiny shoes off to the side. He grinned looking at the shoes. She didn't like them shiny? Bullshit. She didn't *want* to like the things that reminded her that he was something new for her. But she *did* like him and all of those things about him. It shouldn't surprise her that she was going for something different, something unique. Everything about her was unique.

He pulled the comforter and sheet back and then slid her over and started to cover her again.

She stretched and her eyes fluttered.

"Hey," he said, bracing a hand on the mattress beside her.

Her smile was soft and quick. "Hi."

"How are you feeling?"

"Sleepy." She reached for him though.

He let her pull him down for a kiss. He meant to keep it short and sweet but, well, that was probably never going to be the way he kissed Kennedy. She ran her hand up the back of his head and into his hair, opening her mouth for him with a little sigh.

He kissed her deeply, wishing like hell they could have just come straight up here after dinner. He could still feel the hot silk of her pussy around his finger, and he wanted nothing more than to make her call out his name again the way she had in the bedroom earlier.

He'd loved everything about touching and tasting her so far, but he needed to hold back here or he was going to be hurting all night. He was not having sex with her when she was drunk.

Bennett pulled back and looked down at her, loving the pink in her cheeks and the way she smiled up at him.

"Come here." She started to slide over and realized she still had her dress on. She sat up and reached for the zipper.

She was out of the dress a moment later, tossing it to the floor, sitting there in only her bra and panties as if that was the most natural thing. She held the sheet up and slid over.

Bennett climbed in, knowing that he was playing with fire. He wouldn't have sex with her tonight, like this, but being pressed up against her nearly naked body all night was going to be torture. And he was weak. Very, very weak.

Once he was under the sheet, Kennedy turned toward him, kissing him again and pressing the body he wanted more than anything against him.

He let himself enjoy it for about thirty seconds—probably twenty seconds longer than he should have—before grabbing the gorgeous hips that were wiggling against him and pushing her back, giving his cock some much needed space.

"Okay, girl, that's enough for now," he told her.

She frowned. "What?"

He tried to turn her. At least if he got her back to his front it might be slightly less tempting.

But who was he kidding? Her back to his front would be a very nice position to thrust deep and take her hard. His cock was all for that one.

It didn't matter. Kennedy wasn't letting him move her.

"I want to have sex," she said, trying to kiss him again.

"No." He said it firmly, wrestling with every excuse tripping through his head. He squeezed her hips. "Not tonight."

"But..." She frowned again. "By the tree you said—"

"That was before you nearly drank my cousins under the table."

"Oh, I'm fine." She lifted her hand to wave that away and nearly whacked him in the nose.

He caught her hand, but that meant letting go of one hip, which she immediately pressed against him.

"Ken," he said, firmly, but unable to keep the gruffness from his tone. "I'm not fucking you tonight. Not when you're drunk."

"I'm not..." She wrinkled her nose, thinking. "Fourscore and seven years ago our fathers brought forth, on this continent, a new nation, conceived in liberty, and dedicated to the proposition that all men are created equal."

"What are you doing?"

"Proving I'm not that drunk. I remember all those words and didn't even slur."

She was right. Dammit. Bennett sighed. "Ken—"

"I really want to. *Please*."

Normally Kennedy Landry begging him for something, especially an orgasm that he was all too eager to give her, would have been exactly where he wanted to be. He would have drawn it out, of course. Teased her a little. Made her say please a few more times. But he couldn't play with her tonight. He wanted her too much and she was definitely going to be able to wear him down. He couldn't let her know that.

"No," he said again. "Not tonight. First thing in the morning though? As soon as you have some ibuprofen and I'm positive you're fine, I'll give you everything you want."

Her breathing hitched. Then she narrowed her eyes. "Bastard. You can't talk like that if you're going to leave me hurting over here."

Hurting? She wanted to talk about hurting? He put her hand against his cock. "Yeah, well, we'll be hurting together."

Her fingers tightened around him and Bennett realized he'd made a huge mistake.

Kennedy started to move her hand up and down, but he stopped her before she even got one full stroke in. Still, it was enough to have his balls screaming.

"Not taking advantage of me because you think I'm drunk is a little romantic," she said softly. "I should do something dirty to get you back for that."

His heart rate picked up. He loved this teasing with her. And here were certainly things they could do—well, things that could be done—that wouldn't be sex. She wasn't so drunk that they couldn't tease and play a little.

"Okay," he said. "Then you take care of yourself." He moved her hand to her panties. His heart pounded. Could he lie there next to her while she got herself off?

Abso-fucking-lutely. He wasn't taking advantage of her that way, but she was still getting some relief.

She immediately slid her hand into her panties. Even vodka couldn't dull her natural inclination toward mischief.

"I will, if you will," she said.

"You'll play with yourself, make yourself come, and let me watch if I do what?" he asked, pulling the sheet down so that he could see.

One of her knees was bent slightly, spreading her legs, and her fingers were working behind the silk of her thong. He wanted to kiss that rose on her inner thigh more than he could remember wanting anything in a long time.

"If you get yourself off at the same time," she told him. She reached up and pulled one of her bra cups down, playing with her nipple.

He reached over and pulled the other cup down. God, she was so fucking gorgeous. And this was so hot. "I'm in."

He ran a hand over his rock-hard cock, sighing at the slight relief the pressure gave. But it wasn't enough, of course. But before he could take care of himself, he needed to see all of Kennedy.

Bennett reached over and pulled her thong down, baring her, and her busy fingers. She was circling her clit, slowly, almost leisurely. She was also plucking at one nipple. Her hips moved slightly side to side and stopped only to let him pull the tiny scrap of silk from her legs and toss them to the floor. He also quickly divested her of her bra. He took a second to drag a fingertip over her tattoo from her hip to her knee. He relished the way she shivered with the stroke.

"Now you," she told him, her eyes on the front of his boxers.

He pulled them down, naked with her for the first time, and threw them over his shoulder.

She blew out a breath. "Whoa."

He grinned. "You're drunk." He wrapped his hand around his throbbing cock, loving her eyes on him.

"I'm not *that* drunk. That's a whoa no matter how much I've had." She spread her legs further. "You're *sure* we can't have sex?"

He wasn't. At all. She seemed totally with it.

"I want nothing more than to be buried in you," he told her honestly. "But—"

"This is *really* hot," she said. "I know. I agree."

He huffed out a laugh. He wasn't sure that's what he'd been about to say. "Yeah?"

"I've never gotten myself off while someone watched before," she told him. "This is... yeah, hot."

That decided it. He didn't know—didn't want to know—every detail of the other men Kennedy had been with, but if there was something they could do together for the first time that she found hot, then he was in.

"Show me how you like it," he told her, his eyes focused on all the gorgeous pink between her legs and the fingers that clearly knew exactly what to do.

"Well, usually I use my vibrator," she told him. "It's faster."

He stroked his fist up and down his cock. "I want to see that, too."

"I can go get—"

"Don't you dare," he growled. "Fucking finish yourself off while I watch, Kennedy. Just your fingers this time. Work at it a little bit."

She sucked in a quick breath before giving him a sheepish grin. "I like this work."

She began circling again, rubbing, then dipping her fingers into the sweet wetness beneath. She continued playing with her nipple as well, pinching and rolling, and Bennett made note of what she liked. He continued to stroke himself, slow and easy, not wanting to rush ahead of her, but damned grateful for the pressure around his aching shaft. God, he needed to come and he needed it to be with her, if not *in* her.

"Help me," she breathed as she slipped two fingers inside and thrust deep.

"How?" He was beyond being the good guy who wasn't going to touch her. Whatever she wanted, he was going to give.

"Move so I can see you better."

Bennett got to his knees and moved between her legs. "Better?"

"Oh my God, so much better," she panted, her gaze riveted on his cock.

He liked it, too. From here he could see every hot, sweet, wet inch of her. "You're right. This is pretty fucking hot."

She watched his hand moving. "I want that so much."

"It's gonna be all yours."

"I'm never drinking again," she told him, "if it's going to keep me from that."

He chuckled and stroked faster. "Well, I don't think we have to go crazy here."

"Seriously." Her hand was moving faster. "I'll do anything."

"Be careful, babe," he said, also moving faster. "I'm going to hold you to that."

"I'm going to come, Bennett."

"Yes, honey, come for me."

She arched her neck and a moment later squeezed her eyes shut and gave him a long, heartfelt, "*Ahh*."

Yeah, they were going to work on her being a hell of a lot louder and just what—or rather whose name—she was calling out. Bennett gripped his cock and stroked hard and fast, feeling his climax tightening his balls, the tingling starting at the base of his spine.

Kennedy arched her back like a freaking cat as she withdrew her hand from between her legs. Then she propped herself up on one elbow and swirled her fingers over the head of his cock and he erupted.

"Kennedy!"

"Oh, yes," she said softly as he came over her hand. She followed his hand with hers as he finished stroking himself. "Very, very hot."

He let himself fall forward, waves from his orgasm still rippling through him, and pressed his mouth to hers. She wrapped her arms and legs around him, pressing against his body everywhere she could reach.

They kissed for several long, delicious minutes. Finally, Bennett rolled to the side, bringing her with him, his hands firmly cradling her ass.

"That," she said, nuzzling her face against his neck, "was great."

"It was." Though "great" seemed so inadequate.

They lay plastered together for several long moments.

"Tell me about your foundation," she said against his collarbone.

He took a breath. He really didn't want to talk about his

foundation. Or any of the stuff he'd been talking about all damned night. "Not right now."

"How come?"

"Because that's what kept me from bringing you up here earlier when you were totally sober."

He felt her smile against his skin, but she didn't say anything. Until they'd been quiet again for a few minutes.

"I don't have a thing."

Bennett frowned. "What?" She'd said it very quietly, but he also didn't understand what she meant.

"I don't have a thing. Like your foundation and the environment and all the stuff you do. Or like Tori and Maddie and Juliet have."

Bennett stroked his hand up and down her back. "You do have a thing," he told her.

"Not really."

It was just what Teddy had said downstairs. Maybe they'd been talking about it.

"You do," Bennett insisted. "There's no one like you, Kennedy. You make people happy. You make them feel supported. You're like...coming home. You make me take a big deep breath when I see you and let me just...be happy."

She didn't say anything to that.

"You...you're like your grandpa," he said, feeling the need to go on. "You know how he always sits on that same stool? And he's always got a grin and a story? He'll be the first one to give you advice and to tell you you're being a dumbass, to keep you grounded, but he'll somehow also make you feel like he thinks you're awesome and can do anything. He's dependable, always the same. He's...a rock," Bennett said, as he had about Kennedy earlier. "He's exactly who you think he is and if he tells you something, you know he means it and you can count on it. That's definitely a thing. Something a lot of people can't be."

She still didn't say anything. He wondered if she'd fallen asleep.

"Ken?"

Finally, she sighed. "I don't want to be like my grandpa."

Bennett tried to look down at her but could only see the top of her head. "What? Why not? Thought you loved Leo more than anyone."

She nodded, her cheek moving against his chest. "I do, of course. But he...frustrates me. He's a pushover."

Bennett frowned. "That's not how I see him."

"You weren't there when my grandma broke up with him."

Oh. Yeah. Bennett had come along after the elder Landrys were already getting back together. They'd been married for years. Then they'd split up but had stayed close friends. Leo had moved out but only as far as the trailer behind the house he'd shared with Ellie. He'd even slept on the couch in that house whenever it rained because the trailer leaked. He'd continued to do things for Ellie around the house and help out at the bar. He sat on the same stool that he now occupied, and always had, throughout their breakup. He'd never really left her. He'd just, apparently, given her the space she'd thought she needed.

"He didn't want to break up?" Bennett asked.

"No. Definitely not. I mean, he knew that they were fighting a lot and that she thought she was unhappy, so he wanted to break up if that's what she wanted or what would make them both happy. But he was never going to *leave* her. Not really. He was always going to be there for her, no matter what she needed. No matter what she did. Or who she did." The last few words were more of a mutter.

Bennett tightened his arm around her. "Their breakup was hard on you, I'm guessing."

"I just..." She paused for several seconds. Then she looked up at him. "I pitied him," she said. "He just sat there. Right there at that bar. Slept right outside her back door. Was always there. She knew he would always be there. And she got to do whatever she wanted. And I hated seeing that. I hated seeing him just take it. And I hated feeling sorry for him. He's my favorite person. He's the most loving person I've ever met. He will always put other people first. He will do anything to make people smile. He would do *anything* to keep our family safe. But she just took him for granted. And then he was there when she was ready to come back. Just like she knew he would be."

"Are you more upset that they broke up or that they got back together?" Bennett asked.

She seemed to have to think about that. But finally she said, "Both. But maybe the getting back together. I mean, I like them together. He's definitely happier with her than without. And my family is happier now that they're back together. But...it's like he doesn't have a thing, either," she said. "He's just there. Helping everyone else do *their* things. Why can't *he* have a thing?"

Bennett didn't know what to say to that. Frankly, she had a point. Leo was the guy who built everyone else up to go off and do their things. The family hadn't gone too far from him. His grandsons—Josh, Sawyer, Owen, and Mitch—all still worked in Autre in the business that Leo had handed down to them. His son and daughter still lived in Autre, too, though they worked in New Orleans. He was surrounded by people and friends he'd known all his life.

"Maybe he's doing his thing," Bennett suggested. "Maybe he likes being that rock. Everyone needs a solid place to start from and to rely on when things go wonky. Maybe he looks at it as him having a hand in *all* of those things everyone does. Those are all kind of his thing."

"Did you have that?" she asked. "Were your parents a solid place to start for you to go do all your amazing things? Because they had their own things at the same time."

Bennett took a deep breath and shook his head. "No. I mean, the path was solid if I wanted to follow what they'd laid out. And I did for a long time. But veering off of that got...rocky. Definitely not like Leo, who lets everyone figure their stuff out and is just there, being supportive no matter what."

"You veered off your path?"

"I did."

"Why?"

He took another deep breath. "This is a lot for tonight."

"I want to know."

He really didn't want to get into this. What he *wanted* was for Kennedy to see that she really was like Leo, in all the best ways. Bennett really needed her to be that. That sounded selfish as hell, of course. This wasn't all just about him figuring *his* shit out.

Apparently.

But that was why his gut was tightening and why he suddenly felt restless. He'd thought she was solid. He'd thought Kennedy had her shit together and was doing exactly what she wanted to be doing. He thought she could be that person who he could count on to be there, exactly who he thought she was, who would tell him the truth, no matter how painful, who would be...rock solid.

She didn't sound rock solid right now.

"Let's clean up first." He rolled her off of him and slid out of bed without looking back at her. He went to the bathroom and cleaned up. He was feeling edgy, and he knew it was because Kennedy was revealing some things that he hadn't been aware of. Things that were making him question all he'd been so sure of.

He wanted Kennedy Landry.

But did he want the woman who was lying in his bed right now or the woman he'd *thought* he knew? The one out there right now sounded sad and frustrated about the family that he'd thought was solid and sure. She seemed far less confident than he'd expected and maybe even a little lost. He wanted the sassy, sure-of-herself bayou girl. He'd thought she was a what-you-see-is-what-you-get girl. He'd thought she'd already found her place and had dug her roots in deep.

Now, between what Teddy had said and the little bit of insight she'd just given him, he wasn't sure.

Bennett blew out a breath. Well, this whole trip had been about getting to know one another better. They were doing that. He wet a washcloth with warm water and went back into the bedroom.

She was asleep.

He stopped and just watched her for a long moment.

She was gorgeous. She was also deeply devoted to her family, handled everything anyone threw at her—even the need for shrimp po' boys in the midst of his mother's fancy party—made people laugh and was bluntly honest.

She *was* who he thought she was.

There was just even more there.

And he was an asshole for not knowing that. Or for even wondering about it.

Bennett tossed the washcloth back into the bathroom and headed for the bed. He slipped under the covers next to her and welcomed her warm, softness against him as she cuddled her butt into his groin.

His cock stirred, of course, but he wrapped an arm around her and kept her close.

Kennedy was definitely more open than most people he knew. All of the Landrys were. It was refreshing and he'd fallen head over heels for it all immediately. But it was unfair of him to think that he knew everything about this woman. In fact, this was the first deep conversation they'd ever had. And she was at least half-drunk. Her guard down. It was possible she'd never intended to let him this close.

But then she turned in his arms, snuggled close, put her nose against his neck, and said softly, "Bennett."

Contentment.

The feeling was intense and washed over him and he sucked in a deep breath.

Maybe she didn't mean to let him this close, but she had. And he wanted more.

10

Fuck vanilla vodka and everything that had ever been made with it.

Kennedy groaned as she rolled over. Her head pounded.

Okay, fuck all vodka.

Kennedy put her hands to her head. Dammit. She hadn't been hungover in a long time. She knew better. She knew what her limits were. At least, with moonshine on the bayou. Vanilla vodka was an unknown evil.

Until now.

She squinted at the clock. It was nine-thirty a.m. She looked at the bed next to her. Bennett was gone.

She listened for the shower but heard nothing.

Slowly, painfully, she pushed herself up to sitting and looked around, careful not to move her head too fast.

Nope, he wasn't here.

She heard a chime from the bedside table and looked over. Her phone was there and apparently she had a text.

She reached for it, again slowly and a little painfully.

Golfing. Will probably be a while. Go down and help yourself to coffee and food.

The second text read, *I'll need a shower when I get back.*

Even hungover, her body responded to that. She *was* getting in that damned shower with Bennett in the next twenty-four hours, or somebody was going to be in trouble.

Kennedy ran her tongue around her mouth, trying to clear the cotton out of it. Man, she needed coffee. And one of Cora's hangover cures. She figured Maria had to have those ingredients in her kitchen. She stood slowly from the bed. Okay, her stomach was all right. Her head hurt, but otherwise she was okay. Ibuprofen, a tall glass of *But Did You Die*?—Cora's name for her morning-after potion—and a shower. Then she'd feel human.

And, of course, she could shower again later with Bennett.

She grabbed her phone for music and headed for the bathroom. She braced herself for the lights to come on and let them slowly adjust to the brightness. She stood in front of the shower stall, just taking it all in.

The thing was enormous. And all glass. With lots of nozzles. The huge mirror over the vanity was directly across from it, too, and would let her—or whoever she was with—watch whatever happened in that shower. Her heart thunked and heat tripped through her system thinking about it. Everything from the night before came rushing back. Her and Bennett in his bed. Him listening to her go on about how she felt about Leo and Ellie. Bennett insisting he couldn't fuck her because she'd been drunk. That was unnecessarily gentlemanly of him, and she could honestly say that had been hot, too. And then all the incredible sexiness that came after that. The do-it-yourself orgasms were never as good as the real thing, but yet last night had seemed unbelievably satisfying. It had been deliciously dirty, for sure, but it had also seemed intimate.

She heard her phone ding and looked down. It was another text from Bennett.

Remember what I said about any orgasms that you have without me.

Her pulse pounded. He'd said that he'd tie her to the bed and tease her mercilessly.

Hmmm…

She eyed the shower. He'd never have to know though.

Her phone dinged.

And I will know.

She giggled. Actually giggled. He'd never know, and he didn't even know she was awake and reading these messages right now. But she loved his cockiness and his dirtiness.

She'd already been hot for the guy, but after learning about everything he was doing from running a foundation that took care of the environment, to resisting everyone's attempt to get him to run for office, to building a freaking *island* to help protect Louisiana, she was *really* turned on.

Kennedy would have *never* in a million years guessed that politics and environmental activism and throwing money around like it was beads off a Mardi Gras float would be a turn-on. But it was. Evidently.

Or maybe it was the man, and his intentions, behind it all.

Yeah, it was maybe that. But if she admitted that, she might have to admit that she was falling for him. A little. Maybe.

She reached in and turned on the shower, waited for it to warm up, and stepped under the spray. She'd just clean up quickly now. Yes, she eyed a couple of the nozzles and spent a few seconds telling herself that Bennett would never *actually* know. But in the end, she resisted.

Because she wanted that orgasm from him.

Dammit. He already had her doing what he told her. Or *not* doing what he told her *not* to do, to be more precise.

Still, she soaped up, rinsed off, and stepped out of the shower without doing a thing about it.

She was in trouble.

Ten minutes later, Kennedy was downstairs in a tank top and shorts, her hair in a ponytail, scrounging in the kitchen. It seemed that breakfast had been served earlier, probably before the guys left for the golf course, but she'd slept through it.

Which was fine. All she really needed was coffee, bacon, and some grits. She opened three cupboards without finding anything though. She frowned. Maria was a Cajun girl. She might not live that way now, but there was no way a girl who had grown up in Louisiana gave up grits entirely. She finally found what she was looking for in a lower cupboard back behind the oatmeal and coconut flour. What the hell was coconut flour?

She started with the hangover cure, running the blender and pouring a big glass. She'd drink that while she made everything else.

"Please, please, *please* never turn that blender on again."

She turned to see Charles shuffling toward the coffeepot.

Kennedy's ibuprofen and the twelve ounces of water she'd downed were already working and she grinned. "Good morning, Governor."

"Fuck vanilla vodka."

"Dude. Same," she said sincerely.

"Seriously." He slid up onto a stool, cradling his cup with one hand and resting his head on his other hand. "How can that stuff be so potent?"

Kennedy continued gathering what she needed for the grits. "No idea. At least after a night with moonshine you have some great karaoke on video and probably a story or two about how you won a slam dunk contest or something."

Charles chuckled, then groaned.

"So, no golfing for you, huh?" she asked, assembling the ingredients. Looked like she was making sweet grits for two.

"I don't like golfing on my best day," Charles said, nursing his coffee. "Definitely not today."

While the water heated, Kennedy dug in the fridge, bringing out bacon and eggs.

Charles groaned again as she began breaking and beating eggs.

"Oh, no, you're eating," she said. "You start with the grits. They'll soak up all the alcohol, but then you have to have protein."

He just *harrumphed* in reply.

"And," she said, bringing the glass of tomato juice—and other stuff—to him. He needed it more than she did. "Drink this after your coffee."

"Bloody Mary?" he asked, eyeing it suspiciously.

"My grandma's best friend's remedy," Kennedy said. "Tomato juice, spinach, and cayenne. And a few other things. Worcestershire and salt. Stuff like that."

"Cayenne?"

"Trust me. Natural pain reliever."

Charles tipped back the rest of his coffee and reached for the glass. Kennedy went back to the stove.

"So, Charles," she said, as she stirred the grits and started the bacon frying. "What's the deal with Bennett and his dad?"

Charles didn't reply and she looked over her shoulder. He seemed to be considering his answer.

"What's he told you?" he asked.

"Nothing. I get the definite impression they don't get along. That his dad is disappointed in him not running for office."

"That's part of it," Charles agreed.

"What else?"

He looked uncomfortable. Kennedy stirred the grits.

"Charles?"

"Yeah?"

"These are going to be the best grits you've ever tasted. And they're going to make you feel better."

"Okay."

"Or...they're not."

"What do you mean?"

"I mean, you tell me about Bennett and his dad, or...you'll regret this breakfast more than you're regretting the vanilla vodka."

Charles narrowed his eyes. "You're threatening a governor?"

"No one will be able to prove a thing."

He slowly smiled. "I'm guessing you've gotten revenge on a couple of brothers over the years?"

"And cousins and a grandfather," she confirmed.

Charles blew out a breath. "Okay. But only because it smells amazing."

Kennedy smiled. One thing she was sure of—she was a hell of a cook.

"Bennett always planned to follow in his father's footsteps. Law practice, public office, all of that," Charles said.

Kennedy pretended to be busy cooking. The truth was, she could have made all of this in her sleep. She couldn't begin to count the pieces of bacon she'd fried over the years in her grandma's bar and restaurant.

"But when Bennett was a senior in college, almost done with his political science degree and applying to law schools, someone sent him a packet of information about his father."

"Someone? Who?" Kennedy asked.

"It's never been confirmed," Charles said, studying his tomato juice.

Kennedy watched him for a second. "What was the information? An affair or something?"

Charles looked up. "About ten years before, his father had defended a company that was knowingly polluting some of the rivers and streams. It was a big chemical company and his dad got very rich."

"He won in court?"

"He did. More than he lost, anyway."

Kennedy frowned.

"By Bennett's senior year, his dad was in the Senate," Charles went on. "The materials also showed how that company, and others, helped fund his campaign and several pieces of legislation that his father had introduced and voted for that were helping those companies."

Kennedy saw where this was going. "Bennett had no idea?"

"No."

"What happened?"

"The packet contained tons of stories—many that had been buried—about how the pollution had affected wildlife and communities. Kids who had gotten sick. The immense cost of cleaning it up, which the communities and state governments were stuck paying for rather than the chemical companies."

"How can that be?" Kennedy said. "It was their fault."

"They had an incredibly good legal team."

That was led by Bennett's dad. Kennedy turned to remove the bacon, eggs, and grits from the heat. She started plating everything. "So what did Bennett do?"

"He confronted his father. They had a huge fight. Bennett went back to school, added environmental studies—"

"Biodiversity," Kennedy said absently, her mind spinning.

Charles smiled. "Right. Biodiversity. He added that to his major and finished that in eighteen months. Along with his political science degree. He went on to law school but with a new focus. He was determined to fight the companies like the ones that got his father elected."

"And did he?"

"He did. And he started his foundation. Along with the environmental initiatives, he also bought part of three different newspapers so that he could help ensure that the stories were told and the companies, and elected officials, were held accountable."

Kennedy felt a weird stirring of heat. And it wasn't from the stove. Bennett Baxter was a nerdy scientist...who freaking fought the Goliaths and stood up for what he believed in and put his energy and his time and money where his mouth was. He believed in things. Deeply. He got loud about them. At least loud with money and stuff. He'd even sacrificed his relationship with his dad to do the right thing.

He really was a lot like the Landrys.

She took a deep breath. "And he and his dad don't get along now?"

"They try. But they don't see eye to eye on a lot of things. Bennett has contributed thousands of dollars supporting his father's opponents when they run against him. And, of course, has been the lead attorney in seeking damages against some of Preston's biggest donors."

Kennedy's eyes widened as she thought about all of that. Wow. Bennett was a badass.

"Oh, I'm so glad I didn't—oh, Kennedy."

Kennedy turned to face Bennett's mother. "Good morning."

"I thought that Melinda was still here cooking." Maria looked tired, but she was dressed as if she was on her way to have tea with the queen.

She also made a point of running her gaze over Kennedy's tattoos.

Kennedy smoothed the front of her tank top. Should she have dressed up more to come downstairs? Breakfast was a casual event in Autre. Okay, all meals were a casual event in Autre.

"Sorry. No. She must have cooked for the guys before they went golfing." Kennedy glanced at Charles. "Well, some of the guys." She couldn't help her smile. He didn't look especially governor-y. But it was nice to know that he was a regular guy behind the title.

"You didn't need to—" Maria looked past her to the stove. "Are those grits?"

Kennedy had no idea how to read this woman, so she just went with her default setting—complete honesty. "Yeah. Best grits you'll ever have."

Maria regarded her with narrow eyes. "I don't know. My grandmother was an amazing cook."

Kennedy grinned. "Well, I learned from *my* grandmother, so I guess we'll see." She finished doctoring the grits and dished up three bowls. Then she passed out plates of eggs and bacon.

Maria took the seat next to Charles across the breakfast bar from Kennedy. She dipped her spoon into the grits first. Kennedy actually found herself holding her breath. Maria took a tiny bite, her eyes widened, and she looked at Kennedy.

"They're sweet."

Kennedy nodded. "For sure."

"You put *sugar* in grits?"

"I definitely do for breakfast," Kennedy said.

It was a well-known debate. Many felt that grits were *always* only savory. But she'd grown up on sweet grits for breakfast and found they were perfect with salty bacon.

"I, of course, eat them cheesy, with shrimp, mixed with eggs, with gravy," Kennedy said. "Every other way, too. But I love them sweet."

Maria dipped her spoon again, taking a bigger scoop. "I haven't had sweet grits since I was a kid." She took a bite and closed her eyes briefly. Then she focused on Kennedy. "My *other* grandmother made them this way. She died when I was only eight."

Kennedy smiled. "I love when food can take you back to a good memory."

Maria nodded. She looked like she was going to say something else, but instead she just took another bite and then dug into her eggs and bacon.

The three of them ate and finished off a pot of coffee with

very light conversation about not much at all. They all seemed tired, but it was also a strange combination of people who didn't know each other that well. At least not have-breakfast-together well. Kennedy got the impression that Charles was much more a friend of Preston's and only knew Maria superficially.

When they were finished, Kennedy started cleaning up.

"You don't have to do that. The kitchen staff will be in to do lunch," Maria told her.

Kennedy shook her head. "I was raised in a bar and restaurant. If someone comes in for the next meal shift and there are dirty dishes in the sink, there is hell to pay. My grandma might just fly up here and slap me if I leave a mess."

Maria clearly wasn't sure what to say to that.

Kennedy turned her attention to scrubbing the skillet.

Finally, Maria said, "Are you and Bennett serious?"

Kennedy looked over at the other woman. Wow. What a question. From his mom, no less. The mother that she'd told about her gazebo-blow-job plan. Strangely, Kennedy wasn't quick to answer. Just last night she'd told Charles that she and Bennett were just messing around. Twenty-four hours ago, she'd have easily said that they were just flirting. Now... Well, she could only be honest.

"Your son is amazing."

Maria looked surprised by Kennedy's answer. "Yes, he is."

"And I want him to be happy. Really, truly happy. Long-term." She meant every word of that, too.

"And that will all happen with you?" Maria asked.

"I think that's possible," Kennedy said, realizing it for herself for the first time.

"Only possible? Not for sure?" Maria pressed.

Kennedy met her eyes. "The more I figure out, the surer I get."

"The more you figure out about Bennett?"

Yes. But, not just him. Maybe it was getting out of Autre and her circle of family and friends. Getting outside her comfort zone where things were easy and routine and she didn't have to think about things very hard.

Or maybe it was the things she was learning about Bennett. But *those* things didn't seem surprising. She hadn't known the details and seeing Bennett in *his* comfort zone had made her look at him more clearly, maybe, but she wasn't shocked that Bennett was a fighter who did the right things for the right reasons.

So yeah, she was feeling differently about her and Bennett, and it wasn't because Bennett Baxter was surprising her. *She* was surprising her.

Kennedy shook her head. "The more I figure out about me."

Maria narrowed her eyes. "You're figuring some things out while you're here?"

"I am."

"So *you* are serious about *him*?"

"I am serious about Bennett being everything he can be. I'm serious about that for myself, too. And if we can do that together, then yeah."

"I see." Maria seemed to be thinking about that.

"Kennedy!"

They both turned toward the new female voice. Jo had joined them. Along with Tawny and Sarah. They were all in bathing suits and carrying towels with sunglasses propped on top of their heads.

"Hi, ladies," Kennedy greeted. She felt that things with Maria weren't quite finished. But this was something that she and Bennett needed to figure out first.

"Want to come to the pool with us?" Tawny asked. "The guys won't be back for a while. We thought we could get some sun and chat?"

Huh. These were people who knew Bennett well. Maybe it

would be good for Kennedy to be friendly. Jo had been sweet all along, and her husband was Bennett's best friend. The other two women were related to him. Tawny had been very nice last night and Sarah had been fine. Kennedy just needed to lay off the voodoo stuff.

"Sure. That would be great."

"Okay!" Tawny seemed pleased. "We'll meet you out there."

The three women left the kitchen and Kennedy looked at Maria and Charles.

"Any tips for hanging out with them?"

Charles chuckled. "I barely know them."

Maria, on the other hand, nodded. "Be yourself."

"They'll be judging me. To see if I'm good enough for Bennett, right?"

"Well, to see if you're a good fit," Maria hedged.

Kennedy sighed.

"But," Maria added, "don't you want to know that, too?"

Kennedy thought about that. Three women closer to her age who knew Bennett well? Yeah, maybe this wasn't a terrible idea. "Okay, fair enough."

Maria gave her a small smile. "Thank you for breakfast."

"I'm glad you liked it."

She nodded, excused herself to Charles, and headed out.

Kennedy turned wide eyes to Charles. "So..."

He chuckled.

"Am I screwed?"

He shook his head. "No. Definitely not. But *I* might be."

"How are you going to be screwed?"

"If Bennett convinces you to move to Georgia, I lose you both."

"Us both?" She was too surprised by his statement to correct the idea of her moving to Georgia. No way.

"I'm thinking you would be fantastic on my new task force looking at tourism in the state."

Kennedy stared at him. “Me?”

“Yes, absolutely.”

“What would that entail?”

“A few trips to Baton Rouge. Sitting at a table with a bunch of other people who know and care a lot about tourism in our state. Talking about ideas to make it all even better, things that are affecting you all, keeping you from doing all the things you want to do. To start with anyway.”

Kennedy’s mind started spinning. What? Her in Baton Rouge? “Seriously?”

“I saw you last night. You were excited and energized about sharing ideas and lobbying for what you know are needs.”

“Yeah, but…”

He nodded when she trailed off. “Yep, that’s how government works, Ms. Landry. It’s made up of the people who just want to make where they live a place they’re happy and safe and proud to be.”

“I never thought about it that way.” Autre was already all of those things to her. But she damned well wanted to keep it that way.

“Well, think about it now.” He saluted her with his coffee cup and then turned and left the kitchen.

———

BENNETT KNOCKED ON THE DOOR TO KENNEDY’S BEDROOM. THE other houseguests were down having lunch or lounging by the pool. They’d said she’d been invited and had agreed to join them, but they hadn’t seen her for about three hours.

She didn’t answer his knock. Was she sick? Had she gone back to bed?

He tried the door and found it unlocked. He pushed it open and peeked inside, not sure if he should wake her. But really wanting to. Or maybe he’d just crawl in beside her. He’d had a late night, too. Though he'd had a lot less alcohol than she had.

But her bed was empty. And made. As if she hadn't been in it at all.

He stepped into the room. She wasn't there and the door to the connecting bathroom was open and the light off.

Where was she?

He headed for his room. He needed to shower and change at least. He'd shoot her a text and—

She was propped up in his bed, his laptop open on her thighs.

She looked up. "Hi." She gave him a big, bright smile that stopped him in his tracks.

She was so damned beautiful, and she seemed sincerely happy to see him.

"Hi." He stalked toward the bed with a frown. "Are you okay?"

She nodded. "Why wouldn't I be okay?"

"The girls said you were going to meet them at the pool."

Her gaze flew to the clock in the corner of the computer screen. "Oh, wow. I totally lost track of time."

She shifted, and Bennett suddenly realized she was wrapped in a towel. There were black strings coming out of the towel that tied around her neck that he assumed were attached to a bathing suit.

He kicked off his shoes and stripped off his shirt and climbed up from the bottom of the bed to stretch out beside her. "What have you been doing that you completely forgot about swimming?"

Kennedy's eyes tracked over his shoulders and chest, making his cock stir.

But she said, "I just wanted to look a few things up and then I got sucked into all this reading. I had no idea I'd been up here for so long. I kept thinking I'd just read one more page."

"What are you reading about?"

"Well, it started with reading about your foundation, actually. Then that led to articles about the loss of land along the coast," she said. "I knew a lot of that but just wanted to read more in depth. Then that led to the engineering along the Mississippi. And that led to looking up Grant Peterson's company. And then I started reading about how Louisiana state government is set up."

Bennett stared at her. Then he looked at the computer. Then back to her. Finally he asked, "*What*?"

Kennedy set the computer on the bedside table and shifted to face him, crossing her legs and leaning in on her knees. The move caused the towel to loosen and fall, revealing that the bathing suit was actually a bikini. And she looked fucking hotter than hell in it.

"Last night, Teddy and Charles and I were talking. And I was thinking about everything all morning. I remembered meeting Grant when he came for a swamp boat tour. He works in Missouri, up where the Missouri River meets the Mississippi. I was thinking that maybe we could talk to him. He knows a lot about the rivers and maybe, I don't know, someone could come up with a way to pick up the sediment that's getting dumped away from the barrier islands and bring it over."

Bennett felt as if she was speaking German to him. Except that everything she was saying sounded like the stuff that he talked to people about all the time. The Mississippi. The sediment. The barrier islands.

But he just was having a hard time processing that he and Kennedy were talking about it.

"I don't understand."

She leaned in, a gorgeous smile on her face. "Surely someone, somewhere, is smart enough and motivated enough to come up with something that would...I don't know...act like a strainer. It could take the sediment out of the water as it goes through. Then they could bring it over to the barrier islands."

He nodded. Then frowned. Then said, "*What*?" again.

"I want to help you. What you're doing with the islands and the coast and the politics of it and your foundation—God, Bennett, it's just all so…amazing."

"Well…thanks. I mean…" He had no idea what he meant.

"I want to get involved," she said. "All of this is really exciting. There are some really big things that need done and…" She took a deep breath. "It's so fucking *hot* that you're the one leading so much of this."

Bennett felt his eyebrows rise. "It's…hot?" His body liked hearing that even as his brain was still trying to catch up.

She laughed softly. "It really is. I thought I was all into big muscles that could build things and get rid of bats and stuff but, turns out, my kink is brainy guys who have so much charm they can get people to give them millions of dollars, which they then turn into these amazing things that are saving the planet." She leaned in. "Saving my home. My family. *Me*."

She put her hand on the back of his head and her lips against his. "I really want to give a blow job to the guy who's going to save Louisiana."

Well, saving all of Louisiana might be pushing it. But he could save a few birds and fish and maybe a village or two. And if the fucking government would get out of his fucking way, he could do a hell of a lot more…

Bennett reined in his thoughts. He had a half-naked woman that he wanted to his *bones*, offering him a blow job. What the fuck did he care about the nesting habits of the Least Tern right now? Except that he still kind of did. He could never completely shake all of that.

Damn. He wasn't sure, Kennedy was *really* ready for him to be his all-out geek self. There was probably a balance between impassioned scientist who read legal briefs in his spare time and the guy she wanted to take her clothes off with.

He was reeling a bit from the idea that all of this was a turn-on for this girl who wore cutoff blue jeans and cussed like a shrimp boat captain and could absolutely get rid of bats all on her own.

He'd, admittedly, kept a lot of this from her because he'd figured she'd think it was all... Hell, he didn't even know what to call it. Crazy? She wouldn't have been the first to think the idea of building a barrier island was nuts. Boring maybe? He wouldn't have guessed that water flow and river sediment and the politics of environmental protections would be interesting to her, not to mention a turn-on.

But fuck...if it was? Then he was going to be able to rock her damned world. He could do that dorky-scientist-slash-politician thing all day.

"I have to admit, that's a hell of an incentive to keep working in spite of the set-backs," he told her.

She kissed him. "The idea of stripping you down and putting my mouth all over your body and having you breathing hard and panting *my* name, while there are people all over Georgia and Louisiana who are begging you to work with them and help them with things... God, I don't know, but that just makes me hot and restless and *wet*."

He slid his hand to the back of her neck. "You want *me* begging?"

"I really do."

"And saying your name?"

Her pupils were dilated and she was breathing a little hard. "Definitely."

He pulled on the tie on the back of her neck, undoing the bow and causing her bikini top to drop away from her breasts. He took in the sight, then put his lips against her neck.

"Kennedy, I'm *begging* you to let me make you come harder than you ever have."

She tipped her head back. "Well...okay."

He kissed his way to her collarbone, then lower, over the upper curve of her breast, and then down to her nipple. He flicked it with his tongue, taking in her gasp of air, then sucked. Hard.

Her fingers curled into his scalp and she arched closer.

Bennett pulled back. "Shower. Now."

Kennedy opened her eyes, blinking at him, looking a little dazed. "Um."

He reached behind her and untied the bottom strings of her bikini, whisking the top away from her. "Shower," he repeated, pushing back off the bed and shedding his clothes. "Now."

Her gaze tracked over his body as she slid off the bed and slipped out of her bikini bottoms.

Bennett blew out a breath. "Damn."

She grinned as she started across the carpet toward the bathroom. She grabbed his hand as she passed him, tugging him with her. "I have been *dreaming* about that shower."

"This is going to be the dirtiest shower you've ever had."

"It better freaking be," she tossed over her shoulder.

They stepped into the bathroom and Bennett went straight for the shower, starting the water and adjusting the temperature. He turned back and pulled her close. He took her face in his hands. "You are the most gorgeous, amazing, sexy, funny, sassy woman I've ever been with."

She gripped his wrists, looking into his eyes with a grin that was definitely sassy. "And you're..." But she trailed off and pressed her lips together. She swallowed hard and her grin faded into a sincere look. "You're the first guy I've been with that I actually really, truly respect," she said. She shook her head. "That sounds bad. I don't mean that my other boyfriends have been dumb or jerks. They just haven't been..." She pressed her lips together and took a breath.

Bennett stroked his thumbs over her cheeks. "Kennedy—"

"No, I want to say this," she said, squeezing his wrists. "You are the first guy who's actually been a challenge. And it's not because you're difficult to be with or anything. I mean, I love our back-and-forth stuff and the way I never know what to expect from you. But it makes me feel energized and makes me have to be sharper and more focused. In my usual day, I can just kind of coast through and do things that are so easy and so routine that it doesn't take much brain power. Or heart. But with you, I find that I have to be more on my game and on my toes. And now, being here with you and really learning about the things you do, you've made me look at everything and think that maybe I could be doing more or trying harder or...just *being* more."

Bennett felt his heart squeeze hard in his chest. Holy shit. He was way more than halfway in love with this woman.

"And," she went on, her smile returning, "all of that makes me think that this sex is going to be the best of my life and I'll never want it with anyone else ever again. So...no pressure. But I really need you to rock my world."

He gave a little growl and put his hands on her ass, pulling her against him. "Get in that fucking shower and let me worship you."

Her eyes widened and she nodded slowly. "Yeah. Definitely. Okay."

He lifted a brow. "Kennedy."

"Yeah?"

He tilted his head toward the shower.

She looked at it. "Oh. Right."

She reached for the handle and as she pulled it open, he put his mouth against her ear. "Face that back wall, hands on the tile, legs apart."

She blew out a breath. But did as she was told.

Bennett felt a surge of heat and triumph flood through him. Kennedy was not a woman who anyone bossed around. Unless she let them.

That meant something. She trusted him. She wanted him. She was willing to put her pleasure in his hands.

He intended to prove that was a very good idea.

He stepped in behind her. The water was coursing over her from the rainfall showerhead in the ceiling, wetting her hair and running in slick, shiny rivulets over her skin. She had her hands on the wall and her head tipped forward slightly.

Bennett lifted a hand and traced a single finger from the base of her neck down her spine, watching her skin pebble and her body shiver. He flattened both palms on her shoulders, gliding down her sides, his fingertips skimming the outsides of her breasts, to her hips. He squeezed there, then continued down the outsides of her thighs, loving the feel of her skin under his hands. And the way she just stood still and let him touch her. He moved his hands up and down her thighs, then slid around to the front, stroking up to her belly and then back and forth.

She arched her back, pressing her ass against his cock. He groaned at the contact and flattened his hands on her stomach, holding her still so he could rock into her for a moment. She moaned softly and he put his lips against the curve where her neck turned into her shoulder.

"Fuck, you're amazing," he told her.

Kennedy tipped her head back, letting the water run over her face, her eyes closed. "This is decadent," she said. "I never want to leave this shower."

He ran his lips over the side of her neck, then bit down gently on the top of her shoulder. "Well, you're not going to be able to stay in here after I fuck you so good that your legs won't hold you up."

"Damn," she said on a long, exhaled breath. "*Yes*."

He ran his hands up, cupping her breasts, the hard tips pressing into his palms. He played with her nipples, tugging and rolling, as she circled her hips, moving her ass against his cock. He was aching and loving every second of this. Just having her in his arms, her body all his, to play with and pleasure, was heaven. It felt like he'd wanted her forever.

"Can I touch you?" she asked. "Please?"

Oh, hell yes. Having Kennedy Landry *asking* him permission for something, even adding a please on the end, was almost enough to push him over the edge. He grinned. "If you touch me with your mouth only."

Yeah, he wanted to be dirty with her. Very dirty.

She suddenly spun to face him. "*Yes*," she practically hissed.

"On your knees, darlin'," he said, adding just a bit of drawl to his tone. He'd long ago gotten rid of his accent. His father had insisted that people had too many stereotypes against people who had southern accents. But Bennett could definitely turn it on when needed.

Kennedy got on her knees, but of course she made that something a little more, too. She slowly slid her body down his, the water making the move slippery and even hotter.

She knelt before him, her hands on the back of his thighs. Bennett braced his hands on the wall behind her, bending over, and keeping the water from hitting her directly.

She didn't tease or even work up to anything once she was in front of his cock. She leaned in, dragging her tongue from the base to the tip and then swirling around his head.

Bennett swore. He had to move his feet apart to steady himself and realized the slippery tile on the wall was going to be no help if his knees gave out.

"Suck me, Kennedy," he ordered, his tone low and firm.

She did. Eagerly it seemed. She opened her mouth and took him in, sucking, then moving up and down his length. She teased him with just her tongue and mouth for several long, hellish but heavenly minutes. Bennett grit his teeth, watching her work up and down his cock. He took it for as long as he could. But he refused to end it all like this.

He wrapped his hand in her wet hair, gathering it back and tugging her mouth away from his aching shaft. He stared down at her, breathing hard. Her cheeks were pink, her eyes filled with lust. "Come here," he said gruffly, urging her to her feet.

She stood and he pressed her into the wall, kissing her deeply. He tore his mouth away a few seconds later. "I need to fuck you."

She just nodded.

He gave a low groan. He did love her submissive. "Do I need a condom? I'm totally clean. I haven't been with anyone since I walked into the office in Autre and saw you for the first time. But I'll do whatever you want."

Her eyes widened slightly, but she wet her lips. "I haven't been with anyone else since I met you, either. I'm clean. And I take a shot for birth control."

He didn't pause to reiterate any of that. He turned her and shifted to the right. He reached past her and angled one of the nozzles to hit her inner thigh. He ran his hand down to cup her pussy. He pressed his middle finger deep, sliding easily into her wet, heat. He stroked her. "You ready?"

"So. Ready." She pressed her hands flat against the wall.

Bennett stroked once more, trailing his finger over her clit, his cock hardening even further when she bucked against his hand.

He slid his hand to her right knee and lifted it, opening her legs and moving her in front of the wall nozzle so the water stream would hit her clit directly.

"Oh, *God*." Her head fell back on his shoulder.

Bennett bent his knees and then slid home.

11

It was so freaking good. Kennedy almost wanted to cry.

Bennett was filling her from behind while the most glorious shower she'd ever had the pleasure of stepping inside massaged her clit perfectly.

She couldn't really hold on to anything. The walls were far too slippery, and she was standing on only one foot while Bennett held her other leg up. All she could do was let him hold her up and let the pleasure course over and through her.

"Play with your nipples," he said gruffly against her ear.

Oh, hell yeah, she could do that. She let go of the wall with both hands, lifting them to her breasts. Her entire body was supported by him now. She was at his mercy. And strangely, she had absolutely no trouble just letting go and letting him take over.

She tugged and rolled her nipples, the action making her pussy tighten. Bennett groaned behind her, the sound vibrating through her since they were completely connected.

"You feel fucking amazing," he told her.

"Ditto." She took a deep breath. "Definitely ditto."

Then he started moving.

Bennett pulled out and then thrust deep, seemingly hitting every single nerve ending in her body all at once.

Kennedy gasped. "Oh, yes. Do that again."

He chuckled, rough and low. "Honey, there's not much that could keep me from doing that again." He did. "And again." He did it again.

Kennedy felt her body tightening. "*Bennett.*" She let her head fall forward, arching her back and pressing back against him as much as she could.

He groaned and thrust harder and faster.

He filled her and as the water vibrated over her clit, her orgasm came spiraling toward her and then broke over her like a wave. "Bennett!"

"That's it," he praised gruffly. "That is fucking *it*."

But instead of continuing to thrust, he pulled out and spun her around. Then he lifted her against the wall. She wrapped her legs around his waist and he slid deep again. The fit was so perfect, so full, so hot, so...everything...

Dammit, she really was never going to be able to have sex with anyone else ever again.

That thought came at her fast as he thrust again. Maybe that wasn't so bad. She could do this with this guy over and over again.

"Oh, God." She moaned as the sparkles of pleasure kept raining down with the water.

He pinned her to the wall, his hands between her ass and the hard tile. Then he pumped into her, his eyes locked on hers, until she felt a second orgasm climbing through her.

"Bennett. Please." But she wasn't sure if she was begging him to keep going or to stop. It was almost too much. Then again, if he stopped, she was going to cry.

"Again, Kennedy," he said between gritted teeth. "Let me feel it again."

"I just... I need..."

"What. Tell me," he said sharply.

"Harder." She said it softly.

But he heard her. He definitely heard her. His jaw tightened, he squeezed her ass, and he went harder.

"Yes!" Her orgasm rose up and she wasn't sure the first one had even completely finished. Everything in her tightened and clamped down.

Bennett roared her name and came a second later.

Kennedy squeezed her arms around his neck and legs around his waist, hugging him tightly as he leaned into her, panting. Slowly, he loosened his grip and she unwound herself, sliding to the floor as he pulled out.

He braced a hand over her head and stared down at her. "Well...damn."

She smiled and nodded, running her hands up and down either side of his face over the scruff there. "Yeah."

He reached to the side for the soap and without saying anything more, they washed each other, head to toe, shampooed their hair, and then stepped out to wrap up in towels.

They went straight to the bed and climbed in together. Kennedy rolled to her side to face him. He did the same.

They just lay looking at each other for a few minutes.

"I want to date you," he said, after a long silence.

She gave him a smile. "Okay."

"In Autre."

She lifted a brow. "Just in Autre? Because the mini quiches here—"

"Everywhere." He didn't smile.

Kennedy got serious. "Okay," she said sincerely. She put her hand against his cheek. "Very okay."

"And no one else."

Her eyes widened. "You better not fucking date anyone else."

"I meant you."

"I don't want to date anyone else." No one else would ever measure up again. That was a truth she was going to have to get used to.

"Good."

She started to lean in to kiss him, but he said, "And you should know that I'm only dating you long enough so that it's not a huge shock when I propose."

Kennedy pulled back. "What?"

"I want you. I want Autre. I want the bayou. For good."

Kennedy blew out a breath. She knew she should say that was crazy and how could he know that? But the words wouldn't come. Maybe because it didn't feel as crazy as it should. "Okay," she said softly.

Emotions flared in his eyes. "But you should also know that I don't want politics. I don't want to run for office in Louisiana, either."

She swallowed. That one wasn't as easy to agree to. "You're amazing. You're everything that *should be* in office."

He squeezed her hip. "I'm serious. You have to be okay with that."

She narrowed her eyes. "Maybe *you* have to be okay with me believing in you and pushing you to do more."

Bennett cocked an eyebrow. "You would try to talk me into it?"

She lifted a hand to his chest and rubbed back and forth. "I would. I mean, you can't run for office in Louisiana until you live there for two years anyway."

"Kennedy—"

"And—" She scooted closer and put her lips against his chest over his heart. "I have an argument that no one else has used with you."

He groaned, clearly knowing where this was going.

She kissed him. Then licked. Then moved lower and licked again.

His hand went to the back of her head and he curled his fingers into her hair. But he didn't stop her. "Kennedy. That's not fair."

"It's for the good of Louisiana," she said, kissing down his ribs. "I can't build an island to protect it. But I can incentivize the guy who can."

"I'll build the damned island anyway."

His breathing was getting a little ragged and Kennedy grinned against his stomach.

"Well, you know how hot I find that," she said. "Imagine what you could talk me into if I'm calling you Senator in bed."

He groaned.

She licked just below his belly button.

"Or Governor."

"Ken—"

There was a sudden loud knock at the door. They both froze. Kennedy lifted her head. Bennett covered his face with his hand.

"*Nooo*," he groaned.

"Bennett?"

It was Maria. Kennedy rolled away from him, clutching her towel around her. Well, crap.

"Not now, Mom!" Bennett called.

"Yes. Now. It's an emergency."

With a muttered curse, Bennett sat up, pulling his towel around his waist. He started for the door but stopped to look back at Kennedy. "This negotiation isn't over."

She laughed. "I'll bring my argument to this table any time."

Bennett blew out a breath and went to answer the door.

"Bennett, I—" Kennedy heard Maria start. Then an, "Oh."

"Just took a shower, Mom. What's up?"

"The catering truck for tonight turned over on the highway.

Everything is ruined. We'll have to cancel tonight. Can you help me make calls?"

Kennedy got out of bed, making sure the towel was tight around her, and moved in behind Bennett. Out of Maria's line of sight.

"Calm down," Bennett told his mother. "There has to be something else."

"I've called two other companies. No one can do it on such short notice."

Maria didn't sound good. But there was no way Kennedy was going to risk peeking at her. Or even coming out from behind Bennett.

"Well, then we'll...figure something else out," he told his mother. "Can we just do cocktails or something? Everyone will understand."

"I am not throwing a *dinner party* without *dinner*, Bennett," Maria replied coolly. "And there's no way Melinda is prepared to make a meal of this size for this many people."

"How many people?" Bennett asked.

"Fifty."

"Well, let's order pizza," he suggested.

"You want to order *pizza*?" Maria asked. "For your father's retirement party?"

Kennedy rolled her eyes. It was a solution. It just wasn't a great one.

All they needed was a bunch of great food and...that was really all they needed. Her family had been throwing parties for fifty or more every weekend for years. Okay, and beer. That was a staple.

"Pizza is good," Bennett was saying. "Everyone likes pizza. And we can get... salad."

Kennedy sighed. "Crawfish boil."

He glanced over his shoulder. Then her words sank in and

he grinned. He reached for her wrist and pulled her around. To face his mother.

"Kennedy," Maria said with a sigh.

"Hi."

Maria's lips pinched.

"A crawfish boil," Bennett repeated. "That's perfect. It's different and fun and easy." He looked at Kennedy. "Is it easy?"

She nodded. "Relatively. Very few ingredients and no dishes required."

Maria's lips pinched even tighter.

"I'm a great cook," Kennedy told her. "But the only things I can do quickly, easily, and in that quantity are grits, gumbo, and crawfish. Gumbo will take too long and grits are not really a whole meal. But a pot full of crawfish, corn, potatoes and sausage, along with a few sides and some beer, and you're set."

Maria ran a finger over the center of her forehead, as she'd done the first night. "You want me to have a crawfish boil in my backyard for my husband's retirement from the Senate?" Maria asked.

"You can have it in the front yard if you want," Bennett said.

Kennedy pinched him. Even she knew when not to be sassy.

"Bennett," Maria started.

"We'll take care of everything," Kennedy heard herself say. Maria looked surprised. But it was the grin Bennett gave her that made Kennedy nod. "If you'll just turn it over to us, we can definitely throw together a party for fifty in time for the guests to arrive. It will be...bayou chic."

Maria's eyebrows shot up. "Bayou chic?"

"Sure," Kennedy said, already regretting it. "A great combination of you and Preston's backgrounds and lives. Casual but elegant."

She had no idea how to pull this off.

"You can do that?" Maria asked.

"Sure." She really didn't know. Ellie and Cora could help her with the food via phone, but she was going to have to tap into other resources for the ambiance. But she smiled. She had Maddie and Juliet. They were both city girls. Or at least had been for a while. Maddie's grandmother in California, where she'd lived for over a decade, had money. Juliet's dad was a big investor and they even had a yacht. Those girls could surely help her figure out how to decorate so it looked less like Ellie's place on the bayou and more like a place Maria Baxter would be seen.

But it would *taste* like Ellie's place on the bayou. And Kennedy knew from experience that once people started eating, everything else became less important.

"Fine." Maria lifted her chin. "It's all in your hands." She shot her son a look. "I'm trusting you with this decision."

Kennedy gulped.

She did not think that Maria was referring to his decision to throw a crawfish boil tonight.

Bennett knew very well how quickly things could get done if you were willing to pay for it. The Baxter credit cards could absolutely get things done quickly.

But Kennedy Landry could get things done quickly, too. And without interest.

She'd had gotten dressed, pulled her hair up, and parked herself at the breakfast bar in the kitchen with her phone, a pad of paper, a pen, and all of the Baxter's guests gathered around.

Kennedy's first, and only, phone call had been to Autre. Of course. As she talked to Ellie, Cora, Juliet, and Maddie on speakerphone from Ellie's, she made lists and wrote instructions on the notepad, then tore the pieces of paper off and handed them to the people around her.

Kennedy had told them that they needed everyone on deck to help Maria and Preston pull this off, and everyone had been more than willing to help. Bennett had caught his mother off to one side looking misty-eyed and a little awed. He wondered when the last time was that Maria Baxter had asked for help. Did she realize that she did have actual friends, people who wanted her to succeed and be happy?

Bennett's heart had swelled when he realized that Kennedy was the one showing her that. Because of course she was. She was a Landry. They might know crawfish boils and airboats and the bayou like no one else, but their true specialty was friends and family.

Kennedy and Bennett had gone out to find the right pots for the boil and to choose the crawfish and pick up the needed spices. Duke and Jo had been sent to find the corn and potatoes. Even Duke's mom and Bennett's grandmother had been given a task—finding the tablecloths for the tables and enough small hand towels for everyone attending. Then Kennedy instructed them to wet and roll the hand towels and arrange them in a bucket of water with lemon slices. It was, evidently, a classier way for everyone to keep their hands clean than just paper napkins and was, thanks to Juliet saying, "You know, like they do in first class when you fly." The Landrys didn't know. So she'd explained it directly to Maria, who definitely knew.

Jo, Sarah, and Tawny were now sitting at the picnic tables filling the mason jars with a mix of water and essential oils—that they'd been sent out to procure earlier—with a floating candle on top. Apparently, they were not only pretty but also worked as a natural bug repellent. Bennett knew that had come from Cora.

His cousins, Steve and Brian, had been in charge of getting two "old-looking" wheelbarrows and "nice-looking" metal buckets. The wheelbarrows were now filled with ice and one held the bottled beer, while the other held bottled root beer and cream soda. The metal buckets were going to be placed on the tables for the crawfish shells and corn cobs. At this moment, Steve and Brian were painting crawfish on the sides of those buckets. Apparently, they hadn't been "nice looking" enough. At least, according to their wives.

Within a few hours, six big, wooden picnic tables had been delivered to the backyard, crawfish were boiling, beer was chilling, and the entire house smelled like heaven.

In addition to the macaroni salad, coleslaw, and cheddar biscuits she'd put together, Kennedy had insisted there be dessert and that it fit the theme.

"Pralines," Bennett had heard her say to Ellie. "Those are quick and easy. If we're doing mini peach pies in mason jars, we'll do something else that's simple." She paused to listen. "Well, or cookies. Pralines seem more in theme, but cookies are okay, too."

Bennett stepped into the kitchen. "Bananas Foster."

Kennedy looked up at him. "What?"

"Peach pie and Bananas Foster. A little bit of Georgia and Louisiana."

Kennedy frowned. "Bananas Foster is a lot more difficult than pralines. Which are definitely Louisiana."

"Sure. But you can do more than pralines." He stopped in front of her. "Bananas Foster is more...and you can handle it." He leaned in and braced his hands on the counter on either side of her hips. "Besides, lighting that all on fire? How cool will that be?"

Kennedy seemed to search his eyes for a moment. Then she said, "You think so?" It was clear she was talking to Ellie and him.

Bennett nodded. "I do."

She sighed a second later. Bennett assumed Ellie had agreed with him.

"Fine. Bananas Foster it is."

Bennett grinned. He wouldn't be able to eat it, but he was going to love watching her present that to his mother's guests. He leaned in and kissed her. It was quick and sweet, and he especially loved the stunned look on her face when he stepped back.

Right into his mother.

"Mom. Sorry. Didn't know you were there."

Maria looked from him to Kennedy. "It's all coming together."

"It is," Bennett said. "It's going to be great."

Maria stepped around him, directly in front of Kennedy. She put her hands on Kennedy's shoulders, looked her in the eye, and said, "Thank you so much. You are saving the evening. I don't know why you would work this hard for me. But thank you."

Bennett was staring at his mother. That was possibly the most sincere thank you that Maria Baxter had ever given anyone.

"You're welcome," Kennedy said, putting her hands over Maria's. "But, just so you know, I'm doing this because you care about it, and Bennett cares about you, and I care about Bennett. So"—She lifted a shoulder—"I care about this, too."

Maria was quiet for a moment. Then she nodded, let go of Kennedy, and reached for an apron. She put it on and said, "I'll peel the peaches. Unless you'd like me to do something else."

Kennedy smiled at her. "That would be great."

Bennett had left the kitchen feeling flummoxed. And happy. Very, very happy.

"This is going to be fun," Duke said, climbing down from the ladder where he'd been hanging up the last of the twinkle lights and looking around the yard.

"You think so?" Bennett looked around, too. It looked great and he loved a good crawfish boil. But he was biased.

"It's going to be hilarious to see if these guys can actually seriously talk business and deals when their hands are covered in crawfish and butter," Duke said, nodding. "Plus, who isn't happier when they're eating pralines?"

Bennett chuckled. "All good points."

"And Kennedy is saving your mom's ass. That's going to get her huge points."

"I don't care if she has points," Bennett said with a frown.

Duke laughed. "Liar."

"I want Kennedy, no matter how Mom feels about her."

"Okay," Duke agreed. "But it definitely makes it all easier if she likes the mother of her grandchildren."

Bennett felt everything in him react to that and couldn't reply immediately. He had no idea if Kennedy wanted to have kids, and it wouldn't matter if she didn't. He wanted *her*. Everything that came with that was just icing on the cake. But, yes, he did care a little about how his mother felt about her. Not just because it would make his life easier if the two main women in it got along, but because he'd like to think that his mom would trust him to know what was right for him. In the woman he spent his life with. In the career he spent his life on.

"If my mom doesn't like Kennedy, that's on her. Not Kennedy," Bennett told his oldest friend. "She's the most genuine, warm, funny, sure of herself woman I know." She got it from her grandmother. Bennett had heard everything Kennedy had said about feeling bad about how Leo had stuck around and put up with a lot from Ellie. But Bennett got it. Women like them were rare and once you had one, letting go was impossible.

"Kennedy's awesome," Duke agreed. "And Maria might be imposing and particular, but she's also smart. She won't want to lose you over this. Not now."

"Not *now*? What's that mean?"

"Now that she's seen that Kennedy really does have your back and will do whatever she can to make things work for you."

Bennett nodded. "Yeah. She will have my back." Kennedy definitely seemed to have his back. She was downright enthusiastic about the politics and his foundation. She wanted him to do even more than he was doing. And with her there pushing, encouraging, and being turned on by it all, he might just find himself with a political campaign after all.

Kennedy Landry was a little imposing, too.

EVERYTHING HAD TURNED OUT PERFECTLY.

Well, perfect was in the eye of the beholder, Kennedy knew. But this was a damned good crawfish boil. The people attending might not think that dinner table centerpieces should be metal buckets with crawfish painted on the sides or that the air should smell like cayenne, garlic, and lemon.

But they'd be wrong.

Kennedy stood to the side of the serving table where people could help themselves to salads and bread before taking their seats at the picnic tables laden with crawfish, sausage, corn, and potatoes.

Of course, she'd had to tell them all that they were to serve themselves before sitting. Apparently this crowd didn't do buffets.

While *her* usual crowd would have died seeing the actual glass plates being used in the yard and the rolled-up, lemon scented hand towels for washing up. The Landrys and their guests used paper plates and a garden hose.

But the point of the evening was truly the same as all the

parties at Ellie's. Great food, good friends, laughter, and memories.

Kennedy had definitely rolled her eyes at the group she was feeding tonight, but she had to grin watching them. Several of them were trying to use their forks for the crawfish, and she'd had to open the tops of the beer bottles for two of the women, but three of the men had realized they needed to get rid of their jackets and their ties, and two of the women had gone to find ponytail holders to hold their hair back while they ate. They were catching on quickly. They'd all donned their bibs without complaint, and it had only taken one bite for them to all be enthusiastically digging in.

"Oh, for heaven's sake!"

Kennedy swung around as Maria Baxter rose from the head of the table.

"You all are ridiculous," she told her guests.

Then she kicked her shoes off. The expensive Louis Vuittons fell into the grass, the white bright against the deep green. Sure, the grass was expensive, too—at least the landscaping and upkeep of it—but it was still grass.

Kennedy's eyebrows rose as everyone stopped eating and sat up straighter, focusing on their hostess.

"You don't eat crawfish with a fork," Maria informed them. "And this isn't lobster." She shot a look at William Ray, Georgia's Governor, who was sitting just to her right.

"You gonna show them how to twist and suck, honey?"

This came from Preston Baxter and Kennedy felt her eyes widen. Teasing? Flirting with his wife? In front of esteemed guests? And acting laid-back and happy about eating crawfish in his backyard?

Damn, it was possible that she'd underestimated Bennett's father as well. He was, after all, one of the men who'd tossed his jacket and tie onto the patio furniture before grabbing his plate.

"You know it," Maria said, giving him a grin.

Kennedy found Bennett. He was standing a few feet away, also observing the party rather than partaking just yet. She'd learned from Ellie and Cora that you always made sure your guests were served and happy before sitting down yourself. It looked like Bennett was doing the same thing. She loved the idea that he felt like this was *their* party. She gave him a smile and he gave her a wink.

He looked so hot tonight. He was wearing a black button-down dress shirt, open at the collar and no tie, with the sleeves rolled up to his elbows. With that, he had on black dress pants and black shoes. That were shiny, even in the dusky evening illuminated by the setting sun, candles, and twinkle lights. He was also wearing his glasses. Kennedy could only assume he'd put those on and given his shoes an extra few buffs to torment her.

It was working.

But her attention was quickly pulled back to the hot science nerd's mother.

Maria held a crawfish up. "Okay, first step—twist the tail." She did. "Peel the tail." She did, tossing the remnants into the bucket in front of her. "Eat the tail." She also did that after dipping it into some of the special sauce Kennedy had made. "Then," she said, holding up the rest of the crawfish. "You suck." She did, sucking the juice and some of the remaining meat out of the shell. Then she tossed that into the bucket as well.

Kennedy gave a little shudder. She wasn't a crawfish sucker. But the rest of her family loved it.

Maria held up her messy hands. "If you don't want to get dirty tonight, you're in the wrong place."

There was a beat of silence, during which Kennedy assumed everyone else was thinking *who is this woman and where is Maria Baxter*? Just like Kennedy was.

But then Preston gave a low whistle, and the rest of the table applauded.

Maria gave them a smile—the biggest Kennedy had seen so far—and took her seat. Somehow, even having just sucked a crawfish and with juice all over her hands, looking like a queen.

Kennedy watched as the rest of the guests dug into the food, with their hands, and conversation and laughter started bubbling up. It was stupid, but for just a second, Kennedy had to blink her eyes rapidly.

"I need to talk to you."

Suddenly Bennett was beside her, grabbing her hand, and starting around the side of the house.

She hurried over the grass with him. "Bennett, what's going on?"

But he didn't reply until he had her around the corner and backed up against the bricks. He braced his forearm on the side of the house and settled his other big hand on her hip. "You did something romantic," he said, running his palm up and down over the fabric of the second dress Maria had bought for her. "So I have to do something dirty."

His gaze was intense and with his big, hot body so close, Kennedy felt her breathing quicken. "I thought that was just my thing. To punish you."

"Guess not." He slid his hand up and down. "It's *our* thing."

Kennedy felt her heart thump at that. They had a thing. She liked that. A lot.

"Wait, I did something romantic? That doesn't sound like me." Yep, a little breathless-sounding.

"Stepping up to help with this party? Helping my mom out when she hasn't exactly been sweet and friendly to you?" He leaned in until their noses were almost touching. "And knowing that you actually did it all for me? That's romantic."

"Huh." Her hands were flat on the bricks behind her, but her whole body felt like it was arching into his. This guy had an incredible effect on her. One she wasn't sure she was ever going to get used to.

"And," he told her, brushing his lips over hers. "Watching you out there? The way you were watching everyone else, clearly hoping that they not only liked the food, but that they were also having a good time? And then the way you smiled when my mom kicked her shoes off and twisted the tail off the crawfish? You like them."

He ran his hand up to cup her face. "And you're fitting in. Without even really trying. You just...do. You came to a strange place, so unlike your world, sat down with people so unlike *you*, and you made them smile, you made them feel comfortable, you took care of them."

Brushing his thumb over her bottom lip, he looked into her eyes. "You helped make last night fun for my cousins, you nursed Charles' hangover, you made my mom grits like she had when she was a little girl, you learned everything you could about my foundation, you stuck up for Autre and the tour company with the governor, and tonight you fussed over everything from the candles to the desserts. You touched every single thing here and made it warm and delightful and—" He dragged his lips to her cheek. "—delicious."

His thumb skimmed over her cheek and then he lifted it to his mouth. Clearly, she'd had a smear of something there.

"Sweet. You are so fucking sweet even when you're being sassy and smart-assed. I'll never get enough of you."

Kennedy managed to drag in a deep breath even as her chest tightened and her heart pounded. Holy crap. This guy. He saw her and he appreciated her. And vice versa. She'd never had this before. This mutual respect and affection that went along with the good times and hot sex. This was...everything.

She had to blink fast again as emotions threatened to overcome her. "And you haven't even tasted my Bananas Foster yet."

"No." He paused. "Can't."

"Can't?"

"I'm allergic to bananas."

Kennedy shook her head. "What? Then why did you ask me to make it?"

"Because I knew you could do more than pralines. I want you to always do everything you're capable of."

Whoa. She blinked again. What was with all of this emotion swirling around inside of her? "Well, just so you know for the future, I make a kick-ass crème brûlée. You should ask for that next time."

He gave her a funny little smile with an expression that was full of emotions she couldn't name. He nodded. "I'll do that."

"And now *you're* the one being romantic," she told him, sliding her arms up and around his neck and pressing close to him.

"Huh. So we're going to have to do dirty things to each other," he said. He ran his hand down to her hip again.

Then lower to her thigh, rubbing over the soft fabric of her skirt.

This skirt was also longer, probably to help cover her leg tattoo. But she didn't blame Maria. Eventually, she'd come around. Or she wouldn't. Kennedy could wear longer dresses when she was here in Georgia with Bennett's family. What she wore wasn't who she was. She'd used her black clothing, tattoos, and piercings to make a statement after her years as a pageant queen. And she loved her combat boots. And tattoos. But she'd already realized this weekend that who she was could best be expressed in conversation and with ideas and with actions. She was a smart, passionate woman, who knew a lot about the bayou, loved Louisiana, and who could make people listen to her. She was also a woman who would step up and do what needed to be done even if the person she was helping didn't deserve it right at that very moment.

Bennett started gathering her skirt up and Kennedy reached to help him.

He gave her a wicked grin as his hand found bare skin. He ran it up her thigh to her hip.

Where he discovered that no matter what her dress looked like and who picked it out, she was still going to do whatever she wanted deep down.

"No panties?" he asked, his voice a little growly.

Her nipples beaded at that tone and the look on his face. "Oh, oops."

"Oops, my ass," he said, definitely growly this time, just before he took her mouth in a hot, deep kiss.

As his tongue stroked hers and she lifted on tiptoe to get more fully against him, he slid his hand to cup her, sliding a finger deep, with no warning. Not that she needed any. She was already wet and *needed* that finger right there. He pumped deep, then rubbed the pad of his thumb over her clit. She gripped the sleeves of his shirt and took a quick deep breath.

When she had her bearings again, kind of, Kennedy slid her hands down his sides, feeling the hard planes of his torso behind the expensive fabric of his black dress shirt. She ran one hand down over the front of his fly, relishing the hard steel of his cock behind the black dress pants, too. Sliding her hand up and down, she breathed in deeply of his cologne, and though she couldn't see them with her eyes closed and his mouth doing delicious things to hers, she pictured the black shoes. The *shiny* black shoes.

"You should know better than to wear dress clothes to a crawfish boil," she told him, as he slid his mouth to her neck and she unbuckled his belt, unzipped his pants, and slid her hand in against hot, hard man.

"These are my backyard party dress clothes," he teased.

"I've seen you in jeans and T-shirts," she told him, ending

with a little gasp as he curled his finger just right. "I know you can pull that off."

"Well, this is a pretty fancy dress you've got on, too," he told her.

"Yeah, if you tell my family I wore this to eat crawfish, I'll deny it. And make you pay."

He chuckled, rubbing a lazy circle over her clit. "We'll keep each other's secret then, okay?"

She lifted her head from where it had tipped back against the bricks and met his eye. "We've got each other's backs."

"We do," he agreed sincerely.

"Great." She squeezed his cock and then gave it a long stroke. "Now get me off so I can get back to the party."

He groaned. And did exactly as she asked. She came hard and fast as he whispered dirty, romantic things in her ear. She reciprocated. And then covered for him when he slipped into the house to change his pants.

Fortunately, like any good, nerdy politician, he had plenty of black dress pants in his closet.

"I HONESTLY DON'T KNOW HOW ANY OF YOU KEEP GETTING elected."

Everyone at their end of the table, that was now devoid of crawfish and instead set with plates that had only remnants of the peach pie and Bananas Foster, looked at Kennedy.

She was sitting back in her chair next to Bennett. Their fingers were linked between them and she couldn't remember a time she'd felt so contented. Even in Autre. That was home and she always felt contentment sitting around with her family by the water after a great meal. But this was different somehow. Being with her family, who loved her unconditionally, was one thing but being accepted into a new group that was just getting to know her, was something else. It gave her a sense of accomplishment. Or something. That wasn't quite the right word, but she felt like a success here. These people didn't have to like her or listen to her. But they did and were.

The man across from her and Bennett was Michael Elbert, the Mayor of Savannah. He laughed. "What do you mean?"

"I'm just sitting here listening to you all talk and you have almost nothing in common with the people who elect you and who you represent," Kennedy said, lifting her shoulder. "I don't understand why they keep voting for you all. I mean, you're nice enough," she added quickly. "You're clearly smart and, I assume, you actually want to do good things for your cities and states." She glanced around the table. She wasn't just referring to Mayor Elbert with this observation. Somehow all of the politicians in the group, along with Teddy, had ended up down here. "But you have no idea what it's like to just be a normal person."

"So what's it like to be a normal person in the small towns on the bayou?" Governor Ray asked.

"Why don't you come down and find out?" she asked him.

He nodded. "Maybe I will."

"You should. That's the best way to see what's really going on."

"We do go out to our communities," Charles piped up from across the table and down. "We go to local events, hold town halls. We want to hear from people and see those towns."

Kennedy shrugged. "I'm sure you do. But you're my governor, Charles, and I've never seen your face in person until I came here."

He lifted a brow. "I can't *make* you come to my town halls."

"But I didn't even know you had one near me," she said.

Charles glanced at Teddy. Teddy just grinned and lifted his beer bottle.

She felt Bennett lift her hand and press a kiss on the back of it. She gave him a smile.

"Bedtime," he mouthed.

The conversation continued around her and she felt her body stir. But she shook her head. "Not yet," she mouthed back.

Did she want to go upstairs with Bennett to the bedroom with that big bed with the silk sheets and the attached magical shower? Of course. But she didn't feel quite done down here.

He lifted a brow. "No?" he asked softly.

"Just not yet," she whispered. "I'm enjoying this."

He looked around the table. He seemed bored. But he probably heard this type of conversation all the time. When he looked back at her, he sighed. "Okay."

She grinned. "You can go up without me. And send me texts trying to tempt me up there while I hang out a little longer."

He gave her a slow grin. "That sounds like fun."

"It does."

He stretched to his feet, slowly letting his fingers slide through hers. Then he leaned over and gave her a kiss. "See you soon."

"You think so?"

"I'm going to pull out all the stops."

"I can't wait." She loved playful, sexy Bennett. This was definitely a win-win.

"Goodnight, everyone. It's been a very nice evening," Bennett told the group.

Everyone gave him their goodnights as well along with a promise for lunch from Mayor Elbert and an invitation for him and Kennedy to join Governor Ray and his wife sailing sometime soon.

Yeah, Kennedy wasn't going sailing. She knew about boats, and the only ones she liked were airboats and pontoons.

She watched Bennett walk away, feeling that warm blanket of contentment settle around her again.

Okay, maybe she'd go sailing. For him. Once.

She sighed. Or as many times as he asked.

This weekend was proof that she would do just about anything for him. And that maybe it wouldn't all totally suck.

Bennett Baxter was something. He had a lot of important things ahead of him. He needed a Leo. Someone who would be there, behind him, encouraging him, loving him, no matter what.

Kennedy felt a streak of *oh crap* go through her.

Loving him?

But yeah. She was in love with him. And other than his uncle Teddy, he didn't really have someone there telling him that he was doing the right thing and was amazing and should keep going and that they were there no matter what.

Yeah, he needed a Leo. He needed *her*.

She was definitely stuck.

But she wasn't sure she minded the idea so much anymore.

12

Bennett rolled over and reached out.

The other side of the bed was empty. As it had been last night when he'd fallen asleep.

But he could smell her. Kennedy's scent filled the air.

He rolled to his back and opened his eyes, blinking. The sun was up, but it wasn't very bright through the east windows yet. What the hell time was it?

He heard footsteps and looked toward the bathroom door.

Kennedy was crossing the room, pulling a brush through her long hair. She was clearly showered and was wearing a dress he'd never seen and that was definitely not hers. No way. It was red. He'd never seen Kennedy wear red before. No, they hadn't known each other long enough that he'd seen her entire wardrobe. Probably. But the black tops, dresses, shorts, and pants were all...black. Red didn't fit. It was too bright. Plus, the dress was very brunch-with-his-mother rather than bayou-badass. Though her tattoos did show with the capped sleeves and the skirt that hit her midthigh.

"Hey," he said, his voice still rough from sleep.

She turned with a smile. "Hey."

"What's going on?"

"Breakfast."

"Oh."

She came toward the bed and climbed up onto the bottom, sitting on her heels. "Just a few of us. Charles wants to go over some plans that we talked about last night in more detail."

"What's with the dress?"

She looked down. "Oh, it's your mom's." Kennedy grinned at him. "She loaned it to me."

"For breakfast."

"Yes."

"With Charles."

"Right."

"In my mother's kitchen."

"No."

Bennett frowned. "No?"

Kennedy smiled and ran her hands over the skirt. "We're going downtown somewhere. Michael is coming, too, and is having a couple of people from his office join us to help fill me in."

Bennett pushed himself up to sitting. "What the hell are you talking about?"

"I'm going downtown to breakfast to talk with Charles and Michael more about getting involved in Charles' reelection campaign. Michael is having some of his people join us so I can ask them questions since Charles' people are in Baton Rouge. But I'll meet them when we get back."

Bennett just blinked at her.

Kennedy tipped her head. "Oh, I guess you had already come upstairs when we started talking about that."

"Um. Yeah. I guess I had." Bennett shifted. "You're going to get involved with Charles' reelection campaign?"

She smiled again, brightly. She looked excited.

Dammit.

"They think that's a good way to get me started learning the ropes. And, obviously, he needs people all over the state. I can help talk to people in our parish in the small towns about his plans and stuff. There's nothing like having one of your neighbors or someone you can really relate to telling you about his ideas and plans and listening to what they're concerned about."

Bennett sighed. "Sounds like they gave you the full spiel."

She frowned. "It's not a spiel. We were talking about how I should get involved and that's what I realized."

"How you should get involved helping Charles connect to the small-town bayou people that he needs to get reelected," Bennett said, not even trying to hide his disgust. He pushed the blanket back and swung his legs over the side of the bed. "You've been here for less than forty-eight hours and he's already got you working for him." He looked back at her as he stood. "Or, I should say, volunteering, right? You're working for free?"

Kennedy scrambled off the bed, too, also frowning. "I'm *helping* him. No, it's not paid. But it's like an internship. I need to learn how this all works, and being in the field will teach me a lot."

"Why do you need to learn how this all works?" Bennett asked. He pulled a T-shirt out of his suitcase and yanked it over his head.

"So I know what to do when it's my turn to do it."

Bennett pulled his jeans on and turned to face her. "I told you I don't want to run for office. Not here. Not in Louisiana. I want the bayou. I want Autre. I want my foundation." He blew out a frustrated breath. "I want *you.* I love that you believe in me." He took a step closer to her. "I love that you were able to fit in here and learned more about my life and what all is involved in my past. And now. But I don't want to run for office. I don't need a campaign manager or whatever you're looking to learn." He stopped right in front of her. "I was hoping, actually, that you'd work with the foundation with me."

Kennedy folded her arms, keeping a space between them. She lifted a brow. "And what would I be doing with the foundation? I'm not a scientist or an engineer."

"You'd help with...phone calls and the mailing list. Setting up functions where we show people what we're doing. We could take them out on tours and show them the bayou and the islands and what we're working on."

"So...I could be your secretary."

Bennett winced. "That's not what I'd call it."

"Your assistant then?"

"Um..." He really thought that yes was the wrong answer here.

Her eyes narrowed. "You wouldn't be asking me to send you files?" she asked.

"I would...not do that," he decided right then and there.

"Because, as my past emails to you have said, I'm not your fucking secretary."

"Right. I know."

She dropped her hands but moved to the dresser and stepped into a pair of red heels that he'd just noticed. Those had to be his mother's, too.

"Well, then I guess it's all a good thing I wasn't talking about you running for office and that I'm not going to breakfast to learn how to be your campaign manager." She turned to face him.

"Then what are you going to learn?"

"What it takes to be a candidate."

Bennett stared at her. "A...candidate? For office?"

She lifted her chin. "Yes."

"*You*?" he asked. Then dialed back the disbelief in his tone. He still felt it, but he was a smart guy and the tightening of her lips meant she wasn't loving his reaction. "You want to run for office?"

"I'm going to start off on Charles' task force for tourism. I'm going to help with his reelection. But yes, I'm thinking about it. Being a state representative from our parish could be really fun and rewarding."

Bennett took all of that in, holding back his initial reaction. He was sure that showing his shock was not appropriate. But Kennedy Landry? The sassy, tough, bayou girl was going to run for public office? He had not seen that coming.

"I had no idea that you would be into all of this," he finally said. "I'm just a little surprised."

And worried. Because public office would take her away from Autre.

Baton Rouge was only a couple of hours away, and state representatives, of course, spent a lot time back home, but they also spent a lot of time in the state capitol. She wouldn't be at the Boys of the Bayou. Even when she was home, she wouldn't be in the office answering phones and scheduling tours. She wouldn't be hanging out at Ellie's bar or relaxing on Ellie's front porch swing or lounging around a bonfire at a crawfish boil. She'd do some of that here and there probably, but it would be part of her bigger role as a representative, not just the girl he was in love with and wanted to drink beer and flirt and dance with before taking her home to make love all night.

Fuck.

He'd wanted her here this weekend to show his family that he was serious about giving all of this up and going down to the bayou to lead a simpler, happier, quieter life.

Now Kennedy was all wrapped up and talking about a lifestyle opposite of all of that.

"Why are you surprised?" she asked.

Her arms were crossed again, and Bennett knew that was a sign that he'd best tread lightly. "Because you're..."

"What?" she pressed when he trailed off. "I'm what?"

He let out a breath. "Bayou." He had to be honest with her.

"And what does that mean?" she asked, her spine straightening. "Simple? Poor? Uneducated? Because I'm kind of all of that. I like things straightforward. I like when people say what they mean and mean what they say. I didn't go to college. I don't have yachts and diamonds."

Bennett straightened, too. The thing he loved best about Kennedy, and the Landrys in general, was their honesty. It was the fact that he knew if he asked them a question, they'd tell him the truth. If they made him a promise, they'd follow through. If he was screwing something up, they'd let him know. He owed that to Kennedy, too.

"Yes," he said. "Yes, that's what I mean. But in every possible good way, Kennedy. You aren't like the politicians and businessmen and women. You're not trying to always make a buck, to make a deal, to make yourself more important. When you meet people, you want to know them and listen to them because you're sincerely interested."

He took a deep breath. "You're not trying to figure out what they can do for you, how they can help *you*, how you can sell them something, or talk them into something. When you go to work in the morning, it's with the goal of making the people you encounter happy and comfortable and helping your family be successful, but you're never thinking about pushing or selling or manipulating."

He shook his head, amazed by her all over again as he said these things out loud. "You know that what you have is enough. When you go home at the end of the day, it's to enjoy your family and to help take care of them. They all know that you're there for whatever they need and you take care of a bunch of stuff they don't even know they need."

Kennedy just looked at him for a long moment. Then she took a deep breath and nodded. "Yeah. You're absolutely right."

Thank God, she understood.

She grabbed her purse off the dresser. "And all of that is why I would be a great state representative."

Then she turned and headed out the door.

"You could only handle her for three days?"

Bennett sighed as Sawyer, Owen, and Josh Landry pulled out chairs at his table at Ellie's and sat. He'd been expecting this.

"You cost me twenty bucks," Owen said. "I really thought you'd be able to handle Ken for four days."

"No one handles Kennedy," Bennett said.

"Just so you know, I really thought you'd make it all five days," Sawyer said.

Bennett looked at Josh. "You were the big winner then?"

Josh nodded. "I'm forty bucks richer because you came home early."

Bennett rolled his eyes.

"Hey, Leo had you coming home Saturday."

Bennett sighed.

"Okay, look, Baxter, we need to talk," Owen said. "We can't take it anymore. You have to fix this."

"I've tried." Kennedy Landry was as stubborn as she was sexy and sassy. She'd decided she was angry with him for not believing that she should run for office.

And she was making him pay.

Not by yelling at him. Not by crying. Not by dumping gumbo on his head.

It was way worse than that.

For one, she wasn't speaking to him. She wasn't even making eye contact with him when he came into the room. He was tempted to grab her and back her up against a wall and *make* her look at and talk to him, but he was quite sure that his nuts would be feeling it for a week if he did.

But worse than pretending that she couldn't see or hear him, was that she was making her family miserable. And making sure they knew it was because she was pissed off. And that she was pissed off because of Bennett.

The Landrys did crazy, over-the-top, make-sure-everyone-knows stuff when they fell in love. They also, apparently, did that when someone had wronged them.

"The coffee *sucks*," Owen said. "I mean it *sucks*."

"I think she put dirt in it. Literally," Josh said.

"You all drink it with chicory in it," Bennett pointed out.

"Don't you ever fucking insinuate that chicory and dirt are similar," Owen told him crossly.

Bennett felt his brows rise. He would have expected Owen to defend the local specialty coffee, but his annoyance was clearly turned up a notch. And likely because he was lacking caffeine.

Making her family take sides was one thing. Making them actually miserable and pissy and no fun to be around was something else.

Kennedy was clever.

"And when I made a point of getting to the office before she did the other day to make the coffee," Owen went on. "She came in, saw it, marched right over to the pot, and dumped it out."

"You can't get coffee in here from Ellie?" Bennett asked.

He knew all of this was designed to make *him* miserable. If the Landrys were unhappy, he was unhappy. If they knew that their unhappiness was because of him—worse, if they knew their coffee was bad because of him—he was going to have no allies.

"We can't be traipsing up and down from Ellie's all fucking morning," Owen said, again more irritable than usual.

"Well, especially when she's working our asses off," Josh added with a frown. "She's booking us tours back-to-back and completely filling our boats. I barely have time to breathe."

"And I'm sleeping like shit on top of it," Owen said. "She called me at three a.m. to get a possum out of the pantry."

"There was a possum in Ellie's pantry?" Bennett asked, already knowing the answer.

Owen glowered at him. "No."

"Same here, except that she came over banging on our door," Josh said. "Claimed that some guy was sneaking around their backyard."

"Didn't that wake Tori up, too?" Bennett asked.

Josh gave him a look that said, *Man, are you stupid*. "Of course it did. So then she was sleep deprived and a little crabby the next day. And guess who gets the brunt of that? The guy living with her."

"What did she do to you?" Bennett asked Sawyer.

The big man gave a disgusted snort. "She got Leo drunk and sent him over to my house to sleep it off."

Bennett blinked. "She got Leo drunk?"

"She did. She's about the only one who can."

"Leo is a difficult drunk?" Bennett asked.

"Leo is a chatty drunk," Sawyer said. "And nostalgic. He'll go on and on about old stories. Loudly. For *hours*." Sawyer frowned at him.

Bennett knew chuckling was *not* the right response, but he had to fight it.

"I guess I'm learning just what a handful she can really be," he said.

"You think she's a pain in the ass when she's just her usual, smart-mouthed self?" Josh asked. "She is the *worst* pissed-off female in the family."

"You've been back from Savannah for four days," Owen said. "*Four days*. We're *dying* here."

"I haven't had good grits, gumbo, or catfish since you fucked up," Josh told him.

Bennett had initially thought it was just *his* food Kennedy was ruining. Leo had quickly informed him otherwise. She was spending more time in the kitchen with Ellie and Cora for the specific purpose of making her family's food terrible and then claiming that she was too emotionally distraught to focus on the cooking. Because of him. That part was unspoken, even when they *begged* her to give up the cooking.

"You can't make your own food? *At all*?" Bennett asked them.

They all just blinked at him as if they didn't understand the question.

"And your mother and grandmother would just let you starve?" he pressed.

"I mean, I can make peanut butter and jelly," Owen said. "But man, that's bullshit when there's perfectly good sausage and catfish right over here."

"Maddie doesn't cook?" Bennett asked of Owen's girlfriend.

Owen leaned in. "When there's perfectly good sausage and catfish *right over here*?"

Right. Well, he couldn't argue with that. Ellie and Cora's food—especially Cora's food—was amazing. Almost as good as Kennedy's. When she wasn't trying to torture everyone.

"This is all very immature," Bennett said.

"Oh yeah," Josh said. "Super petty. She prides herself on that."

"You *have* to fix this," Owen said as Cora set plates of fried shrimp and fries in front of them.

They all eyed it suspiciously.

"You're keeping her out of the kitchen at least *some* of the time, aren't ya, Cora?" Owen asked.

Cora gave him a wide-eyed innocent look. "Who?"

Owen sighed. "Never mind."

Cora turned away, but not before Bennett caught her smile. So the Landry women also banded together. Another thing that was good to know.

Sawyer pushed his plate away without even sampling anything. "You do have to fix this. That's why we came to talk to you. Beyond the coffee and breakfasts and lunches, it's now going beyond the family. Earlier today *I* had to smooth things over with a customer because *she* asked him if he'd ever fucking heard of Google when he asked her a question about the airboats," Sawyer said.

Oh, boy. Bennett ran a hand over his face. For the past few months everyone, especially Kennedy and Maddie, had been the ones doing damage control with customers when *Sawyer* had overreacted and been an ass. Now that Juliet had come to town, Sawyer was getting back to his usual, fun, laid-back self. But it had been rough there for a while.

And now *Kennedy* was the one pissing customers off? He was sure the guy's question had been innocent enough. Or maybe he'd been flirting with her. In which case, Bennett was fine with her being bitchy. But...no, he wasn't. This was their business and she was the main one to interact with everyone. She needed to cool it. At least with the customers.

"So tell me how to fix it," Bennett said. "I've tried apologizing. I've tried talking to her and explaining. I've tried getting her to talk to *me*."

"Talk?" Josh asked.

"Seriously?" Owen added.

Bennett looked at Sawyer. "What?"

"Landrys don't really talk," he said, lifting a shoulder.

"That has *not* been my experience," Bennett said dryly. It wasn't just Leo who could go on and on and on. Nor did they have to be drunk for that to happen.

"Nah, when it comes to *big* stuff, we *show* it," Owen said.

Josh nodded. "And you're gonna have to make it big. That's how we do stuff. Big. Loud. Like jackasses."

Bennett sighed. "I don't have a lot of experience with that."

"We can definitely help you there." Suddenly Leo was there, turning a chair around and straddling it, leaning onto the back of it as if to impart some great wisdom.

Well, Bennett could use some of that. Kennedy wasn't talking or listening. "So, how do I do this?" he asked.

"It's like when Tori stood up at her best friend's wedding and declared her feelings for Josh in front of a whole congregation of people," Owen said. "The hardest thing for her was putting herself out there with her emotions and risking that they wouldn't be returned or that she'd made a fool of herself."

"Or," Sawyer said, "When Maddie did the one thing she most did not want to do and got on an airboat, went out on the bayou, and pulled a gun on a gator for Owen."

Josh nodded. "Or when Juliet faced her fear of the water and went out on a tour with Sawyer and then hung off the end of the dock to rescue Gus."

They were all nodding.

"You have to do something that's huge. Even if it's just huge for *you*," Owen said. "You have to *show* her how you feel."

Leo made a snorting sound and Bennett looked over. "What?"

"Did you notice the thing that all those stories had in common?" he asked.

The guys all looked at each other.

"Yeah," Josh said. "Someone putting themselves out there for the person they loved."

"Yeah," Leo echoed. "The *girls* putting themselves out there for *you* dumbasses."

Josh opened his mouth but then seemed to think about it and shut it again. Owen said, "Yeah, but..." He didn't, however, finish that statement.

Finally Sawyer looked at Bennett. "Yeah, maybe we don't really know what to tell you."

Bennett sighed. Leo laughed.

"I guess I just…" He looked around the table. He thought these guys really might get this. "Every couple needs a Leo, right?"

No one looked confused. But no one said anything, either.

"There has to be that one who is ready and able to build the life. Who can take care of things. Who gets stuff done."

Josh shrugged. "I think Tori and I figured that out together. Hell, we're still figuring it out. We just know we want to be together. But we both take care of things. And each other."

Owen nodded. "Us, too. I'm maybe a little steadier than Maddie, but since she's been back, she's been pretty damned solid on what she wants. I think we're maybe both Leos."

Bennett shook his head. He'd been making this case in his head and heart all along. It had to make sense. "But someone has to be the rock. The one who has it figured out. That one who knows who they are and what they want and can let the other one be the dreamer and the risk taker…" He trailed off. All of those words swirling through his head. "Holy shit," he said a second later.

Leo nodded. "There you go." And he reached for a fry.

"What?" Owen asked, looking from Bennett to Leo and back. "What is holy shit?"

Leo looked at Bennett. "You got it?"

Bennett nodded, feeling his heart pounding.

"*What*?" Owen asked again.

"I'm the Leo," Bennett said.

Leo grinned and grabbed another fry. Clearly, he wasn't worried about what Kennedy might have done to it. Sawyer tentatively took his lead and also reached for one.

Owen shook his head. "You're the Leo? What the fuck does that mean?"

"I'm the one who's figured out what he wants. The stuff I'm doing might seem like a dream and a risk, but...it's really not. Not for me. I know how to get it done. I'm the one who wants the steady, predictable stuff. Who doesn't want the spotlight or the headline and can just be behind the scenes. I can be the rock." He looked at Leo. "Right? Kennedy needs to be the Ellie."

Leo just smiled.

Owen nodded. "Oh. That. Sure."

Bennett looked at him. "Really? Just like that? It's obvious?"

"Of course. We're all that for our girls."

Josh nodded. "Yep. We're..."

"Home," Sawyer filled in. He met Bennett's eyes. "Our girls came here, needing something. They found it here with us. I mean, they balance us out, too, and give us plenty. Hell, Juliet's already home to me." He got a goofy grin on his face that Bennett would have never believed if he hadn't seen it himself. "But yeah, we gave them a place where they could settle."

"It's confusing," Josh added. "Because Kennedy was the one already here and you're the one who came in. But yeah. Now you're gonna be the one she comes home to and that helps settle her."

Bennett swallowed hard. "She's always seemed settled."

Owen snorted and finally gave in, reaching for a fry. "Nah. I mean, she's always here but that's not the same as being settled. Being content. Knowing that you've found your place. She hasn't had that."

Bennett marveled at how laid-back these men were even when discussing big, deep issues like this.

"That's why she's always turned me down when I've wanted her to do more with the business. Maybe buy in. Or go to school and get a degree. Or *anything.* She knew that Autre and Boys of the Bayou wasn't everything she wanted," Sawyer said, happily digging into the shrimp as well.

Apparently, Kennedy hadn't made this food. Or at least she

hadn't messed with it. Bennett wondered if that meant she was moving past the tormenting.

"You tried to get her more involved here and she always resisted?" Bennett asked.

"Sure. She's as much a part of Boys of the Bayou as any of us. But she didn't want to take more on officially. I think maybe she always knew that there'd be a time when she'd want to try something else."

Bennett blew out a breath. "This might not work out. This might not be what she wants." He wasn't sure how he felt about it all, actually. Did he want Kennedy to become a successful politician? Could he be a politician's spouse?

But the answer was easy. Of course he could. Whatever Kennedy wanted, he'd be there.

"It might not," Leo agreed. "And that's what Leos are for. To be the place you come home to no matter what happens."

"You think Kennedy will end up coming back and settling down again here eventually?" Bennett asked. For some reason that idea bugged him. He didn't want her to settle for less than what she truly wanted. And he wasn't sure he could just wait around for her to try all this new stuff out the way Leo had for Ellie.

But Leo laughed. "No. That girl's not coming back. At least not for good. Not back to the life she has now."

Bennett shook his head. "So...what do I do?"

"Remember what I told you about the four categories of men in her life?" Leo asked.

"I do."

"Be the fourth kind."

Bennett frowned. "The category *you're* in?"

"Yep. The one who simply hands her the tools she needs, keeps her company while she's taking care of what she needs to do, and makes her push herself harder than she thinks she can."

Bennett stared at the older man. Slowly he started nodding. Yeah. He could do that. He could be Kennedy's Leo.

KENNEDY FELT HER GRANDMOTHER MOVE IN BESIDE HER.

"You know I'm not going to let you keep ruining my food," Ellie told her, plucking the clove of garlic out of her hand.

"I'm not doing anything to the customers' food," Kennedy said. She'd never do that.

"Yeah, well, I can't have my customers sitting around listening to the guys complain' about their food. It's gonna start to rub off."

Kennedy set her spoon down. "I know it's immature."

"It is. But if Bennett wants to have a life down here with you, it's better he find out up front what it's like when you're not happy," Ellie said, grabbing the spoon and bumping Kennedy out of the way with her hip.

"I'm not always like this," Kennedy said, abandoning her spot and leaning back against the counter next to the stove.

"No. You're very rarely scared," Ellie said. "But when you are, look out."

Kennedy frowned. "Hey. What? I'm not scared. I'm mad."

Ellie looked over, her expression a mix of affection and *Come on, girl*. "You're scared."

Kennedy crossed her arms. "I'm hurt. Bennett doesn't think I'm capable of being something more than what he's seen here in Autre. And he doesn't want me to be anything else. He wants me to just be the receptionist at Boys of the Bayou and sit around in the office waiting for him to come flirt with me and take me on big fancy trips when *he* has time or a reason to go. He's going to go out and make the world better and save the environment, while I'm supposed to sit here and answer the phone and order stuffed alligators and dust the fucking shelves."

It wasn't until Ellie stepped in front of her and lifted her hands to wipe the tears off her cheeks that Kennedy even realized she was crying.

"Of course he thinks that. Because that's what you've been doing. Happily."

Kennedy sniffed. "He should think I can do more."

"It's not that he doesn't think you *can*. He didn't know you *wanted* to."

"But—"

"Because *you* didn't know that until you went to Savannah."

Kennedy wanted to protest that, too. But she couldn't. She sniffed again.

Ellie cupped her face. "And now that you do know it, you're scared. Because you can't ignore it anymore."

Kennedy swallowed hard. "I don't want to ignore it."

"You do. Ignoring it is easier. I know." Ellie dropped her hands and took a deep breath.

Kennedy watched her grandmother return to stirring the bisque she was making. She wasn't sure she wanted to get into this. But she wasn't sure she could resist.

"I've been telling myself that I was afraid of being Leo. The one who just put up with everyone else's bullshit. The one who lets everyone take him for granted."

Ellie smiled and nodded. "I know you've been telling yourself that."

Kennedy chewed on her bottom lip, watching Ellie. But Ellie didn't go on.

This fucking family. When you wanted them to shut the hell up, they wouldn't. When you wanted them to talk, they wouldn't.

"But you don't think it's true," Kennedy said.

"Of course not." Ellie looked at her. "You're afraid of being me."

Kennedy had almost been expecting that answer. It still made her take a quick little breath of surprise.

But she let the air out quickly. She'd realized this at some point over the past four days. Being back in Autre after the trip to Savannah had made her feel itchy. She'd felt restless and, yeah, pissed off. Because as she sat in front of the computer, answering the phone, interacting with the people the way she always had, she'd started to feel discontented. And that made her mad. She wanted to just be fine in Autre. She wanted to just be there for everyone else.

But now she knew there was more. She could do more.

She loved Boys of the Bayou. She was proud of it. It was a fabulous company run by people she loved with all her heart.

But she could do more than answer phones.

A fact that she'd been happily ignoring for a while now. A couple of years, if she was honest.

Now she couldn't ignore it anymore. Now she'd gotten a taste of the *more*. And now she was unhappy. Mad.

But not at Bennett. Not exactly. Yes, she'd been a little hurt by his surprise that she was going to start working with Charles. But she'd realized what Ellie had just said out loud on her first day back in Autre. Bennett had been surprised by her interest in politics.

But not as surprised as *she'd* been.

And she was mad at herself.

She didn't like feeling insecure and restless. She'd liked feeling like she was the Leo of the group. The settled one. The wise one who saw the big picture and could appreciate the simple things in life. The one who was there to help support everyone else.

She wasn't Leo. Not deep down.

She was Ellie.

"Do you know why I'm scared of being the Ellie?"

Ellie paused, then took a deep breath. She gave the pot another stir and then set the spoon to the side. She turned to face Kennedy.

"Because I upset everything and everyone when I decided to change things up."

Kennedy nodded. "But that's not all of it."

"Okay."

"Because it didn't work out." Kennedy took a deep breath. "You upset everything and everyone. But we...adjusted. Kind of, at least. And then—" She shrugged. "It didn't work out. You came right back to where you started. It was all for nothing."

"Oh." Ellie moved in close. "Honey, is that what you think happened?"

"Isn't it?"

"No." Ellie gave her a small smile. "Not at all."

"You...were with another guy."

Ellie nodded. "Trevor was...mostly a mistake. But he was a mistake I had to make. I just made it...out of order." She shook her head. "I didn't make a lot of mistakes..." She frowned, as if thinking. "I didn't make *any* mistakes before I met Leo."

Kennedy tried not to laugh, but she couldn't hold back the soft chuckle. "Seriously?"

Ellie grinned. "Seriously. Mistakes are what happen when you try new stuff and take chances. I didn't do that before I met Leo. So, I started thinking that maybe I hadn't lived enough before I settled down. Because I hadn't done anything big and crazy and hard on my own. So I took those classes in New Orleans and met Trevor and made new friends and—"

"Classes?" Kennedy interrupted. "What classes?"

"I took those business and marketing classes. At the community college. Oh, and the burlesque classes."

Kennedy shook her head. She'd known about Ellie's fascination with burlesque and had even gone to one of the clubs in

New Orleans with her a couple of times. "You were taking *college* classes?"

"Yeah."

"But..." Kennedy frowned. "You didn't change anything in the business afterward?"

"I didn't."

Kennedy frowned. "Why not?"

"Because I learned that I liked what we were doing and how we were doing it."

Kennedy shook her head. "So..."

"Okay, I know that sounds like that was *another* thing I tried but then ended up in the same place I started." Ellie moved in and took one of Kennedy's hands in hers. "But that's not really true. I realized that if you never do anything new, you never learn anything. And learning things changes you. Even if those things aren't what you intended to learn. You're never the same after an adventure, Kennedy." She tapped a finger over her heart. "In here you change. And in here you change," she said, tapping her temple that time. "I had to learn some things—make some mistakes—on my own. I thought." She gave a soft laugh. "The thing is, once you have Leo Landry in your life, you're never really on your own again."

"But I'm not Leo. I'm you."

"And now you can try new things and learn new things and have some adventures," Ellie said. "Because your Leo is finally here."

Kennedy instantly felt her eyes stinging with tears. She sniffed again. "I'm not sure Bennett wants to be Leo."

Ellie laughed outright at that and squeezed Kennedy's hand. "Bennett wants to be Leo badly. He just didn't have an Ellie. Until now." She leaned in and kissed Kennedy's cheek. "I love you, girl. And now it's time for you to go out and make some mistakes."

Kennedy laughed and sniffed. "Oh yeah?"

"Yeah, you haven't made a lot of those in your life yet."

Kennedy had to admit that Ellie had a point. "I'm scared."

"I know. Good thing Bennett will be there for you."

Kennedy gave Ellie a hug. "Okay."

Ellie nodded. "Okay." Then she moved back to the stove. "And of course the rest of us, too."

Kennedy stood watching her for a few minutes, but all she could think about was Bennett. And how to let him know that she was doing this Baton Rouge and politics thing, but that she still wanted him.

"I have to go," she told her grandmother, pushing away from the counter.

Ellie smiled. "Kick some ass."

Kennedy didn't ask if she meant figuratively in Baton Rouge, or literally—with Bennett Baxter.

Kennedy pushed through the door and stepped out into the main area of the restaurant. She knew Bennett was there with her brothers, Owen, and Leo. She figured it was about time that they started leaning on him so that their gumbo and coffee would improve.

She took a deep breath and headed straight for their table. When she stopped behind Leo, they all stopped talking and looked at her.

The only one she cared about hearing this was just to Leo's right.

"I'm going to Baton Rouge," were her first words to Bennett in four days.

He nodded. "I know."

"I think I'm going to be great at this. But I'm not sure. Still, I want to try."

"I know."

"And... I want to date you."

His gaze flickered with recognition. He'd said the same words to her in Savannah. "Okay."

"In Autre," she added.

"Okay."

"And in Baton Rouge."

He looked a little relieved. "Okay."

"And no one else."

"Okay."

She looked at him for a long moment. Then she nodded. "Okay." She turned on her heel, determined to go home, get some sleep, go to Baton Rouge tomorrow, and deal with everything else after that.

"Kennedy."

She stopped at the sound of Bennett's voice. Slowly she turned back.

He was standing and holding something out to her. She took the few steps back.

"Are those…my combat boots?" she asked.

"They are."

She looked from the boots to meet his gaze. "Did you shine my boots, Baxter?"

"I did."

It took a second for that to sink in, but when it did, she covered her mouth to keep from laughing. Or crying. She wasn't sure which.

"They don't shine as well as my shoes," he said. "The leather is treated differently or something. We can get you some *good* leather boots."

"If you replace my combat boots with some high-end, hoity-toity brand, you better just never eat the gumbo around here again. It won't be safe for you."

He grinned at her answer. He looked relieved and, if she wasn't mistaken, in love with her.

She swallowed and then said, her voice softer, "I wasn't going to wear combat boots to my meetings."

"But you should. They're you."

And they were shiny. Very fucking shiny.

She felt her heart flip over in her chest. She might not be a Leo, but she was stuck hard to this guy.

Finally she nodded and reached out, taking the boots from him. "Okay. I'll wear them. Thanks."

"And if you need to re-shine them, I remember there was a guy who set up in front of the capitol building—"

"I won't," she cut him off. But she gave him a little grin. "They can wait until you get there."

Bennett gave her a single nod. "Sounds good."

She didn't confirm that he would come or ask *when*. She didn't ask how this was going to work.

He would be there. She knew that. That was all that mattered.

TWO DAYS LATER, KENNEDY STOOD UP FROM THE CONFERENCE table in the Louisiana State Capitol building, having never felt more tired in her life.

She'd scrubbed airboats—*once,* before refusing to do it ever again. She'd helped repair air-conditioning units. She'd refinished her grandmother's dining room table. She knew how to work.

And she'd never been more fatigued than she was after sitting all day long in meetings.

All. Day. Long.

Inside.

With a fucking sweater on.

She loved air-conditioning as much as the next girl, but damn, she was almost missing the humidity. They kept things cold in those rooms and hallways. Plus, she was barely moving around, and the only sunlight that hit her skin was in the morning on the way from her hotel to her car and her car to the building and then again when she left to go back to the hotel.

The hotel. The lonely, boring, empty hotel.

She'd so far resisted calling Bennett. She wasn't sure why. They were together. They'd agreed to date. *In* Baton Rouge.

But she was waiting for him to make the next move. She'd admit it. That wasn't really her style. When she wanted something, she went for it.

But the last couple of days in these meetings had been a little tough on her confidence. She was interested in everything they were talking about and she'd contributed a few ideas. Charles had been encouraging and told her more than once how happy he was to have her there. But she was used to ruling the roost and bossing everyone around. The tour schedule was in her control. How Josh, Owen, Sawyer, and Maddie spent their days was up to her.

Here, she was in way over her head.

"You're doing great." Charles caught up with her as they waited for the elevator. "I know it's a lot to take in at first."

She nodded. "It's a lot. But I'm excited to be here." Scared and feeling like a fraud, too, but she didn't mention that part.

"I promise, in a month or two, this will all feel routine."

A month or two. Right. She was going to be coming back. "I'm sure it will." She gave him her beauty pageant smile. At least she had that to get her through until she felt like she knew what the hell she was doing.

They stepped onto the elevator with a small group. Kennedy was the only one in combat boots. But rather than feeling self-conscious, looking down at the shiny-ish toes of her boots reminded her that she was here because the regular people, the ones who lived on the bayou and in the small towns and who wore boots to go to work needed representation, on the tourism task force and in bigger ways.

The elevator dinged and Kennedy stepped off first.

So when she came up short, everyone else did as well.

"*Bennett*?"

He was sitting in the middle of the main area just inside the front doors. On a stool.

Not just any stool, either. It was Leo's stool from Ellie's. The bright yellow seat and multicolored legs made her heart thump and her eyes immediately fill with tears.

"Hi, darlin'."

Oh, lord, he'd dropped his "g" for her. And he was grinning at her like he'd never been happier to see someone.

She headed straight for him and right into his arms.

She pressed against him, feeling her tears fall. The feeling of *home* was so intense when he gathered her close that she couldn't breathe for a moment.

"Did you have any trouble getting everything in?" Charles asked.

Kennedy pulled back, looking at Bennett for a long, happy moment. Then she looked over at Charles. "Everything?"

The majority of the people who had been on the elevator, many of whom had been in the meeting with her today, had also stopped to see what was going on.

"I brought you something," Bennett told her.

He set her back as he stood and then went over to a silver cart she hadn't noticed sitting a few feet away. As he wheeled it over to her, she saw that it had a gas burner in the middle of it and a pan on top.

Her heart started racing and her eyes widened. "What's this?"

"This is my attempt at doing something big and out of my comfort zone and crazy like a Landry."

Oh boy. Crazy like a Landry could be downright dangerous. There had been feuds with neighboring towns, pseudo-kidnapping, and sheds burned to the ground when Landrys had been crazy in love in the past. Kennedy's eyes widened. "What are you talking about?"

He lifted the lid off of the pan to reveal bananas in the rum sauce that made Bananas Foster.

"Bennett…" She had no idea what else she was going to say.

He pulled a bowl from under the cart and set it on top. There was a scoop of slightly melted ice cream in it. Then he turned the dial on the burner, picked up a glass of clear liquid, and toasted her. "I love you, Kennedy. And I want to be your Leo. I want to be there for you, to encourage you and listen to you and push you. And since you're going to be way too busy to be making the desserts, I'm going to learn to make them."

Before she could say a word, he dumped what was clearly rum into the pan. Flames shot up.

The people around them ooh-ed, but the security guard who came running was not impressed.

"Hey!"

Kennedy lunged forward, covering the pan and putting the flames out while turning the burner off.

"You can't do that in here," the guard said. His hand was on the gun in his holster.

"Whoa!" Kennedy said, stepping between the guard and Bennett. "Calm down. It's okay."

"You can't just come in here and set shit on fire!" the guy said.

"I cleared this with security ahead of time," Bennett said, moving next to Kennedy. "It's just a little rum."

"And fire."

"Matt, he's with me," Charles spoke up.

The guard looked from Bennett to Charles. He frowned. "Governor Arnaud."

"I promise this is fine," Charles said. "I take full responsibility."

Matt nodded. "Okay." But he gave Bennett one last glare. "No more fire."

"You got it," Bennett said, holding up his hands in surrender.

Kennedy frowned and looked closer at Bennett's palms. "What's wrong with your hands?" There were red splotches all over.

Bennett looked down, then turned his hands over. Then sighed. "Hives."

"Hives? From what?"

"The bananas."

She stared at him. "Oh my God. You're *allergic* to bananas!"

How had she not realized what all of this meant immediately? Maybe because she was still so damned happy to see him. And maybe a little stunned that he'd set something on fire for her. That was *very* Leo-like.

"Yeah," he said with a shrug.

"But you still decided to make Bananas Foster for me?"

"Yeah."

"*Why*?"

"I thought maybe it was Landry-like to risk having my throat close up to tell you I love you and want to be with you, no matter how many trips between Autre and Baton Rouge we have to take. And to tell you that I rented us an apartment here so that there's a place we can stay when we're in town rather than a hotel."

All Kennedy really heard was "my throat close up." "You're *that* allergic to bananas?" she demanded. "Your throat could seriously close up?"

He swallowed hard. And she noticed some hives start to appear on his neck.

"I was cutting the bananas quickly and I might have touched my face or something."

She stepped close and unbuttoned his top three buttons.

Sure enough, hives were spreading over his chest as well. "Did you sample the bananas?" she asked.

"Just the sauce."

"The sauce that's been in contact with the bananas?"

He nodded.

"Bennett, this wasn't crazy," she told him. "This was stupid."

"Yeah…maybe it was."

"Are you okay?" He didn't look okay.

"I don't usually handle them this much. I stay away. Worst case, I accidentally get a piece of banana in something I didn't know had it. I—" He swallowed hard again. "I don't normally handle them—peeling and cutting them up and stuff."

"Oh, my God." She took his arm and started for the door. She glanced back at Charles. "Closest ER?"

Bennett tugged on her arm, stopping her. "Hey, you didn't say you love me too."

She frowned at him. "*Now*? You're about to die!"

"Don't let me die without hearing it."

Her eyes went wide. "You're supposed to say you're not going to die!"

He swallowed hard again. "The longer it takes for you to say it, the bigger the risk, Ken."

"Oh for God's sake!" She turned to face him, gripping both his hands. "Yes, I love you. I love you so fucking much. *Please* don't die. I'm not even close to done with you."

He grinned, even as the red blotches seemed to grow. "That's better." Then he swallowed. "We should probably head to the ER now."

Ten minutes later, Bennett had been given a shot and was resting in one of the bays in the emergency room.

Kennedy stood next to the bed. "Wow."

He gave her a grin. "I know Maddie went to jail for Owen, but the hospital is pretty good, right?"

"Maddie went and had coffee with the local cop for about an hour one day for Owen," Kennedy said with an eye-roll.

"But she had a close encounter with a gator, too, right?"

"Who is telling you these stories?" Kennedy asked, leaning onto the railing of his bed. "She shot *near* an alligator that was absolutely no threat whatsoever."

"Juliet almost drowned for Sawyer, right?"

Kennedy shook her head. "Leo's telling these, isn't he? You should know by now to take whatever Leo tells you and dial it back thirty to fifty percent."

"So ending up in the ER really *is* a big deal."

Kennedy leveled him a serious look. "Don't you *ever* put yourself at risk like that again."

"But—"

"I like Bananas Foster," she cut in. "But I love crème brûlée. And pecan pie. And hell, a great chocolate chip cookie even more."

"Seriously?"

"Yeah."

"I can make chocolate chip cookies."

She smiled and leaned over, kissing him softly. Then deeper. When she leaned back, she looked into his eyes. "This was all very *ostentatious* of you."

He chuckled. "You know, I start thinking about sleeping with you and then you throw out a word like ostentatious...and the urge gets so much stronger."

EPILOGUE

Almost Christmas time...

"I wanted to wait until everyone was here and now that Bennett and Kennedy made it back, this is the perfect time."

Josh stood on a chair in the middle of Ellie's and had just shouted for the place to quiet the fuck down. The bar was full tonight, as it always was on a Friday. Kennedy had finished up her meetings early so that they could make it back to Autre for the crawfish boil, but they'd still barely made it on time. She didn't know what exactly was going on, but Josh had texted her three times and Bennett twice, making sure they'd make it back. It was something big.

"If I hadn't had to swing by the governor's office and promise to bring him gumbo in exchange for not arresting you for ignoring his request to wait three days before taking another ship out to Sauveuse Island, we'd have been here in plenty of time," she said softly to Bennett from behind the first ring of people gathered around Josh.

Bennett pinched her ass in reply. "You would have taken

him Cora's gumbo anyway. Don't blame me because you always have 'just one more thing' to tell him. The poor guy is probably relieved you were spending the weekend down here."

Kennedy laughed. Charles was quickly becoming one of her best friends. He was the one that had talked her into her next political step. "You might be right. He's really excited about me running for mayor down here. That will keep me away from Baton Rouge more."

Josh, Owen and Sawyer thought the idea of her as mayor was hilarious, of course, and were already talking about all of the ways they could blackmail and bribe her.

She couldn't wait for them to try.

Bennett hugged her against his side with a chuckle and kissed the top of her head. "I'm not saying this is why he's behind it, but he does like me a lot and I did mention to him that I thought calling you Madam Mayor would be really hot."

She looked up at him with a sly smile. "Yeah, that would be really hot. We should practice that tonight."

His eyes darkened. "Oh, Mayor Landry-Baxter, we can definitely do that."

Landry-Baxter, she liked that. "And you can play being my assistant. And every ten minutes I'll be asking you for files that you don't actually need."

He squeezed her ass again. "Yeah, I'll put my *files* anyplace you want them."

She reached around and pinched *his* ass. "Keep up that attitude and you might just earn yourself a raise."

"But," he added in that slightly condescending tone that always made her want to kiss him until he forgot how to do anything but say, *yes, fuck, Kennedy*. "I do feel the need to point out that if I'm the *assistant*, I won't be using my silk necktie to tie your wrists while bending you over my big mahogany desk." He gave a little shrug.

Heat arrowed through her. Yeah, the day that Bennett's desk

had been delivered to the office space he'd rented in Autre for his foundation had been a really fun day.

"Your dress code for the job will require a silk necktie every day," she told him, wondering if they could sneak out and go to his office right now.

"But assistants don't have offices to put big mahogany desks in. Or big mahogany desks."

"Huh. Does it work if you're calling me Madam Mayor but it's *your* desk?" she teased. "Seems like I'm in the position of power. Maybe I should just take that desk for my own."

He nodded, seeming thoughtful. "I guess you would be in the position of power. Unless..."

She arched a brow. "Unless?"

"I guess unless you're calling me... I don't know...Senator. Or something."

Kennedy pulled back slightly, her eyes went wide. "What? Wait...really?"

He grinned. "It would be okay to practice Senator Baxter, I suppose."

Kennedy stared at him and shook her head slowly. "Yeah, that would definitely be okay." He still had to live in Louisiana for almost two years before he could run for Senate, but the things this man was going to be doing in those two years were going to be impressive as hell. People were definitely going to know him. And love him.

Then she grinned. "Oh, man, Charles is going to owe me five hundred bucks!"

Bennett gave her a little frown. "Why's that?"

"Because we made a bet about who could talk you into running for office first. I told him that I definitely had an unfair advantage, but he took the bet anyway." She laughed. "And hell, if you're going to have to keep running for higher offices than me just so you can keep the 'power' and the big desk...maybe *I'll* eventually run for Senate." There weren't many positions above a Senator. But those positions were huge.

He hugged her close but chuckled. “Don’t get ahead of yourself, Madam Mayor.”

Yeah, that wasn’t a no. Getting ahead of herself was one of the things he liked best about her.

Feeling happy and completely contented in Bennett’s arms, standing in the place that would always feel most like home, Kennedy actually had to blink back tears. She couldn’t let her brothers see them. They already teased her mercilessly about the perpetual grin she wore now that she and Bennett were going back and forth between Baton Rouge and the bayou, spending a lot of time in each place, but always together.

Though they also figured her goofy grin was in part due to her amazing sex life.

They weren’t wrong.

Josh turned to Tori, who was standing at the end of the bar, also waiting for whatever his big announcement was going to be.

“Victoria Kramer, you are the love of my life. The night you walked into my bar on Bourbon Street, my life changed. And I thank God every day that you came back a year later. Thank you for finding me, thank you for loving me, thank you for saving me, thank you for being the best part of every day for me.”

Kennedy’s eyes widened as everyone in the room seemed to gasp at once. Ever since Tori had walked onto the Boys of the Bayou dock, it had been a given that they would get married. But honestly, Kennedy had had no idea Josh was going to propose so publicly.

She should have though. He was a Landry. They did everything big, but nothing more so than love.

Kennedy looked over at Tori, who was staring at Josh with her hand over her mouth and tears streaming down her cheeks.

Josh gave her a wink and then looked over his shoulder. "Come on."

There was a pause and then Juliet exclaimed, "Oh my gosh!"

Everyone looked in that direction. Coming around the edge of the bar was a goat. With a sign hanging around his neck that said, "TORI, WILL YOU..."

An otter followed. There was a piece of cardboard strapped to his back that said, "MARRY..."

Everyone gasped again, but they stayed quiet, miraculously.

Finally, the pig that had been a piglet only a few months ago, came around the bar with a sign that, predictably, said, "ME?"

Tori gave a little half laugh, half sob.

The pig stopped, looked around, and peed.

Everyone laughed. He'd done that as a baby whenever he'd gotten nervous—which had been whenever he was around humans other than Tori—but they'd all assumed he'd grow out of it. Unfortunately, he hadn't. And now it made a lot bigger mess.

Josh looked at Tori with a big grin. "So? What do you think?"

The whole place went crazy with cheering and laughing and toasting.

Which annoyed the hell out of Kennedy.

"Hey!" she shouted. "Hey! We didn't hear her answer!"

Not that anyone thought that there was a chance in hell Tori would say no. Kennedy knew that Tori loved Josh with everything in her. Still, she wanted to see the damned moment completed.

Of course, no one heard her over the noise.

"Hey!" She put her fingers to her lips and gave a sharp whistle. Bennett winced and a couple of people heard and turned, but the room was still full of boisterous, happy noise.

Kennedy extricated herself from Bennett and headed for the kitchen, returning a moment later with a metal pot and a big metal serving spoon. She climbed up onto the bar and started banging on the pot.

Within about seven seconds, the room was quiet and everyone was looking at her.

"If you would all just *shut up* for a second so that Tori can—"

The main door suddenly slammed.

Everyone pivoted to look in *that* direction.

Chase Dawson stood there with a duffel bag over his shoulder and a big bag of what looked to be wrapped gifts. "Uh, hey, everybody." He lifted a hand with a sheepish smile. "Sorry to interrupt."

There was a beat of surprised silence. Then Juliet and Ellie both exclaimed, "Chase!"

His face lit up with a huge grin as two of his favorite females rushed him, grabbing him in a joint hug.

"I thought you were stuck in traffic," Josh said as everyone called out greetings.

"I was," Chase said over the tops of their heads. "Sorry."

"I would have waited."

"Well, go on now," Chase said motioning for Josh to continue. "I'm here for about two weeks."

That got another squeal from Juliet and more questions from Ellie.

Kennedy beat on the pot again. "Hey!" she called. They started to quiet. "Good *lord*, you people are loud." Had she just been away in Baton Rouge with people who took turns and didn't constantly try to talk over the noise of airboats and juke boxes for too long?

Of course, the pot banging made the pig pee again. *On* Tori's feet, who had tucked him between her knees in an attempt to comfort him.

Maddie was holding the otter while Owen had the goat by the collar.

Ellie handed Tori a towel and Kennedy pointed the spoon at her. "You wanna say it quick before anything else happens?" Because it would. This was Autre and the Landry family. Chaos was the norm.

Tori grinned at her, then looked at Josh. "Marry you and get all of *this* all the time?"

He nodded. "Yep."

"Then yes," she said. "Definitely yes."

When the crowd cheered that time, Kennedy made no move to quiet them. She caught her grandfather's eye from where he was standing with Ellie, looking out over the room and the people with a look of deep affection and pride. He was, clearly, exactly where he'd always wanted to be, doing exactly what he'd always wanted to do—loving and laughing with these people. He gave her a wink and lifted his coffee cup—the one he always used, no matter what he was drinking—in a little toast. Kennedy grinned and gave him a little nod, understanding completely what he was thinking. This was good. This was all just so damned good.

"Hey, Madam Mayor!" Sawyer called to her. "Get off that bar! You might be big and important in Baton Rouge, but around here, you're still one of us."

She grinned and blinked back tears again. Damn right, she was one of them. She always would be. But she'd also win the mayoral election because these people would be campaigning for her and supporting her and telling everyone *else* how amazing she was.

She let Bennett lift her down from the bar, and they moved right into the middle of the crowd of people in the middle of her grandmother's bar.

Her family. Her home. Her soft place to land. No matter where else her adventures took her.

Thank you for reading *Crazy Rich Cajuns*! I hope you loved Kennedy and Bennett's story!

If this is your first trip to the bayou with the Landry family, be sure you check out the rest of the **Boys of the Bayou series!**

If you've been along on the ride the whole time, I've got one more chance to visit Autre!

There's a Christmas story starring Chase Dawson and Bailey Dixon too! Be sure to check my website for more information about **Must Love Alligators**!

And don't miss the **Boys of the Big Easy series!** More hot, charming southern boys and the sassy, strong women who are their perfect matches!

The book list of all of my hot, funny Louisiana stories follows!

Thanks again for reading! I've loved my time with the Landrys and I consider Louisiana a second home... I can't tell you how much I've loved writing the Boys of the Bayou and the Boys of the Big Easy! Thank you for reading and loving these books!

Find all of my books... and plenty more quirky small towns... right here!
www.ErinNicholas.com

MORE FROM ERIN

If you loved Beauty and the Bayou, don't miss the rest of

The Boys of the Bayou

My Best Friend's Mardi Gras Wedding

Sweet Home Louisiana

Beauty and the Bayou

Crazy Rich Cajuns

Must Love Alligators

And there's more Louisiana fun in the

The Boys of the Big Easy

Easy Going (prequel novella)

Going Down Easy

Taking It Easy

Nice and Easy

Getting Off Easy

Eggnog Makes Her Easy (Christmas novella)

If you're looking for more sexy, small town rom com fun, check out the

Billionaires in Blue Jeans series!

Diamonds and Dirt Roads

High Heels and Haystacks

Cashmere and Camo

And much more at

ErinNicholas.com

ABOUT THE AUTHOR

Erin Nicholas is the New York Times and USA Today bestselling author of over thirty sexy contemporary romances. Her stories have been described as toe-curling, enchanting, steamy and fun. She loves to write about reluctant heroes, imperfect heroines and happily ever afters. She lives in the Midwest with her husband who only wants to read the sex scenes in her books, her kids who will never read the sex scenes in her books, and family and friends who say they're shocked by the sex scenes in her books (yeah, right!).

Find her and all her books at
www.ErinNicholas.com

And find her on Facebook, Goodreads, BookBub, and Instagram!

Milton Keynes UK
Ingram Content Group UK Ltd.
UKHW041814150923
428743UK00018B/275